THE JUMP POINT

Hartley James

Prologue

No one knew where the Sirona came from, or where they went when they were done. Some speculated that they had a homeworld, but others were not so sure. Whatever the case, we knew that when they appeared above our worlds with their offers of trade, we were powerless to do anything about them.

Their great, silver ships materialised out of the void over many of our worlds. Their technology was so far advanced, and yet they seemed interested in the insignificant things we had to offer. We knew there was little we could do to send them on their way.

After a time, their invisible hand became too strong. The Combined Council of Worlds was formed to inject order. Wherever the Sirona had been, disorder and social decline could be found. We didn't know why or how, but the implications were clear. Though the CoCee studied the Sirona and their technology, we came no further forward. Their culture remained an enigma. Dealing with one Sirona was like dealing with any other and may as well had been, because the individual Sirona knew all the dealings of the others. We were perplexed. The things that caught their attention and the scheme behind what they did lay beyond our comprehension. Much later, we began to understand.

Those things wrought by the Sirona were deep and dark. And some became known only years after they happened, obscured by our divisions and our separate ways. One such was Lantana, The Cradle.

Lantana was designated a crib world: a vast sociological experiment established some generations past by a collection of academic renegades from the established orthodoxy. The Lantanans called their world The Cradle. The basic tenet of its foundation was the development of the individual in mind and body. The fundamental axiom was the conscious limitation of technology.

Throughout its brief history, The Cradle had little interaction with the other worlds. Its inhabitants maintained a fierce protectionist policy. The world was not technology free — far from it — but they purposely limited its use. Where the mind and body could do something, the Lantanans believed the mind and body should. Their social order, their training, all the pedagogy was based around this principle.

Lying at the cornerstone of this regime, was a series of enhancements introduced by neural surgery. Shortly after their first year of life, neural extensors were implanted in the young Lantanans, linking the two hemispheres of the brain. These organic implants grew and developed with the normal maturation to adulthood. The pathways, coupled with the unorthodox disciplines and training resulted in a different mode of thought; a new lateralism and perspective found nowhere else in the system. It gave the emerging Lantanans a capability to view and analyse things in ways unfamiliar to the rest of the system.

Because of The Cradle's isolationist policy, few outside knew about or experienced their perspective or their program of social engineering. For years, it remained a zealously guarded secret.

Numbers expanded in the initial stages of The Cradle's foundation, but the growth stabilized once it reached what the leaders deemed was optimum. The Lantanans held no illusions about their vulnerability or the reality of external threat. Defence of personal freedom was recognized and guarded as was the latitude to pursue their own ideals. They became a hermit world to guard that freedom.

They kept so separate from the rest of us that no one knew when the great silver ships appeared above Lantana. None saw the devastation. Nor did anyone know why it occurred — not even the survivors, few that they were.

Chapter One

Mahra cursed to herself. Damned port security. The voyage could have been a lot better. How was she to know about the security crackdown? The confusion at the port on check-in should had alerted her, but it didn't. Well, despite the trouble, she was here now, in yet another unremarkable hotel room, on yet another world. Nothing changed. One world was much like any other these days. One city the same as the next.

She spat on her whetstone and drew it in long even strokes across her blade edge. The flat, sheenless surface felt good resting across her thighs. Wherever she was, she always had her blade. She had made sure of it after her years without. This was her ritual, her daily meditation. The rhythmic motion helped focus her in that small, quiet place, where she could think unsullied by the day's tensions. Despite the years that had passed, she kept to the Old One's teachings. They sustained her alertness and sharpness; attributes that kept her on top in her line of work. She didn't even feel the cold when she was occupied with her blade, and cold it was. Miserable excuse for a place. Miserable excuse for a planet.

"Oh well," she said to herself. "Better here than nowhere."

Chutzpah, her small furry companion, chittered on her shoulder. The grey bush of his tail flicked up and down, expressing his annoyance.

"I know, I know. You're hungry. Come on, we'll get you something to eat," she said, and nuzzled the side of his head.

She sighed, stuffed the whetstone back into the pouch at her belt, and drew herself to her feet. Chutzpah teetered on her shoulder, then righted himself, claws scrabbling and then digging into the cloth at her shoulder. He stuck his tail out to counterbalance. It was most unlike him not to sense and anticipate her moves. He had to be out of phase. Perhaps it was simply the cold.

Mahra sheathed her blade, slipped it back over her right shoulder and stooped to toss her pack onto the bed behind her. She flipped open the tabs, upended the pack, and let the contents spill out across the covers. After some shuffling through them one-handed, she located the bag of coz nuts and pulled out a small handful. Chutzpah caught the scent and strained forward, nose aquiver. She placed a small pile on the chair next to the threev, and leaned her body forward to allow him to jump from his perch.

"There you are, Chutz," she told him. "But that's all. They've got to last. Don't know when next I'm going to be able to afford some more."

She scratched the space between his ears with one finger, as nut held between his forepaws, he cracked noisily into the tough shell.

The hotel was a little less salubrious than she'd have liked, but Mahra was currently between contracts. She slowly turned and took stock. Fairly sparsely appointed. Not even a sim set. Sure, it had a threev, but where didn't? There was not even a remote for it. Still, it was about as much as her card could bear at the moment. She was counting on the fact that, even now, it would take a week or two for any registrations to get back and blow her limit at Credit Central. By then, she should have picked up something, even if it was only a short-hop sign on. Even with that, she *should* be able to spin it out until something more solid came along. She didn't like the *should* though. New Helvetica was a nice enough place she supposed — for a fridge world. She wasn't exactly part of the resort set though. Brightly coloured therm wear didn't really suit her, or most of her purposes. Besides, Chutzpah's claws would have made a mess of it. But she was here now, and hopefully something would come of it before her funds ran out.

The New Helvetians were an austere race. En masse they seemed to have a penchant for shades of grey or brown; clothing and buildings and personality. There was no such thing as a rich comedian on New Helvetica, unless he or she were a tourist. Most of the New Helvetian population made their living on two major industries; tourism and tech. The former she could really do without. The latter was the reason she was here.

Since the Twelve-Day War, the New Helvetians had remained visibly unaligned. Their emotionless character and apparent calmness made them excellent negotiators and an entire offshoot industry of diplomacy and business had grown up around this talent. The truth was, that despite their professed neutrality, New Helvetica didn't really care which side it played, as long as there was a profit in it. They specialised in the sort of tech that made money — weapons tech and info tech. Either one fostered vested interested. If not caring which faction they supplied from one moment to the next constituted neutrality, then neutral they were. Despite the tripartite signings at the Combined Council, Mahra knew they still dealt on every side. The Council and intrepid journalists had been trying to prove it for years.

The three major interest groups of the CoCee preached reduction on the one hand, and made their deals in private on the other. At least at this stage, they were all sitting down at the same table and actually talking. Not that she had any real interesting in what they were talking about. What she was banking on, and with what she knew, her particular skill set, Mahra stood a good chance of being able to pick up something as a fall-out of the New Helvetian subculture. For the moment, she had no concrete plans to speak of, but she was a believer in the principle that opportunities were made — they didn't just happen. If her voyage in had been any indication, however, she had a bit of work to do to change her luck. And she had better start doing so soon, because she was here with no idea how she was going to earn a few creds.

For a start, she could check the bulletins and see if there was anything worthy of attention, but she doubted it. The sort of contract she was looking for was not the type that usually found its way into the open media or message boards. The less reputable bars and clubs around ports often provided her with the leads she needed, or at least snippets that would act as starting points. But she was not that familiar with New Helvetica, and she had to start somewhere.

Chutzpah sat happily tearing out the flesh of a nut. He'd probably curl up where he sat and sleep when he got through the remainder. As usual, with these colder resort worlds, the heating tended to be a little too high and the room's stuffy atmosphere was conducive to drowsiness. Mahra couldn't afford to let herself succumb to the temptation to settle back and relax. She had work to do. She searched about the small room for a temperature control but to no avail. Same old story. She flicked on the threev and browsed the bulletin boards. After a few minutes, she decided there wasn't going to be anything there, so she flipped over to the news channel. Lead item was the expected retaliation attempted by the Warriors of Heaven against the Laizmuth and consequent upgrading of security at all ports.

"Yeah, yeah. Tell me about it," she muttered at the screen.

The only other item that caught her attention was a brief mention of a rumoured corporate courtship between the information giant Interworld Logic Systems and the biosystems company Germ Cells Inc. System-wide business giants flirting with each other was not so unusual, but what did ILS and GCI had in common? She thought about it for a few moments. Something was not quite right about the pattern. It was clearly time she did a bit of digging.

She sifted through her belongings again and pulled out her palm comp. From time to time, it struck her as interesting that the technology had never got any smaller. She often spent her energies thinking about it. Despite the amount of time since her early years, tech still fascinated her. Perhaps it had been those years spent without it. Perhaps it was the questions Aleyin had left with her.

The trend toward miniaturisation had halted abruptly with the realisation that such things were always going to be limited by the human physique. As voice activation and response had proved impractical with the strictures of both privacy and intrusion laws, size became limited by the fact that there was always something that needed to be pressed or swiped by a finger. The end of the human digit became the limiting factor. Screen size had also been a problem until the introduction of holo displays. Now the display could be zoomed to whatever size was comfortable. There might be a little less resolution, but not enough to really impact on the utility. Until the holo screen, portability had been limited by access to a hard screen, or the use of a detachable. Of course, there had been the inevitable flirtation with implants, but for some reason, that had simply trickled away, as far as she knew.

Mahra keyed the sequence, and the screen took shape in the air above the edge of her hand. Index — Infonet — Business, she drilled down through the pictographs and started her query. Mahra had long ago found that it saved her a great deal of time, and more importantly, expense on the nets, to have pre-set parameter groups she could overlay onto the search maps. These had been built up over the last few years and they served her well.

Knowing the scan would take a few seconds, she let her attention wander over the rest of the bulletins, just in case. Finally, the screen flashed at her, indicating completion, and she cut the threev so she could devote her attention to the results. She had to rely upon her intuition, and her hunches were best formed without distraction.

There were several categories to choose from and she scrolled through them to try and pick up some linkage — some connecting thread or background — that might lead her in the right direction. The task was made more difficult by the interwoven structure of ownership and interests. Each of the two companies had holdings in a dozen different areas and there was a trail of subsidiaries stretching down through level after level across virtually all the known worlds. Each subsidiary in turn had its own stakeholdings in other operations. Nothing matched the patterns. The link just didn't seem to be there.

Somewhere at the back of her mind, something pushed to came forward, to snag her attention. Mahra had learnt to rely on these feelings, but she still needed to pin it down, to give it some shape. She normally did some of her best work at night, but this time perhaps she was just too tired. It wouldn't come, and she could feel there was no profit to be had in pushing at it. She bit her lower lip as she pressed the save sequence, turned the display off, and tossed the unit back on the bed. Let it come of its own accord if it was going to.

She had the ready solution to her mood. She pulled her blade from its sheath and tested the edge. The first principles of her years of training; mind, body, and blade sharp — each relying on the others. She pulled off her clothes and boots, moved to the room's centre and lowered the blade point to the floor, concentrating her energy. Suddenly she spun the blade up and caught it as she moved into the first of her positions. Throw, catch, weave. One continuous fluid motion. Spin and catch hand to hand. She was thankful for the lofty ceilings characteristic of these old colonial worlds.

She felt the stretching of her body and reflexes as she pushed herself further. Many a time her life had depended upon both. She couldn't afford to let herself get lax. Once was enough. That time, she had been going through a particularly down period and she had indulged it. The medics had carried her from that port bar, and she still bore a scar on her left forearm to remind her what could happen if you let yourself slip.

By the time she had completed the sequence, her firm muscles were slick with the gleam of sweat. She finished as she had started, in the fighting stance, legs slightly spaced, breasts rising and falling with her breathing. She touched the matte black blade to her forehead, then slipped it back into the sheath in one motion, her thumb tracing the edge as it slid into place.

That was enough. She could put her mind to the thing that was nagging at her tomorrow. Maybe she'd find a lead, maybe she wouldn't. All she wanted to do now was wash off the stink of her travels, grab a few hours rest and start afresh in the morning.

□

The bar was packed. People pushed and jostled through the crowd, arms laden with drinks, and tried to manoeuvre their way back to their companions. The sound system blared the latest crash number and stirred her lower body with a heavy pulsing bass line, but it did little to distinguish itself from the people noise, their individual voices raised to make themselves heard above the din. Across one side a wall-high holo-screen writhed with the intertwined forms of naked flesh — coupling or dance, she couldn't quite tell. The air trailed ribbons of fragrant smoke and laughter. It didn't look like the sort of place that would be good for business, but then, you never knew. It would do for the time being.

This was already her third night of bar hopping around the port area, and it had produced little or no result. Mahra was becoming despondent. Chutzpah was unimpressed, and made his feelings known by nipping at her ear. She turned and snarled at him in reprimand, but he merely bared his teeth back at her. She could sympathise with the way he felt but she snapped back anyway.

"Just put up with it, will you? We have work to do." She turned back to scan the unpromising crowd of revellers.

By leaning right across the bar, she finally managed to attract the barman's attention. She held up one finger and gestured with her other hand. The barman raised his eyebrows and nodded, before moving further down the bar to pour the large mug of foaming brew. He returned and slapped it down in front of her and took her proffered card. He keyed the amount and swiped the reader. Then, giving the card a cursory glance, he flipped it back to her, where it landed in a puddle of the spilled drink. Mahra slid it from the damp surface and wiped away the wetness on her thigh, before slipping it away again. She suppressed an inward sigh of relief and let her breath out slowly. So, she hadn't broken the bank yet.

She really couldn't expect anything better from the barman, she supposed. After all, she didn't look like a resorter, and she wasn't likely to spend or tip the way they did. And he was right, she'd probably nurse this particular mug for some time if she ever found a booth or table. She turned, and propping her elbows on the bar, scanned the room for opportunities.

Mostly, the bar was full of resorters. A la mode clothing, flashing teeth and jewellery, and laughter that was just a little too loud. Damn, but she hated that sort. There were a few navy types though, and one or two others she couldn't pick immediately. Any of them might turn out to be useful. There were, after all, two possibilities here. The first was to get a line on something, or a contact. The other was the hope of acquiring a hand weapon. The blade was good enough. It would do the job if it came down to it, but it could also leave her vulnerable. There was hand to hand, but there was also the possibility of being picked off at a distance by some clever fellow with a range weapon; a prospect she didn't exactly relish — not that it was likely to occur in a place like New Helvetica. The world was known for its layers of regulations and the fines that went with them.

Travel regs these days meant that it was becoming increasingly difficult to move from world to world fully armed, and the inner-system worlds tended to have a more stringent policy about bearing weaponry unless you were fully certified and had the legitimate permits. That Mahra wasn't certified didn't really concern her. The permits were exceedingly difficult to acquire unless you knew the right people. Strangely enough, you didn't need a permit for a blade. People just didn't carry them anymore.

It was no different on New Helvetica where the flaunted wealth of the resort set would make easy pickings for a fully armed street thug. Usually she could get away with her blade, and, if it came to the worst, she could use it, but there was still that odd occasion where she felt she could do with a little extra security.

She spotted a vacant booth and slipped between the crowded bodies, careful not to spill any more of her drink than the barman had already. She took up position in preparation for a long night of watching and waiting. She slid along the padded bench seat, settled herself in the corner and placed her mug in front of her. She made sure of Chutzpah's perch before she nestled back. One arm, she draped across the back of the booth, the other across the table surface, hand encircling her mug. It was not the most comfortable of positions, but it afforded the best view and left her right arm in a position where her blade was close to hand.

Chutzpah assessed the situation, and deciding that there would be no further movement for the time being, clambered down the front of her tunic, using his claws for purchase. Settling his hindquarters in her lap, he stretched up, one paw on either side of her throat, almost as if embracing her. Within moments, a low rumble emanated from deep in his chest as he watched her, face upturned and nostrils flaring with his breath.

Mahra put her watching reflexes on automatic. She let her eyes scan the bar and its inhabitants with half her attention and allowed her thoughts to wander with the other. She trusted to her perceptions to alert her as well as her empathy with Chutzpah's moods and impressions. Chutzpah's continuous rumble seemed to assist, with its almost hypnotic quality tuned to the rhythms of her body and brain. The symbiosis had been there always, but it had grown from the early beginnings. She felt as naked without Chutzpah now, as she did without her blade. Somehow it was like the link she used to have, so long ago, with the Old One, and then with Aleyin after that, but in other ways it was different.

The zimonette was an interesting creature, little understood by the few who knew anything about them. There was precious little available from those that did. One school of thought held that they only gave the pretence of sapience and that attributing any rationality to them was pure anthropomorphism. Mahra was inclined to disagree with that analysis more than just a little. She and Chutz had been together too long, and she had seen too much to make the mistake of down-playing his abilities. Just because the zimonette had not, as a species, developed a tool-using and structured society, did not, as far as she was concerned, deny the powers of cognitive thought. Let the academics hold their theories, she was quite happy with her own.

"Isn't that right Chutz?" she said and stroked the length of his back with the ends of her fingers, right from the place between his shoulders down to the base of his tail. Her stroking intensified the rumbling. "We could tell them a thing or two."

She had met Chutzpah on a garden world aptly named Paradise because of its lush verdure and teeming life. The world had been designated a sanctuary and was relatively unsullied by human contact or exploitation. Mahra had wound up there by accident and in very poor circumstances. She had been lucky to survive the landing, and if it hadn't been for Chutz, she probably wouldn't had made it. He had found her on the forest floor when she could walk no more, wounded, and fevered. He located food for her, and eventually, when she had understood, led her to water. He had also kept the less desirable inhabitants at bay, guarding her sleeping form.

Eventually, she had been located via her distress beacon, but that was nearly two months later. By that time, she had fully recovered, Chutzpah and she had the beginnings of their long-standing bond already in place. When she had finally shipped off Paradise, he had come with her. She didn't know why, nor could she fathom the workings of his mind, but he had been with her ever since.

That had been in the early days when she was still raw and naive about many things. Now she had been through a little more, Chutzpah with her, and both had become somewhat more jaded over the course of time.

Chutzpah continued his steady regard of her face and slowly blinked his eyes as if in confirmation.

She smiled at him for a moment before focusing once again on the bar population. The resort crowd was thinning now, to be replaced by a few more navy types and those others whom she couldn't put a label to yet. She found this often happened in places nestled around the port as the evening wore on. The resorters tended to drift off to parties or dinners or shows, to leave the other, more regular patrons to make up the numbers. Because of its proximity to the port, this place could turn out to be more useful to her than she had hoped.

A few green-suited technicians started to wander in with the regulars and merchanters, as well as one or two dark-suited militaire — shipboard militiamen who rode with the large freighters and passenger liners. She didn't envy them their jobs. She had done her stint in that line too.

Boring as hell, but the pay was good. It didn't matter if it was a long or a short haul. The job always seemed to be the same. The problem was that it was necessary. With the combination of both the boredom, and the number of creds one could earn, it was a recipe for port-side disaster. There was nowhere to spend the earnings on long haul flights so the militaire generally wound up with a lot of money and little satisfaction. It encouraged them to let off a little more steam than normal once they finally hit a port, especially if they'd just came off a particularly long haul.

The few who appeared were not exactly making their presence felt, so she assumed they were only local short-hoppers. The greetings and signs of recognition that passed around the bar confirmed that impression. There were the inevitable one or two glances over in her direction, but nothing too overt. The glancers were probably based locally and had partners or lovers to return home to, after they loosened the joints. No, there was little to be concerned about there. She could have probably handled most of them on her own if required.

The problem was that it didn't offer much in the way of a potential contact. If something didn't eventuate soon, she'd be forced to move on and take her chances elsewhere.

She lifted her mug and was in the process of draining the last of its contents when the low rumble in Chutzpah's chest abruptly stopped. She looked down to see him craning back over his shoulder, eyes fixed on the door.

"What is it Chutz?" she murmured, following his gaze.

At first there seemed to be nothing to capture the zimonette's attention. The usual assortment of individuals circulated round the bar and the booths. A few wandered out the door, only to be replaced by more of a similar type. But Mahra had long ago learnt to trust the signals given by her small companion. His intuitions were uncannily accurate. After a few moments, the crowd by the door parted unconsciously to admit a newcomer. When she at last had a clear enough view, she knew why the crowd gave way.

The new arrival stood out without trying. He was a good head taller than the majority of those already inside the bar and the navy types and techs give way, consciously or unconsciously deferring to his greater size. There were a few smiles and nods of recognition as he made his way to the bar, with a smaller and rounder companion following in his wake. The shorter one wouldn't normally warrant a second glance, but the tall one naturally drew the eye as the pair moved through the room. There was no need for them to signal for the barman's attention. He was there waiting with a smile to take their order as they reached the bar. *Nice for some*, she thought.

These two were obviously known. The tall one ordered kahveh and stood surveying the bar as he waited. His companion signalled a mug and the barman moved back along the bar length to fill the order.

They were an unusual pair, she had to give them that. The tall one was clad top to bottom in black except for the boots, and the boots themselves were enough to attract attention. They were deep, blood red and rose almost to his knee. Black and white designs worked up and down their length forming intricate patterns. By narrowing her eyes a little, she could pick out what appeared to be intertwined serpents. Long black curls fell to his shoulders framing a moustachioed face, highlighted by vivid green eyes beneath a finely etched brow. His companion, by contrast, was swarthy, overweight and wore eye lenses beneath his more standard navy crop. The spectacles were no fashion statement either. They were thick and heavy, magnifying the eyes behind them — eyes that flickered nervously around the room. There must have been some reason why he wouldn't have opted for corrective surgery. It didn't exactly look like they were an affectation.

Their drinks arrived and the two stood there, leaning across the bar in conversation, the taller one stooping a lot

more to bring himself into hearing range of his companion.
As they talked, they sipped at their drinks, the short one
cradling his mug in thick pudgy hands, the tall one sipping
daintily at the hot kahveh, watching the room in the mirror
behind the bar, eyes always on the alert. No, not your
normal porters these ones. His roving gaze paused once,
twice, in Mahra's direction as they surveyed the reflected
room, then he bent and muttered something to his
companion. The short one looked back over his shoulder
and pushed his heavy lenses further up his nose before he
peered across the room. He caught her in that magnified
gaze for a moment or two, said something to his partner,
then gave a dismissive shrug before turning back to his
brimming mug.

Mahra, pretending not to have noticed, focused her
eyes on another part of the room, fixing her face toward a
huddle of people near the door. This allowed enough of an
angle so that she could watch the pair in her peripheral
vision. They continued their conversation, with the taller
one passing the occasional unsubtle glanced her way in the
reflected image behind the bar.

Uh-oh, here it comes, she thought, as the tall one
finally turned and looked unabashedly straight at her. His
gaze travelled up and down as if sizing her up. His
companion turned and watched, a wry expression on his
face. No, there was no doubt about it, he was about to make
his move. The flamboyant stranger sauntered across to stand
over her booth and looked down at her with an obviously
practised, but very charming smile.

"I couldn't help noticing, Mez. It's an interesting pet
you have there. I was over there, debating the matter with
my companion. Now would you be kind enough to help me
out by settling the argument. It's a zimonette is it not?" he
asked in a lilting, musical accent.

His voice was deep and full, but the inflections made
it seem a little gentle. As he spoke, he smiled, one eyebrow
rose in query. This close, he wasn't bad at all. If he was

trying to pick her up, she might even be tempted. Chutzpah, at the first sign of the intrusion had scuttled up her shoulder and stood tensely poised, ready for action and obviously objecting.

"Yes, zimonette, and no, pet he is not," she replied, putting a slight hardness to the last few words just for good measure. She wanted to see how much of a challenge he really was.

Up close, the stranger was a lot younger than she at first presumed, but the air of self-assurance seemed to be at odds with his apparent age. She could see a strip of white hair running through the dark curls at the top of his head. It began at a ridge of slightly reddened skin that continued in a line that slanted across his wide forehead. The large moustache was curled upward at the ends, and he smoothed it with the tip of his finger and thumb as he stood watching her.

"Ah, it has been a while since I've seen one of those, you see? Therefore, the debate. You're not a local." It was a statement rather than a question.

"Well, we'll certainly have to give you points for observation there," she answered wryly. He ignored the sarcasm and continued.

"Listen now, I hate to be forward, but would we be intruding if we joined you? You're alone, are you not? Let us buy you a drink perhaps."

Why not? she thought as she pursed her lips. She pretended to be thinking it over as she looked him up and down. She also made sure she did it in the same fashion that he had done it to her earlier. Then, adjudging that her point had been made, and that there had been enough of a pause, she shrugged and signified her assent. She tapped the rim of her mug with her finger.

At least the pair's intrusion would pass the time, and if this pair turned out to be a waste in other ways, she could always keep an eye on the rest of the bar. The man, however, looked like he might be interesting enough to provide a snippet or two of useful information. She sized him up some more, while his attention was distracted by signalling to his companion to get the drinks and to come and join them.

He was indeed tall, and looked reasonably fit with it. If nothing else, it could almost be worth an evening's dalliance. She couldn't pick the accent, and that bothered her. Accents were something she was usually good at.

As his companion arrived with the drinks, the tall one swept her a mock bow.

"Allow me to present my companion, Jayeer Sind. Travelling companion, accomplice, and comp man extraordinaire. And I, who have the pleasure of standing before you, I am Timon, Timon Pellis ... Mez ... "

"Mahra, Mahra Kaitan ... and this, is Chutzpah," she said giving the zimonette a reassuring scratch under the chin. "Thanks for the drink."

The pair slipped into the booth facing her. She couldn't help thinking what odd companions they made for each other.

"Well Mez Kaitan, um ... Mahra, if I may...?" She nodded. "What brings you to the lovely world of New Helvetica? Pleasure is it ... or perhaps, might I venture, profit?" he asked, giving her a smile.

She noted that when he smiled, he turned up one corner of his mouth more than the other, making it a lopsided grin, further accentuated by the large sweeping moustache. He brushed back his hair as he spoke, to further reveal the red line that passed up across the skin of his forehead. It looked like a burn of some sort — perhaps a legacy of some old combat. The music's intensity had died down a little by this stage, no longer pandering to the resorters. Thankfully, it now provided a subtler background to their conversation.

He was certainly a charmer this Timon Pellis, which was more than could be said for his companion. Chutzpah didn't seem impressed though. He still sat tensed upon her shoulder, looking from one face to another.

"I didn't exactly have any plans, per se, Mezzer Pellis," she replied warily. "Just what you might call 'passing through.'"

"Well ... I wouldn't think that pleasure would make you carry a blade either," said Pellis carefully, following the curl of his moustache with thumb and forefinger. "Are you working?"

"Currently I am, what you'd call, between contracts," she replied, wondering where this might be leading. "You're pretty direct, Mezzer Pellis. Why do you want to know? What is your interest, anyway?"

Pellis looked down and toyed with his mug. Sind just sat watching with his eyes magnified many-fold through those thick viewport lenses. After what seemed like an eternity of silence, Pellis looked up, pursed his lips for a moment and answered.

"Experience has shown me that one who wears a weapon of any sort is either in employment necessitating its carriage, or has the skill to use it and might need to use it. Now we've already established that it is not employment. So, I have to make the other assumption. Are you any good with that thing?"

"I manage," answered Mahra, in a measured voice.

"Uh-huh. And would you have any skills in any of the other, uh, shall we call them, manual arts?" he asked, once more smoothing his ample moustache. He fixed her with a calculating look.

"As I said, I manage, Mezzer Pellis."

"Now please. Call me Timon. I'm not exactly one for formality. But, anyway, that is beside the point ... I'm not going to ask you for references ... No, what I mean to say is, have you done any ship work?"

Ah, at last this is starting to get somewhere, she thought.

Pellis continued. "No, excuse the awkwardness of my phrasing. Let me put it this way. Would you be looking for something?"

"I just might be, Mezzer ... uh, Timon. It depends. Yes, sure, I've done my share of shipboard work. I've had a few militaire runs among others. Why, what have you got on offer? I assume you *do* have something on offer."

Pellis was on the verge of answering when the silent Sind, who up to this point had not made a move, gripped him by the shoulder and gestured with an inclination of his head toward the bar. Pellis frowned and looked from Sind to Mahra and back again. Sind raised his eyebrows and again inclined his head in the bar's direction.

"Yes, all right. Excuse me, if you would, for a few moments. We just have to sort a little something out," Pellis said, sighed, and slid across the bench after Sind, then followed him over to the bar.

There was an animated discussion. Sind stood with hands outstretched, palms upward. Pellis alternately pointed with his finger and chopped the air with one hand. Mahra strained, but couldn't hear what passed between them. Finally, the matter seemed to reach resolution. Sind nodded his head twice in quick succession and Pellis clapped him on the back with one hand, and gestured back to the booth with the other. Pellis almost propelled the smaller man toward the table as they moved back to re-joined her. Pellis slid his long body into the booth, and Sind sealed the gap with his more rotund frame.

Once settled, Sind removed his lenses, pulled a kerchief from the pocket of his coveralls, wiped them, mopped his forehead, and replaced the lenses on the bridge of his nose. Returning the kerchief to its place, he fixed her with those too-large eyes. Pellis gave her that disarming smile, yet again revealing his perfect teeth before starting to speak. She imagined him winning the confidence of many with that smile.

"We have to apologise to you, Mahra, but once more my worthy partner here has corrected my impulsive ways. My friend Jayeer here is the restraint in our operation. The voice of caution and good sense. He tempers my head-strong nature with a little logic and a lot of common sense. It is my fault, you see. I tend to rush into things. From time to time to my cost, I must admit. But, enough of that. It is true that we — that is Mezzer Sind and myself — may had something to offer, but first we would like, or at least want to ask you to tell us a little about yourself. Who you are. What you are. You know, simply things like that." The last he said with a grin, obviously to put her at ease.

"Uh-huh," she replied, reaching up to scratch Chutzpah between the ears. "And what do I get in return?"

"Ah, surely, a fair question. For a start, we'll keep that mug full for as long as it might take, and in return we'll also tell you what we might be offering. That is, if it's worth telling. Does that sound fair?"

Mahra looked slowly from one to the other, pressed her lips together, and equally as slowly, nodded. She lifted her mug and took a long swallow to give herself breathing space in which to consider her options. What to tell? What not to tell? Taking a deep breath and licking her lips, she decided to start.

"As I said, I've done my share of militaire. Short hops usually, but there have been one or two long hauls in there. I even ran as a merc for a while. Won't tell you who for. You don't need to know that. Don't like the mercenary game though. Too much political ideology and I'm not too hot on that sort of factionalism. A few years ago now, I did some bodyguard work as well, but that was pretty boring. Basically, consisted of standing round all day looking tough. Left that one because the individual concerned finally ended up making unreasonable demands. Wanted me to do more with his body than just guard it, and quite frankly, I wasn't interested. Since then, well, my last four contracts have involved courier work. You know, sensitive stuff. There are a few others besides that, but that's about it. What more would you like to know?"

At this point the silent Sind decided to make his presence felt. His voice was soft, the words slightly accented in a manner that suggests Andaran origins.

"Your homeworld?" he asked, and she could feel the probe in his voice.

"Unimportant, Mezzer Sind. I'll tell you what you need to know and not a shred more."

"Family?" he fired back.

"No, at least not any more. And I don't want to speak about that either if that's okay with you?" she said pointedly. She took another swallow from her mug, and wiped her mouth with the back of her hand.

"Any legal problems?"

"No, none to speak of."

"Attachments?"

"Two arms, two legs ... a zimonette."

"Attachments?" Sind repeated, stolidly ignoring her reply.

"No, if we don't count Chutz here. He's the only attachment I need." She scratched the underside of his chin to reinforce the point and just to make sure any negative feeling he was getting didn't upset him too much.

"All right then. Skills," Sind asked and sat back with his arms folded across his ample middle.

"Hmm, what would you like? ... Small arms. Hand to hand. Range weapons. Explosives if necessary. Some comp..." Sind snorted and Mahra ignored the sound and continued. "Tracking. Flying if I have to... do you want me to continue?" she asked.

"No, no. I think not," interrupted Pellis before Sind could reply. "I believe you've covered all the information we require, to now. Is that right, Jay?"

"References?" said the smaller man, unwilling to be distracted.

Mahra laughed out loud.

Timon gave an amused snort.

"Right you are," he said. "And I suppose that it is only right and just that we fulfil our part of the agreement. Now ... what can we tell you?"

Pellis paused for a moment, framing his words as he sat back, cupped his hands behind his head, and stretched his legs out beneath the table.

"You see, Mahra, my partner Jayeer and myself we're in, well, a funny range of business. You might say we are in the import-export trade. We ran into a little bit of bother on our last haul, got a little banged-up. As a result of those, um, unfortunate circumstances we're short a member of our crew ... Now it's not only free trade that we're involved in, you see. A bit like yourself in that respect. So, because of our unplanned vacancy, we're looking for a bit of an all-rounder to temporarily fill the hole in our number. Someone to pick up the slack you might say. It sounds as if you've got the range of skills that we need. So, if you're interested in such a role, say so and we can discuss a few more details. If not, we might as well call a stop to the proceedings here and wish each other a very good night. Well ... what do you say?"

"Mm-hm. You have my attention." She tried not to sound too eager. "Please continue."

"All right then." He smiled, looking pleased with himself. "We have ourselves a ship. Our ship. Right now, she is in need of a little repair. We expect to have her back in a serviceable state in about ten days or so. As soon as she is ready, we'll be shipping out. It doesn't matter where at this stage, but it's neither a long haul, nor a short hop. We'll be running silent as is our habit. Generally, we're able to come and go as we please on New Helvetica."

Mahra involuntarily raised her eyebrows. Movement in and out of New Helvetica, as they pleased, and, with their own ship. Things were looking better and better.

"If you're still interested, you can join us on a trial contract basis. We'd pay you twelve hundred creds for the first haul. Subject to a satisfactory conclusion, we'd offer the possibility of a bonus and re-negotiation after that. The contract would be settled here on New Helvetica between ourselves, so, totally, and legitimately free of tax creds. Now, don't get me wrong. You'd be expected to pull your weight on board. We don't carry useless loads or unnecessary weight — if you get my meaning? No obligation on our part at all. If it turned out to be the case and there was a port handy ... well and good. If there wasn't ... no obligation. Is that very clear?"

"Yes, it's clear." She tried to appear as unfazed as possible and ignore the implied threat. "Um — what about equipment?"

"You would bring what you have. We also have a fully stocked armoury on board, so that is not a problem. All ship's property. Your pet ... sorry ... your companion, can bunk with you. Hygiene would be your responsibility though."

"What about a life-box for him? He is not exactly going to fit into a suit, is he?"

"No ... I take your point. We don't have one. Not part of our standard carriage you see. Fair question. I suppose we can buy one," said Pellis, shrugged, then turned and scowled at Sind as he received a kick under the table for his efforts. "There you go again, Jay. Having a go at my generous nature. Well, too bad. I've said it. It stands."

Sind merely humphed in reply and crossed his arms tighter across his chest.

"So, Mez Kaitan. How does it sound so far? Interested?"

"Well ... to be honest ... more than interested, Timon. More than interested. If you want to, you can count me in."

"All right, it's settled then. We can meet together again the day before we depart. Give you time to settle in."

"Um ... Timon, there's just one small matter ... " said Mahra with a little hesitation. "I'm running a little short and...."

"Oh, is that all that's bothering you. Look, I'll give you five up front if that's the case."

For this, Pellis received an elbow in the ribs. Sind shook his head and muttered to himself. Pellis ignored him, and continued speaking. "Give me your cred number and I'll have the transfer done first thing in the morning."

"Look, I really appreciate this, Timon. Have you got a comp to take down the number?"

"No, no. No need for that. Just tell it to Jayeer. I've never known the man to forget a number yet."

Mahra groped around and fished out her card. Painfully she read off the numbering etched into the surface. She tilted it from side to side to catch the light. Sind looked at her as she said it, merely blinked twice, then looked away without saying a word.

"Well then. We're agreed," said Pellis, and flashed her a smile. "Come on, Jay, we have things to do. We'll meet again in a ten-day."

Pellis and Sind slipped from the booth and turned to make their way to the door.

"But where…?" said Mahra as they turned, remembering that nothing had been said about the location.

"Oh yes. I nearly forgot. Dock D9. You'll recognise the ship," said Pellis as he walked toward the exit. Mahra raised her hand in farewell to the retreating backs.

Yes, she thought, *We're in*.

She might like this Timon Pellis. His easy charm and casual manner had won her over almost immediately. She was not so sure about the other one, Sind, but perhaps in time. Pellis was right. Sind certainly lent reserve and restraint to the proceedings — and more than a little. The two had been arguing again all the way to the door. Well, for what it was worth, it looked like she might be in work again. In many ways, it all sounded too good to be true. She could save her enthusiasm though. And if it all worked out in the morning, she'd have a ten-day to spend amusing herself with a cred balance, and not having to worry about whether the next meal might blow her limit.

She settled back into the corner and smiled. She could check if things were all on the level tomorrow. She'd know then if the cred transfer had been made. If it had, then things were going to work out. If it hadn't she'd lost nothing. Simple as that. Just then, she had a thought. This Timon Pellis had seemed pretty relaxed about accepting her say so. No tests, no verification. She wondered, briefly, what was up with that. A little too easy. But then she sat back, shaking her head. It didn't serve to question good fortune too much.

"What was say we play at being tourists Chutz?" she said scratching him under the chin. "Would you like that for a change?"

Chapter Two

Valdor Carr stood staring out across the lights and cold through his own reflected image on the window pane. He really did love this cut and thrust. He smiled to himself. Just as well nobody *else* could see through him in the same way.

He took a large mouthful of brandy, and ran his fingers through long, dark hair highlighted with grey. Valdor Carr was not exactly what people call good looking, but with his high cheek bones, hawkish nose, and dark brooding eyes, he was certainly striking — the sort of man who stands out in a crowded room without really trying. He could fix somebody with that stare without saying a word and make them question, make them doubt. And he used it to good advantage, often.

He stood surveying for a few minutes longer, mulling over the day, as his breath condensed on the glass and gradually fogged his reflection. He had crucified Masterin in the boardroom that afternoon. It had taken the minimum of effort, and he'd taken immense pleasure doing it; undermining the bargaining position and manoeuvring the terms of surrender. He traced his finger over the cool granite sill, playing it over in his head, before taking a final swallow.

The long, black, fur-trimmed coat swirled around him as he spun and strode to the large wooden desk that dominated the room. His desk. His room. It was all his — won by hard work and subterfuge. Valdor had a knack for such things. Life was an arena of thrust and counter-thrust, never letting the guard down; or only enough to make the opponent over-commit. And Valdor was a key player. His current position was neither gained easily, nor rapidly, and he suffered the inevitable losses along the way, but it was a position worth taking the time to savour now. He loved what he did and if it won him few friends, so what? He spent a few more moments musing before taking his seat.

Valdor liked to own, but at the same time he didn't like to be seen owning. Being obvious about such things made you vulnerable. A good deal of the landscape that stretched out beyond his window bore his marks, but invisibly. He acted as a silent partner in a number of organisations, ostensibly allowing others to perform the dealings that are, in truth, his own. Neither did Valdor Carr play politics, at least not openly, but he was a master all the same. His minions are many and varied, and only a scant number knew that he owned them. They might suspect, but in the end, that was good enough.

It was a relatively easy thing to maintain that anonymity. To know that you could control and manipulate the lives of the faceless, and the not-so-faceless masses, and yet have them completely oblivious to it, made it so much sweeter. He hated to think of ever losing it.

Carr Holdings was, on the face of it, a small operation, but, if any had ever mustered the nerve to follow the data trails they would have been in for a rude surprise. There had been a CoCee appointed corporate investigator once, who had done just that, but he developed a severe personal crisis at a crucial juncture. He was forced, unfortunately, to withdrew from his duties. At about the same time, several files and, strangely enough, all their backups had gone missing from CoCee archives. Such untimely coincidences.

Valdor smiled at the memory and trailed his fingers over his desk surface.

There had also been that private investigator hired by a rival company. The man now worked for Valdor, full time. There was always a price. Not necessarily a price measured in monetary terms, but a price all the same. Valdor was well aware of what his own personal price was, all the same; purely and simply it was power. But he didn't really believe there are any with enough of the stuff to tempt him anymore.

He came from a family firmly entrenched in the middle echelons of society, on a moderately well to do, but mainly agricultural world out toward the system rim. The world produced export goods; primarily system-wide exotica like kahveh. Ninety per cent of the system's populace started their day with the infusion and the Kalanian Black Mountains provide a leaf prized for both flavour and strength. The socially acceptable stimulant had become the major basis for virtually the entire world's economy. Kalany also produced other export products, such as the exotic spices suited to grow in the warm and humid climate, but kahveh was the mainstay.

Valdor hated Kalany.

His upbringing was usual enough for someone from that particular social stratum: a good family; a modest, but comfortably appointed home; parents who instilled in him all the good and worthwhile values, as they saw them. And the plantations, stretching out across the foothills — the leaves fading from deep red to burgundy in the wavering summer twilights. And there were two things Valdor really detests in life. One was a sedate rural lifestyle; the other was heat. He visited his family from time to time, but invariably within one or two days, he became so bored, and so uncomfortable, that he had to drag up some excuse about appointments, or work, and leave. Certainly, he felt some attachment for his parents, for all his family, but their world was just so different, so removed from his. Thoughts of

Kalany brought back the memories of years of frustration and yearning; longing to get off world and away to somewhere with at least a touch of action and excitement. It was always hard to return to a place where you spent so much of your youth aching to get away. So, he would be dutiful later; he'd visit his parents in a month or so. There was plenty of time for that.

He placed his glass down on his desk's broad surface. The empty glass would be picked up and cleared away sometime during the night by one of the faceless staff who quietly saw to his needs. Always without fuss, the way he liked it. He hasn't got time to be bothered with trivialities. It was time now to do some serious thinking.

He strode round the desk and settled himself in the large wing-backed chair that sat behind. The chair was an affectation he knew, but it served many purposes. It enforced the subconscious power relationship with any who sat opposite, prompting the symbols of authority and position. Its wings enveloped him when he wished to be alone with his thoughts. Sometimes, after a particularly long session, or even in the middle of one, he could sink back into the padded comfort to doze, but mainly he used it to cut distractions. The wings blocked movements in the periphery of his vision, made by staff, or others, that otherwise dragged at his attention and disrupted his chain of concentration. Right now, he needed to concentrate.

He'd been caught up the last few days in his own machinations and has not had the time to play in the outside world — the real world. Internal power struggles all too often become the focus and they sapped his attention, leaving him out of touch with the movements of things outside, and outside, things always occurred rapidly. Sometimes too rapidly.

He placed his palm on the recessed panel cut into the desktop's black expanse and tapped out the boot sequence with his fingers. The comp was keyed to both his palm and a precise pattern only he knew. Sometimes he thinks that the level of precaution is a little paranoid, but he preferred to be sure. The screen irised into existence above the desk. Lightly, he tapped the end of his middle finger into a faintly edged depression on the desk surface to initiate the update sequence. Colours, graphs, figures, and notes sprang into existence, scrolling rapidly across the screen. His practised eye scanned the sequences, skimming the surface of the information, finger poised, ready to hit pause if anything snagged his attention.

The displays showed the usual assorted details: power bases, shares, holdings, profit and loss, mergers, acquisitions. Nothing really there to excite his interest. He noted that one or two newer projects could do with a little bolstering. Patchy performance here and there. His lack of personal attention over the past few days shows. Things never work as well if you leave them in the hands of subordinates. There was nothing there that really required personal intervention — nothing that couldn't wait. He'd been doing well enough, he thought, but it is all gloss, no real pressure. Perhaps it was time for a little bit of exploration, a little bit of diversification.

He tapped his finger and the rapid information march abruptly halted. He chewed thoughtfully at his thumbnail for a moment letting his gaze wander about the room. Maybe it was time for a visit to the city. He could do with some loosening up. It would be good to spend some time watching the passing parade and breathe a little air and space. From time to time, he forgets himself in the confines of his personal accommodations and loses touch with how it really is outside. First, however, there is something he has left until last on purpose, just to tease himself. He needs to check the progress of his current obsession.

The beauty of this one, for Valdor, is the contradiction it presents. Interworld Logic Systems and Germ Cells Inc. are probably the two most visible corporate giants in the system. Yet he has his finger in both. Every time a board member of either as much as hiccups it is newsworthy. The challenge is to move their plans in the right direction — his direction — without being seen to do so. And there lay the true challenge.

From time to time, he felt the urge to tell someone what he's doing, to confide in someone close, but that urge always passed quickly. Besides, there really isn't anyone close. No one at all. There are none who can satisfactorily fill the role of Valdor's confidant anyway, and there's no point in breaking open such a flawless effort simply for the sake of a little massage to his ego. Perhaps one day, but not now.

ILGC will be the new banner; he has already decided — Interworld Logic and Germ Cells. The new corporation will be huge, spanning several worlds and a diversity of interests and all for one small overlap of product and strategy, the bio-comp. Valdor had a hunch about this one. Biological components and hard comp architecture. He was sure, deep inside, that this is the way, but it needed a little encouragement from the right direction. Both ILS and GCI have made forays into the area in the past but each of their strategic visions is too limited to make real progress. Throw the two together and it has the potential to be a whole new game. Valdor intended to be the architect of that change. Now, he needed to see how it was going.

He hit the key sequence. Pictographs were replaced by words and the words are underscored by figures, all mapping the pathways of his intent.

"Very pretty, Vald' Carr."

"What?" Valdor's breath exploded with the word.

"These figures," continued the heavily accented voice from beyond the screen's scrolling patterns.

"But how did you ... "

Valdor lets the question trail off as he readjusted his perspective to focus beyond and through the holo display, to the voice that issues from beyond it. He stood then.

"Questions are not — is not — important," said the carefully enunciated voice. "We have interest in what you do — here, Vald' Carr. We wish your — attention."

Valdor narrowed his eyes and tapped the sequence to clear down the screen. As the images faded to nothing, his eyes widened again, for there, sitting across from him, was a Sirona. Never mind the failings of his careful security. Never mind allowing himself to be caught so unawares. It was a Sirona. Eyes still wide, he took a slow, deep breath and attempted to regain a little of his composure while his mind raced.

Seeing a Sirona was a rare event at the best of times. To say they had a low profile is an understatement of the highest order. But, here on New Helvetica, in his own inner sanctum, sat a member of the strange race. Quickly he ran his mind over what he knew of them. Not a lot, really. Of course he recognised them from the pictures and the occasional newscast.

The short humanoids make their rare appearances, occasionally popping up in system, in their strangely shaped, silver ships with offers of trade of one form or another. It was usually for goods or objects that make very little sense to those who really think about it, but it's always at just the right time. Nobody really knew where they come from, or for that matter how exactly their ships get them there. Some say that the Sirona have long ago ceased to have a home world and all they did was travel from system to system and trade, fulfilling their own purpose — whatever that might be.

The last report Valdor remembers, was when they showed up a couple of years ago on his own home world, and the political scandal that ensued. At the time, there had been a mysterious blight that afflicted all the rich kahveh crops on Kalany. The research to locate a cure was mammoth, but to no avail. The public and authorities had naturally poured funds into the effort, as the crops were the world's life blood, but the search was fruitless.

And then the Sirona arrived.

Their offer was simple and apparently straightforward in the end. They offered a trade. They would provide a cure for the blight. In return, all they wanted was the contents of the National Kalanian Museum of Art. No negotiations, no deals, just a simple clear-cut trade. That was the way they operated. The ruling council at the time had decided to go with the offer. The economy was under threat. There was no visible reprieve and as far as Valdor was concerned, they took the right decision. There were many now on Kalany who are not so sure. Public outcry was long and loud. There were voluble discussions of moral responsibility and natural rights. Much indignation and several resignations later, the outrage subsided, but the deed was done and there was no going back. In Valdor's view, Kalany was prosperous enough to rebuild an art collection. As far as he's concerned nothing was truly irreplaceable.

The Sirona's large head was tilted slightly to one side, observing. Its fingers are steepled in front of its lips and it appeared almost to be reading his thoughts.

"We have — offer — of trade," it said carefully.

Naturally, thought Valdor.

"You have for us — something. We have something good for you ... perhaps. Yes?" The Sirona moved its head slowly from side to side, but its eyes never left Valdor's face.

Valdor was confused. His thoughts were racing double time, and he tried desperately to focus them. Sure, there were many things he had, many things he had access to, but what was there in among all of it that could possibly interest the Sirona? Added to that, he had no idea what the Sirona might have that could interest him. Slowly, he sank back into his seat.

"Fine, let's just move back a step, shall we?" said Valdor as calmly as he could manage.

"Apology. Your meaning not clear," the Sirona said, tilting its head back and looking ceilingward as it searched for each word.

"Well ... first, you appear to know who I am. So, if we are to deal together, let's establish a couple of points. You're traders, right? You can understand that, the need to put rules in place, a basis for negotiation. So ... who the hell are you, and what precisely do you want here?" Valdor said clearly, leaning forward a little to add emphasis, the last words coming from between closed teeth.

"Ah ... understanding. You call me Tarn. Name is — unimportant. Trade important. We — offer trade."

This was maybe starting to move in a direction that Valdor could begin to understand. He was still confused, but he could feel a hint of his self-composure starting to return.

"Listen Tarn — or whatever you call yourself — what can I possibly have that you can want? Hmm? And for that matter, what could you have that might possibly interest me?" he asked. Better, Valdor thought, to feign ignorance of the multiple possibilities.

"Perhaps there are things that you — would know. Many examples are available?" the Sirona answered.

Valdor had to concentrate carefully on the meaning of what the creature is saying. It placed emphasis in all the wrong places as it spoke.

"Such an — example." the Sirona continued. "A new substance. Recreational. This — just one example. There is much — the Sirona — could offer."

"Well perhaps there is ... um, Tarn. Perhaps there is. So, let's presume for the moment that I might be interested. Let us talk in the hypothetical. Sorry ... let us talk possibilities. What is it you might want from me?"

"So — the matter — in question? You — Vald' Carr — have interest in something that is important for — the Sirona. The two you were watching. They that you — push — together. The ones—on your display," said the Sirona. It kept its unblinking gaze on him as it illustrated by moving outstretched hands together with fingers splayed. "This the Sirona want. This *we* want."

"I'm not quite sure I understand you," said Valdor, furrowing his brow. "Tell me exactly what you mean. Another way perhaps? Different words."

"Yes Vald' Carr. It is — not so hard. The two you — watch. On the holoscreen. They move together. *You* do this. This will happen. The Sirona see this. But the Sirona — want *them*. We want Vald' Carr to — shape — this for the Sirona."

Valdor stared. Slowly he moved his hand up to cover his mouth, to mask some of the reaction he feels, making a show of rubbing his upper lip in thought. The Sirona's large head tilted again to the side, watching him as if assessing the impact of its words. Hidden beneath the shielding hand, Valdor chewed at his lower lip and tried to come to grips with what he has just heard. He narrowed his eyes briefly as he thought, still watching as the Sirona's fingers moved, touching the fingertips of its other hand in seemingly ordered patterns.

Valdor was off balance in a way he has not been for some time. There was too much out of place here, too much already out of his control. For a start, there were only one or two who had any knowledge of his involvement in the ILS-GCI merger, and he believed he could trust *them* to keep their mouths shut. His net was one of the most, if not *the* most secure in the system. It couldn't possibly have been breached. Or could it?

No, there's no way anyone could know about his involvement unless he wanted them to, let alone the Sirona. But and it was obvious, the Sirona had found access to the information by some means. A Sirona sat across from him expressing clear knowledge of his most intimate dealings. Not only that, but it was telling *him* that they are to be controlled by *them*. He realised he had to collect himself, and fast. The pause became longer, until, finally, the Sirona spoke again.

"Vald' Carr. We give you — time to — consider perhaps. Yes? We trust — discretion."

Valdor could do little more than watch as the Sirona clambered down from its chair and stood. Its head barely reached above the desk surface.

"Consider well, Vald' Carr. Few options."

The small trader placed one long finger to the side of its nose and then turned and walked to the door. Its body adopted a rolling gait, wide shoulders above the short legs. As it reached up for the door panel, Valdor stirred himself from immobility.

"Wait a moment."

The Sirona's large head turned as the door panel slid open and it stepped out into the corridor.

"We talk — again." it said over its shoulder.

"Wait — "

The door slid shut.

Valdor sat back and stared at the spot where the small alien trader stood moments before. Finally, he let his hand slip from his face to the desk and he let out a long breath. Gaze fixed, he tapped a slow measured beat with his index finger. After a moment or two, he pressed his eyes shut as if to dispel the image of the now-sealed door and leaned back into the familiar security of his chair.

He wanted a drink. Badly.

Chapter Three

"Milnus? Is that Milnus? No? Well, where the hell is he? Find him and put him on ... Milnus, is that you? Good. Well, we have a problem that's what.... No. Get up here. Now!"

Valdor sat where the Sirona left him, elbows on his desk, chewing at the end of one thumb. He stared at the door waiting for his Head of Security to arrive, trying to decide what tone he should use with the man. Milnus was good — very good — and Valdor had not once been let down by him. Before now that was. No, he would be calm and collected. Give him the good grace he deserved. Men as good as Milnus were few and far between.

Valdor was no longer shaken by what had just happened. Now he was starting to become angry, and he was very, very dangerous when angry. When he became this angry, he ceased to be emotional. He became cold, calculating, and rational, and heads rolled.

The door panel slid open and Valdor lowered his hand to the desk, palm flat on the smooth, dark surface.

"Come in. Close the door behind you. Come and sit down, Milnus," Valdor said, indicating the chair opposite with the forefinger of his other hand, voice showing no trace of the fury that now boiled inside him.

Milnus did as he was told. He was in the same spot as the Sirona had been mere minutes before and Valdor couldn't help replaying the image in his head. He banished the thought with a quick shake of his head and studied the man opposite.

If there was any way to describe Milnus, it would be that he was grey. His closely cropped hair was grey, his eyes were grey, and the sallow flesh stretched taught across the bones of his unremarkable face had an almost grey tinge. He had the sort of face that was so easily forgotten. It was long, thin-lipped but with no real distinguishing feature to mark it out from the hundreds of faces you might see every day. The man was neither good looking nor ugly and he clothed himself the same way, unobtrusively in neutral colours. He really was the archetypal New Helvetian. If there was ever a cause to attract closer scrutiny though, there was one thing that was noticeable — his eyes. They were the colour of steel with about the same amount of warmth. He sat across from Valdor, hands carefully folded in his lap, back straight and eyes blinking once or twice as he waited to hear why Valdor had summoned him.

"All right," Valdor said. "Can you tell me precisely what just happened?"

"I'm not sure I understand the question, Sir," said Milnus. His response was measured with a slight narrowing of his eyes and just the trace of a frown.

Valdor stared across at him. Forcing control into his voice, he explained just as carefully.

"What the question means, is that *we*, meaning you and I, have just had a breach of security ... and *I* want to know why. Forgive me if I'm wrong, but I'm led to understand that security is your responsibility."

Milnus narrowed his eyes still further and pursed his lips before replying.

"Who?" he asked, with a sense of threat pregnant in the solitary word.

"That's what I want to find out, you idiot," spat Valdor losing some of his reserve.

"I'm sorry. Not who ... then how?" Milnus asked, tilting his head back slightly. His nostrils flared, as if already catching the scent of his quarry.

Valdor paused for a moment, assessing, before he answered. Milnus obviously knew nothing of what had just happened, and that was strange in and of itself. The man seemed to have eyes and ears everywhere, in places that sometimes even surprised Valdor himself. Well, if he was going to find out what was going on, Milnus was the one to do it for him.

"*How* is simple. I just had a visitor. A visitor I did *not* invite. I also had no notice of this visit, nor any idea of how it happened. Now, there's only one way I can see for that to occur, and that is if that visitor had some assistance getting in and out of here ... am I right? See to it."

"May I ask, Sir, who this visitor might have been?"

"I thought we were done," said Valdor, then just as quickly reconsidered. "It was a Sirona," he said, and paused for the expected reaction.

The only sign of surprise was a slight flicker of Milnus's grey-white eyebrows.

"I will attend to it Sir," he said, standing. "May I leave now?"

"Yes, yes. Just see to it."

Milnus spun on his heel and left the room, the door panel sliding shut behind him. For a moment Valdor experienced flash of doubt. That slight movement of Milnus's eyebrows could have indicated surprise, but it could also have meant disbelief. It was improbable for a visitor of any sort to waltz in unannounced and unnoticed to one of the most highly secured establishments on New Helvetica. There was one way to be sure.

As a habit, Valdor kept recordings of all the rooms in his urban fortress, especially his own. It allowed him the luxury of replaying meetings at his leisure. He could study people's reactions and the subtle nuances of meaning that those reactions lent to statements and to promises and deals.

This one thing had helped him build an armoury of knowledge about the individuals he dealt with and the way they themselves dealt. It also gave him practice reading people and the unspoken signs they gave. That, in turn, helped him to better control his own, for he could watch himself in action and learn by his mistakes.

His comp was set up to catalogue and scan these digitised images, searching for anomalies by taking random selections of the periods when he was absent. All calls in and out were monitored in the same fashion. It provided him with an extra level of security above what was already the best security force on New Helvetica, and it gave him eyes and ears throughout his domain.

He keyed the comp and set the replay — his office, one hour earlier. He watched as the images formed, saw himself gazing out the window, turning to the desk and accessing the backlog of comp work. Then nothing. The image was blank.

"No, dammit," he hissed between clenched teeth and slapped his palm down. He couldn't have miskeyed.

He replayed the sequence again, starting from the same point. Again, the same series of moves, and again the image faded to nothing. He noticed this time, however, that the indicators at the screen's base remained, marking the time and the location. The blankness continued as the seconds ticked over. Then, just as suddenly as it disappeared, the image coalesced, revealing him sitting at the desk in an otherwise empty room, staring at the door with a dumbfounded expression on his face.

Seeing that look of stupidity on his own face only added insult to injury and he replayed the same section furiously back and forth. The same blank section of recording broke up the continuity of the images over and over. He switched location to the hall outside, but with the same results. The images simply disappeared at precisely the same time.

Now he was angrier still, but worry was beginning to temper his anger. His sanctum had been violated twice, in ways that should just not have been possible. Either the Sirona were very good, or Valdor was losing his senses. Neither option appealed to him very much. For the Sirona to be that good, they would have to have known about the monitoring devices in advance, and that begged yet another question. None of the implications were good.

He set the comp for self-analysis and shut it down. The program would take some time to run and hopefully it would show if there had been any tampering.

Meanwhile, he was going out.

He keyed the com for Milnus.

"Milnus? Yes, listen. I want full scan. Security, comp, personnel, the lot. No, I don't care. Just do it. You know how to reach me if anything turns up. I'm going out." He carried on, speaking over any questions that came from the other end, then flicked the com off in disgust.

Yes, time to go out, but not unprepared. He reached into his desk and pulled out his portable com, clipped it to his belt, then reached down and opened a hidden drawer. Sitting in a moulded foam bed lay a weapon.

It was small, ugly, and very effective, as well as being highly illegal. The squat, slot-nosed gun was designed to project thin, chemical-coated slivers of metal. Because of the projectile's size, each cartridge contained about two hundred shots. The chemicals themselves were fast and efficient, ranging all the way from disablement to rapid and painful death. Although not very effective at long range, it was a perfect defence in close, the burst facility giving a wide and rapid blanket coverage.

Valdor slotted in a cartridge from the selection available in compartments in the drawer, and clipped the sliver to his belt beneath the concealing folds of his cloak. He chose paralysis as the desired option. If he ran into trouble, he wanted to be able to ask why, and a dead assailant would answer nothing.

Checking his appearance in the full-length mirror by the door, he flicked back one long, wayward strand of hair and patted it into place. Moistening his lips, and, giving his reflection a sneer just for the effect, he placed his hand on the wall beside the mirror to summon his private elevator. While he waited, he checked his image. He preferred it this way, having his comings and goings unobserved. Always better to have no visible patterns that others could seize on and use. The mirror moved back and sideways into the wall revealing the starkly lit elevator cubicle. Its walls were mirrored also, and Valdor checked his reflection from each side as he stepped in and made his descent. The elevator slid smoothly to a stop, and Valdor stepped out to the street. He drew his cloak around himself against the chill.

The roadway was slick with evening damp. Street lights and advertising holos reflected in sinuous patterns along the length of the widely spaced avenue. Some of the older stone buildings seemed to sweat their collected moisture as the light from his open elevator doorway caught the sheen of the walls opposite. The evening was reasonably mild for the time of year, yet the chill still caught him, fogging his breath, and giving him reason to pull his cloak even tighter. You could taste the cold in the air.

He stood for a moment as the door slid shut behind him, considering the options. There was only one destination he really had in mind — the night quarters. There amidst the babble of porters and partiers he had contacts and it would be good to see some of them. It would help him perform some investigations of his own at the same time.

New Helvetica of course had its own security network, necessitated by its status and ever-changing population. The first line of that defence, was a set of orbital stations that monitored, checked, and verified all incoming and outgoing traffic. Every single ship was, as a matter of routine, identified and checked. Valdor had his own link into the global system that constantly monitored and updated his records. One could always buy the right access if one had the resources. Certainly, he had been out of touch, but not so out of touch as to miss anything as significant as the arrival of a Sirona ship. Such occurrences just didn't happen every day.

There lay the kernel of what was really troubling him. No Sirona ship meant no Sirona. That stood to reason. He pondered this as he strode through the urban canyons that led to his destination — urban canyons that felt like his real home.

The numbers of people on the streets grew as he approached the nexus of the city's night time activity. There were one or two hustlers about, but apart from these, whom he noted as he passed, there was just the normal but varied crowd. The standard resort set's therm wore abounded, sprinkled with the more uniform colours of the portside workers. As he strolled, he felt not exactly out of place, but at the same time conspicuous. He knew he shouldn't. After all, this was home to him as much as the complex of his various holdings.

He was entering the area of the flesh shops, and lurid displays, lighting every angle and shop front, beckoned potential patrons with their hollow promises. The resorter component of the crowd was thinning out here, the balance of clothing identifying more of the portside workers. It was the latter that this section of the city really catered to. The resorters had their own decadences on tap. There were some tourists, habitual sightseers, mixed in with the navy crowd, many already inebriated and rowdy. He often wondered what sort of hollow mentality could possibly fell prey to the obvious came-ons such as those that lit the storefronts hereabouts.

Valdor strode resolutely forward, eyes fixed ahead of him and ignored the milling masses. Looking like he had something to do and somewhere to go always seemed the best means of avoiding these herd animals. He really had little respect for their type — so easily led. He merely wanted to get through them and reach his destination. He curled his lips with distaste as an unsteady porter stumbled against him and, flipping his cloak about him, pushed past.

The cloak was doubly useful here. It kept prying fingers away from his belt, and in a crowd such as this, there was bound to be a few who might chance their arm.

Suddenly, he found his path closed ahead by four thick-set navy types. One guffawed and belched, bringing Valdor's attention to their faces. Mischief worked in their piggy visages as, hands on hips, they deliberately stepped in his path. He tried his usual tactic of pretending to ignore and side-step them, but to no avail. They in turn stepped sideward in response. They clearly meant trouble.

One, the largest of the beef, nudged one of his companions in the ribs with his elbow. The look on his face said it all, but the man spoke a little too loudly just to make his point clear. Valdor needed no help in understanding their intent.

"Well, what have we here mates? Looked like Mezzer Fancy Troos has come out to play with us," he bellowed, looking from side to side at each of his fellow navy types, a broad grin on his face.

Valdor tried once more to step past the four but with even less success. They moved once more to block him, grins growing wider. Valdor sighed. One hazard of dealing in this section of the city. Slowly he looked from face to grinning red and sweaty face, ran his fingers through his hair, smiled sweetly at them and dropped his hand to his belt. He had already marked the one who had spoken as their leader. So, let them see how the body performed without a head.

With a slight backward arch of his wrist, and without even unclipping the sliver from his belt, he fired, hitting the ringleader and his nearest companion in quick succession. The first clutched at his throat and then dropped. Valdor was already walking forward over the first crumpled form, as the other one started to collapse. He continued without a backward glance, ignoring the cries of outrage and consternation that grew behind him. He could picture the dumbfounded looks and the struggle as one of the remaining two fought to hold his companion back. He suspected he might have curbed their exuberance for this particular shore leave. Stupidity got what it deserved.

The two he had shot would be fine, if feeling a little hung-over and worse for wear in about twelve hours' time. Meanwhile, he had somewhere to be, and he couldn't afford to stand around just for the sake of an insignificant disturbance. Let the militaire sort it out, as long as he wasn't there when they did. Some two blocks further down he ducked into a side street just to make sure.

He traversed the length of a few more streets before heading directly to the area he had been seeking. The unremarkable shop front he wanted lay just back from the main thoroughfare on a side alley. It was marked only by one blinking red holo, curved above the opaque windows and open door. *Marina's* the sign proclaimed, shouting the solitary word with carmine flashes the length of the alley. The doorway was hung with a curtain of cut-glass chime beads that belled with crystalline tones as he ducked inside. The reception area was the same as it had ever been, dim glowing red. A long bench ran the length of one wall and opposite sat three selection booths, fitted with holo units. A narrow staircase disappeared into redness at the area's back. He knew only too well the quarters it climbed to above.

Valdor didn't recognise the girl who sat behind the bench, hands busy plaiting a length of shiny filament into her long dark hair. She wore a plain white body suit ideally accentuating the darkness of her skin and hugging her taut and muscular frame. She barely glanced up as she spoke to him.

"Evening Mezzer. Welcome to Marina's. What's your pleasure, dear?" She waited for a response, and when none was forthcoming, continued. "Whatever it is, I'm sure we can accommodate you. Maybe you would like the use of one of the booths to help you choose. Feel free ... if that's what you want."

Her voice was deep and rich, probably enhanced, but the tone was almost patronising and carried a heavy trace of boredom behind the accent. Valdor decided instantly that he didn't like this one; not his sort of style really. Briefly he wondered what had happened to the regular, Jolie.

"No Mez, that will not be necessary. I would like to see Marina," he said in a crisp business-like manner.

"'Fraid that is not possible, Mezzer. I'm sure that one of our selections will be perfectly adequate," she answered, indicating the booths once more with a lift of her eyebrows and a tilt of her head toward the far wall.

"I'm afraid you don't understand, Mez. I'm here to see Marina," he said.

"No, you the one who don' understand. Marina's jus' the name, Mezzer. You catch it?" she said impatiently, rolling her eyes as if she thought he was stupid.

That was enough to set him over the edge. His patience was limited at the best of times and Valdor was used to getting his own way. He certainly was not accustomed to being treated as if he was a little slow on the uptake. He said his next words oh so quietly and calmly through firmly clenched teeth.

"Now, I think you should pay attention to me, you *idiot* girl. I. Am. Here. To. See. Marina. Now get on your com, the one you keep under there, and tell Marina that Valdor is here to see her. Do you understand? And leave that where it is," he warned her, as she drifted her hand toward the drawer on the right. "The com is there," he said pointing. "Now use it!"

The girl reached reluctantly for the com as she studied him. Her other hand still hovered in the vicinity of the drawer. She spoke in muffled tones, never taking her eyes off him, and waited for the reply. Nodding, she severed the connection, replaced the device, and petulantly told him to wait, indicating a chair at the base of the staircase with her head. He took up position, smug in the small victory, and fixed his eyes on the entrance, oblivious to the occasional sneering looked the girl tossed his way as she returned to plaiting her hair.

He didn't have long to wait. The sound of feet descending the staircase announced Marina's arrival moments later. She swept into the vestibule in a diaphanous rainbow cloak, metal strands shimmering with the wind of her passage. She spun around searching for him and moved quickly over to stand over him, arms crossed over her chest as she looked him up and down.

"Well, well. Valdor Carr, you old reprobate. Finally got around to visiting old friends have we? Stand up and let me look at you. How the hell have you been, lover?"

As usual Marina filled the small space with her presence. She was as tough as stone this one. Valdor was sure that it was one of the reasons he liked her so much. He rose and gave her a kiss on each cheek, then waited as she held him at arm's length and inspected him.

"Well, you're still in one piece at least. Come on. Come upstairs and talk. You can tell me why you've suddenly chosen to visit after so long. I assume there's a reason," she said linking her arm with his and leading him up the stairs. "No calls, Bathena," she said over her shoulder as they mounted the stairs. "I'm in conference."

Marina led him along, hitting him with a barrage of questions as they went. To each he gave only monosyllabic replies. She finally gave up just before they reached the door. Palming the lock, she threw the door open, leading him into her private apartments. Valdor, as usual, was a little overwhelmed with Marina's exuberance. Half of it was performance he knew, but after a long absence it was a little much to bear.

The apartments were sumptuous, furnished in the finest style. The decoration was flawless and balanced, exquisitely tasteful in form and line, furnishings, art, and lighting. Marina obviously did very well out of her small business, both the club and her side-lines. Looking at her, it would be hard to pick her for the woman of style she really was.

"So," she said standing back. She placed her fists on her hips and looked at him, top to toe. "Valdor Carr. It has been a while since you've bothered to grace me with your presence. What, more than six months? Still — before we start — what's your pleasure? Kahveh, or something stronger? Whatever you want, dear." She waved her hand in the direction of the well-stocked bar.

"Kahveh will be fine, Marina. Thanks. How have you been? You're looking well. It looks like business is treating you well too. That is, no worse than usual." He scanned the room as he spoke and saw one or two new pieces that added to her collection and confirmed his assessment.

"No, you're right. Can't complain, Valdor," she said, laughing lightly, as she prepared his drink.

To look at, Marina gave little hint of her underlying sophistication and razor business sense. Bright red hair, heavily made-up and loud extravagant clothes by the top avant-garde designers made her seem unsubtle and brash. Not the sort of person to really feel at home with, let alone to be responsible for furnishing apartments such as these. Valdor knew better. Their association went back some years. At one stage they had been lovers, but that was long past. Marina's shrewdness and underlying complexity had always attracted him. By now though, desire had been replaced by admiration and their friendship had blossomed accordingly.

He smiled inwardly with remembrance of times past as he watched her prepare the drinks. She was right. It had been too long.

She returned with glasses for both, settled herself on the sofa beside him, and after handing him his drink, patted his thigh with her free hand.

"Well, my dear, tell me what's been happening. You only turn up these days if there's something going on," she said, with just a hint of reproach.

"I know, Marina. I'm sorry. Time just sort of gets away without one realising it. You know. But you're right as usual. Damned if you still can't read me like a book. I have a favour to ask you." Not even waiting for her response, he continued. "How are your sources at the moment?"

"As good as ever. You should know that, lover." She waved her hand dismissively and smiled. "This, my dear, intrigues me. What is it you want to know? Your network has been as good as mine for some time now. Hasn't it? So, what's happened ... trouble?" There was genuine concern in her voice.

"No, no. Nothing that bad," he said with a slight shake of his head.

Briefly, he recounted the major details of the Sirona's visit. He said nothing of the problems with the security systems or of the details of the Sirona's offer. Not that he didn't feel that Marina could be trusted. It was just the way he wanted it for now. It should give him time to think and sort out his options, and help arm him with a two-pronged attack. Marina's sources were good, and if he had missed anything, she would be bound to come up with the answers. Armed with the right information, he'd be better equipped to deal with them. Give him two or three days, and with Marina's assistance, he should have this little problem well and truly by the bits that counted.

Chapter Four

The ship's hull was long, sleek, and black. It tapered to a thin swept-down nose, cruel and slightly reminiscent of a bird of prey. Aerodynamic swept fins and wings give it obvious rapid manoeuvrability in atmosphere. All the better to shake that annoying pursuit planetside. The dull black hull was uniform, and unmarked, unlike most other ships at dock.

Mahra stood back and looked at it with her hands on her hips. Impressive ... designed not only for planetary work but virtually invisible against the dark backdrop of deep space. She checked the dock number again. 'D9' — yes, that was it all right. The only marking visible was a pair of red lips discretely painted on the tail section. She laughed despite herself.

"Yeah, you can kiss my tail as well, Pellis," she said out loud.

As if in response to her comment, a mass of dark curls emerged from the open lock. They belonged to none other than the moustached face of the man in question. He beamed in greeting.

"Ah, it is. It is indeed. Mez Kaitan. Mahra. The woman herself. I thought I heard someone out here, so I came to have a look. I can only hope your last comment was an invitation," he said.

He flashed her a disarming grin and she blushed despite herself.

"Well come on," he said, beckoning her closer. "What do you think of her?"

He stood proudly in the open lock and gestured along the ship's length with arms stretched wide.

Mahra sucked in her cheeks and slowly, making a great show of it, deliberately looked from one end to the other with an air of appraisal, pausing once for effect before looking Pellis straight in the face and replying.

"Hmm. Not bad," she said.

"Ha! Not bad, is it? She's beautiful. And you know it. Humph. I almost have a mind not to introduce you after a crack like that. Ah, but that would be impolite, wouldn't it? So, let's see ... Mahra Kaitan, allow me to present *The Dark Falcon,* love of my life and glory of my days."

The Dark Falcon. The suitability of the name struck her at once. It had to be Pellis's name for the ship. She doubted it could have come from anyone else. Certainly not the taciturn Sind unless she had severely misjudged him on the first meeting.

Chutzpah also gave the ship the once over from his perch on her shoulder. He chattered softly to himself as his tail flicked up and down with disapproval. He wasn't fond of shipboard travel at the best of times, and she could feel the discomfort beginning to radiate from him. She reached up to give him a placating stroke.

"Well, I guess she'll do in a pinch," she said, smiling. "Whose is the artwork Timon — yours, I presume?"

"Now, why would you think that? Not at all — I inherited her just as you see her now, from an aged religious man who rode in her solely at High Festival. Once a year for planetary pleasure jaunts you understand," he said with a mischievous grin, hands firmly planted on his hips. "Save me, I swear it on my eyes. But enough of that. Plenty enough chatter. We could stand here all day swapping pleasantries. Wouldn't you prefer to come aboard? I think you've probably seen enough of her exterior."

Mahra answered his infectious grin and moved over
to take the hand proffered to help her climb aboard. Pellis's
grip was firm and his hand pleasantly warm. He helped to
lift her the final distance with minimal effort and she pulled
up, finding herself standing only a whisper away from his
face, her hand still firmly held in his. There was an
awkward pause that lasted a moment too long as they stood,
face to face in the shadow of the lock. Mahra felt something
stir within her.

It was Chutzpah who broke the moment, hissing at
Pellis with sharp incisors barred and ears flat back against
his furry head. Timon promptly dropped Mahra's hand and
stepped back a pace. Chutzpah continued hissing at him
from her shoulder, obviously not satisfied that he was
making his point. Timon simply stood, keeping his distance,
and looked from the bristling zimonette's face to Mahra's
and back again with a slightly quizzical smile.

"Come on Chutz. That is enough! You'll have to
excuse him, Timon. He doesn't like being shipboard that
much at the best of times, and he gets a bit territorial when
he's nervous."

"No, no. Don't you give it another thought, Mahra. No
harm done. After all, it's only his way of protecting what's
his. Sure, he'll get used to it all soon enough. Now, you
follow me and I'll show you the rest of *The Dark Falcon*,"

He tilted his head in the direction of the inner
passageway.

"She was a bit banged up after our last excursion, but
here she is now, almost as good as new," he said.

Pellis patted the inner wall affectionately and,
ducking through the inner access port, led the way to the
interior. Mahra listened with half an ear to Timon's running
commentary as she followed him down the inner corridor.

As Pellis led her on the guided tour, she found to her
surprise that *The Dark Falcon's* internals were functional
without being cramped. There was a central passageway
running the length of the craft, large enough to

accommodate Pellis's tall frame, without wasting any of the available space. Doorways ran the length, alternating up and down each side. This was clearly a dictate of practicality. Better to step out of a doorway without the risk of colliding with someone emerging from a door directly opposite. There was no real indication of the function of the rooms lying behind them, but Mahra presumed she'd became more familiar with the layout in time. Pellis chatted on as he led her on his tour.

Her quarters would be closest to the lock, first in the line of fire in the event of trouble. That figured. Sind and Pellis were quartered toward the front with easy access to the bridge. It all made perfect sense. Each living quarters sported its own sanitary amenities, a luxury rarely found on a ship this size. There were communal facilities, showers, and sanitary units toward the rear but she doubted they really served any useful purpose. The ship had been remodelled at some stage and these remained as an oversight of that process. The armoury was opposite her own quarters, again, obviously with easy access in mind.

The spare cabin and her own were separated from the front by a fully stocked and convenienced galley and rec room. It was plain that very little expense had been spared in the fitting of *The Dark Falcon* and Mahra was suitably impressed by what she saw. Her appreciative noises only served to fuel Pellis's enthusiasm as he guided her from section to section.

Access to both the drive rooms and the cargo hold was via the passageway's rear. Timon skirted over the details of the propulsion units, that particular area obviously being outside his expertise. He skimmed over the more technical aspects wherever possible, but did so without losing too many of the details to leave her groping for function and purpose. It was at least enough to get her started.

Roughly an hour since her entrance and two areas of the ship remained unseen. Pellis looked her square in the face with an appraising eye before speaking again.

"Yes, I think you'll do, you know. Well, we've neglected a couple of important things. I'll give you a choice. Either we break now and replenish our energy with a fine mug of kahveh — finest in the system even if I do say so myself — or we can continue. The decision is yours."

"Thanks, Timon, but I'd prefer to see all of her. We can take a break afterward, before I get settled in."

"Right you are," he said with a tilt of his head. "You had best follow me then."

He beckoned for her to follow up the passageway, coming to a halt at a series of steps moulded into the side wall toward the front. They led upward to a small portal set into the round ceiling, just wide enough for one person to squeeze through.

"Up there. Battle pod. You can get the feel of it a little later. No trouble about the facilities. She's state of the art. Holo links to all external sensory input. Totally shielded. Scares the hell out of me it does. But that one's your baby. You've probably not had the opportunity to see its like, but Jay assures me there's nothing to it. I'll take his word for that. If you have any questions about it, you can get him to tell you what you need to know. All right? Now come on with me and we'll show you the heart of this baby."

He led the way forward to where the passageway swept upward in a reasonably steep curve ending in a smooth doorway with a bank of controls at one side. This was the entrance to the flight deck, the ship's nerve centre. Pellis tapped a sequence on the panel and the door slid open to reveal a cubicle large enough to hold four people standing in comfort. One wall had a set of storage lockers, the opposite wall was featureless apart from another bank of controls and a com unit built into the surface. Pellis tapped a sequence too fast for Mahra to follow and the outer door hissed shut behind them.

She realised at once that the cubicle was, in reality, another lock. It was a funny place to have one. She decided to hold her questions until she was a little more aware of the set up. Her unspoken queries were brought to an abrupt halt as the inner door slid open to the control room beyond.

The flight deck, like the remainder of the ship, was well appointed. Ensconced in the middle sat the squat form of Jayeer Sind surrounded by a series of colourful holos. He muttered to himself as he looked from one to the other, totally absorbed in the reeling figures and schematics. All around, view screens dominated the walls, showing the tiers of ships surrounding them in the dock. Echoes of the smaller displays scrolled across the view, superimposed on the images of the outside world. Timon strode over to the central couch and glanced at the displays before clearing his throat. Sind's gaze flickered up briefly then returned to the figures flowing past him. Timon cleared his throat again, then shook his head.

"Jay, my friend, we have us a visitor. Could you drag your attention away from your infernal readings for a moment or two?"

Sind's gaze flicked back up to Pellis's face then over his shoulder to Mahra, a frown etched above his thick lenses. He gave a humph of acknowledgement before turning back to stare at the flickering holos.

"Is that it? Surely you can muster a little more civility than that, my friend," Pellis said.

"Look Timon, some of us have work to do," muttered Sind. "If you can leave me in peace, I can get this done and that will be an end to it. If, however, you choose to keep on interrupting, it will never get finished. I will talk to you when I'm through here."

"Uh-huh," Pellis answered with a resigned tone. "Come on, Mahra. Let's leave him to it. He's hopeless when he's in this frame of mind. Come and I'll make you that kahveh."

Sind ignored them as they made their way from the flight deck and the door hissed to a seal behind them.

"You'll have to forgive him, Mahra. He's a bit precious about his beloved systems. We've just had a refit of sorts and he wanted to be sure everything was functioning to his satisfaction. He never trusts a dock crew — ever. Not that I blame him. So, let's go and see what we can do about that kahveh."

He led her from the lock, down and along to the galley and rec room.

Mahra was beginning to feel more and more at ease with Pellis. She appreciated his easy-going attitude and attendant wit. Perhaps, she thought, the casual demeanour could begin to grate after a while, but to be fair, she had only really seen one aspect of the man. If the circumstances had been any different, she might be tempted. He was attractive in an odd sort of way, but in the current circumstances, she had to put that thought to one side.

The ship was fitted to a comfort level that would make this sign-on more than tolerable. If things didn't work out, she'd at least end up with a few creds to spare and she'd have earned them without too much effort or discomfort. She was a bit concerned about the potential for trouble between Pellis and herself though. The incident in the lock was enough to set alarm bells ringing, albeit small ones, and she really didn't want to find herself in the enclosed space of a ship this size with any potential for awkward circumstances. She simply didn't want to complicate things. She'd just have to be careful and see how it worked out.

Chutzpah's tension didn't do much to allay that feeling of caution. He always radiated his moods and sometimes it was a little difficult to distinguish between what were natural feelings within herself, and those that arose from her empathy with Chutzpah. Perhaps it wasn't always so much of an advantage being so close to him.

Pellis busied himself making the promised kahveh as she seated herself and let her gaze wander across the comfortable facilities. Chutzpah clambered down from her shoulder and skittered off to explore on his own. She wasn't concerned about his little foray. He wouldn't stray too far, and he was clever enough not to get himself into trouble, especially on board ship.

Pellis completed his preparations and placed a steaming mug in front of her, before sitting opposite, hands cupped around his kahveh. He blew on the contents before taking a tentative sip. Mahra lifted her own and took a swallow herself, nearly gagging as the acrid brew struck her palate. It was a few moments before her coughing subsided enough to allow her to speak.

"Fire, but that's strong!"

"Aye, sorry, perhaps I should have given you warning." Pellis grinned over the rim of his mug. "We like things with a bit of taste aboard the old *Falcon*."

"Well, I guess I'll get used to it."

There was an awkward silence as they each sipped at their drinks. The taste was not so bad once she became accustomed to it and anyway, as she had said, she'd probably get used to it.

"So, tell me, Timon, how long have you had *The Dark Falcon*?"

"Hmm, I suppose it would be nigh on a ten year now. She is the same ship I started with, and she's had a few modifications since I, um, acquired her. Seen a few scrapes too, she has. Still, long enough," he replied, his eyes focused somewhere in the middle distance. "We've seen us a few sights in our time."

"Well from what I've seen, she is a fine ship, Mezzer Pellis."

"That she is." He smiled with obvious pleasure.

"So how did you get into this game?" she asked, genuinely interested, and hoping to flesh out the picture of the man.

"Ah now, that's a bit of a long story. You see originally — when I was growing up — "

He was interrupted by a cough from the doorway. Mahra turned just in time to see a frowning Sind looking sternly in Pellis's direction, shaking his head. Pellis merely shrugged, but the intrusion seemed to have had the desired effect.

Sind passed a hand across his forehead, shook his head again and walked past the table to pour himself a mug of freshly brewed kahveh. In passing, he shot a glance through narrowed eyes at Pellis, who lowered his own gaze and started examining the backs of his hands where they lay on the smooth table surface. She didn't know whether Sind thought she was stupid or whether he just didn't care that she saw his signals.

Sind poured himself a mug and carried it over before plumping himself down on the chair between the two of them.

Peering through his thick lenses, he gave Mahra an appraising looked that started at the top of her head and worked its way slowly down her neck and arms, to her hands cupping her own mug in front of her. She matched the stare and managed to force herself to smile in response. No use in getting off on the wrong foot, if it wasn't already too late. Sind snorted quietly to himself, pushed the lenses up his nose, and turned to Pellis.

"They seem to have got it right this time, would you believe? Small wonders will never cease. Haven't checked the pod yet. No doubt there's bound to be something there."

"Hmm. There's quite a share of new kit there. It would pay to give it a thorough going over," Pellis replied thoughtfully.

"As if I was not going to," Sind snapped back.

"Now, did I suggest that you wouldn't?" Pellis smiled at him, Sind's testiness rolling past him as if it didn't exist. "And there you go again, ignoring the virtues of cultured intercourse, my friend. Shouldn't you be welcoming our new companion aboard?" The smile never left his face.

Sind glanced in Mahra's direction, snorted, and turned his attention back to his kahveh.

"Mezzer Sind," Mahra said, deciding she had to be the one to initiate interaction with the surly little man, "I'd be interested to see the battle pod's workings, if you're going there to do some tests. It wouldn't hurt to start becoming familiar with its operations. So, if you don't mind if I accompany you when you go — "

"Look ... Mez Kaitan ... " he said, then moderated his tone to one of mere condescension. "You're here on trial only. And I might add, against my better judgement. No one will be going anywhere near that pod until it has been fully checked. I do *not* want anyone, and that includes you, blowing a hole in the docks because they don't know what they're doing. You, for one, will not set foot near it until I say so. And the same applies to *anything* on the flight deck. Understood?"

Mahra swallowed. She obviously had some work to do.

At that moment, Chutzpah, who had become bored with his explorations for the time being, chose to make his return and leapt up on to the table right in front of Sind. Sind flinched backward with a start, upsetting his steaming kahveh in the process. The scalding liquid slopped over the table edge and right into his lap. He leapt up with a cry of pain, his hands patting furiously at his coverall legs. Chutzpah, startled by his sudden action and the noise of his cry, immediately leapt into attack mode, and, tail bristling, jumped straight for the small man, spitting, and hissing.

"No Chutz!" cried Mahra, realising what was about to happen.

Sind gave a shriek of horror as he looked up to see the furry projectile contact his chest, giving him a closeup of sharp-toothed, spitting malevolence. Chutzpah, reined in by Mahra's command just in time, bounced off Sind's chest, and in one hop jumped from the table to Mahra's shoulder, curled his tail about her neck and sat peering around the edge of her face, fur still bristling.

"Fire!" yelled Sind. "And keep that damned creature away from me as well." He spat the words at her, turned and stormed from the room.

Pellis, who had been sitting wide-eyed biting his lip, exploded in laughter. Chutzpah merely sat on Mahra's shoulder as if nothing had happened, shaking one paw to rid it of the spilled kahveh, then proceeded to lick it clean. It was some time before Pellis regained his composure, and wiping a tear from his eye, could speak again.

"Oh, poor Jayeer. He seemed a little upset."

"Oh, Fire!" said Mahra. "I hope he had — "

Pellis shook his head and smoothed his moustache, still chuckling.

"Don't you worry about Jayeer. He isn't what you'd call the cheeriest of fellows at the best of times. That was not what I'd refer to as the best of starts though." He chuckled again. "Oh, the look on his face! Look, he's not the happiest of fellows, but he's good. Damned good he is. You'll just have to tread a little carefully over the next few days. He'll come around. If you're good at what you do, he'll respect you for it. That's all you need to know…."

His voice trailed off. He was obviously thinking about something. "Anyway, I have a few things to attend to myself. You remember where your quarters are? Right. I'll leave you and your little grey friend there to get yourselves settled in. I'll look in on you a little later to see how you're getting on. Meanwhile, I'll see if I can't smooth things over with Jayeer."

He drained the last of his mug, and with one last chuckle, headed for the door.

"Again, welcome aboard, Mahra Kaitan," he said, as he paused in the doorway, then stepped out into the corridor.

Chapter Five

The Cradle

Mahra stood, hands on hips, legs slightly apart, staring across the rolling foothills to where the peaks, ice-toothed, clawed at the pale sky. Her breath fogged in the chill afternoon air and her eyes stung with the wind. She told herself that it was the wind that brought the tears close to spilling over. She knew it was the Old One's time. She knew it, and yet she had promised herself she would not weep. Strength was important as she'd been taught, and she would not show weakness. Not now. Especially not now.

She looked across to the large, bronze coloured bowl set into the pale-grassed hillside. Within it, burning steadily, the Flame of Life. The rising heat distorted the jagged symmetry of the mountains behind. She could smell the fragrant flames, even from here, touched with the hint of herbs, and something else, something sharper.

Fourteen years. Fourteen revolutions of the world about the sun and this was her first time — her first experience of a passing. She wished it was someone more removed so she might at least be able to distance herself. She took several slow, deep breaths and tried to compose herself, to hold off the threatening tears. If they came, she knew she would not be able to stop them. She would have to go and see him soon and she had to be ready. She mustn't let him see. To go and sit with him. To talk for the final time. To feel the frailness of his palm against her brow. Carefully, she evened the pace of her breathing and sought the still place within her. After a moment, she felt the relaxation seep into her body and her mind. Now. Now, she was ready.

She touched the fingers of her right hand to her forehead then lips. She moved her hands cupped, outstretched toward the Flame of Life in the traditional gesture of respect, then turned and moved back down the slope toward the rude dwelling that served as home for both of them. She wrapped her arms about herself and bowed her head slightly as her bare feet padded through the yellowing grass. She kept her eyes fixed upon her feet and the blades springing up beside them as if by doing so she could avoid the inevitability she knew was to come.

Mahra's eyes took a few moments to adjust as she entered the gloom of the darkened dwelling. She stood waiting as the familiar sparseness took definition, then stepped, almost reluctantly, toward the Old One's doorway.

He was already old when Mahra was assigned to him; but his frail form belied the strength and power beneath. Others went through tutelage with him before her — several others — and she knew from his reputation when she first went to him that he would be wise in the ways of teaching. Others had told her, and she had assumed that they were true. Her assumptions had been right, back then. Now, after the years spent together, it was time to move away from him, to break the bonds of dependence and establish her own self-sufficient life. She just wished that it could happen another way. It was too soon, and she didn't want it this way. Taking a breath and biting her lower lip, she entered his room.

The Old One lay on the narrow bed with his head propped up on thin cushions, just enough to raise his line of sight. His thin frame jutted with angles through the translucency of pale skin making him seemed roughly hewn from pale stone or shell. There was no movement, and for a moment Mahra's heart caught, a deep cold chasm opening in the pit of her stomach. No, it could not be; she had waited too long. She started to feel waves of despair sweep down on her but then she sensed something. His eyelids flickered, trembling, then slowly, slowly they rose. After a moment's pause, his ice-blue eyes, slightly clouded now, tracked wearily across the room to where she stood, framed in the doorway. His chest rose with a long hesitant breath, faltering as he held it for the briefest instant before speaking.

"Come. Come closer, my child. I have waited for you. Almost too long I fear," His voice carried only traces of the strength she had known.

She moved up to the bedside with dragging steps, her head slightly bowed. But why should it be so? How could she be reluctant to meet his eyes? Instead, she fixed her attention on the too-pale flesh of the hand that lay outstretched on the covers. She could map the tracery of his veins and the sharp definition of bone and sinew beneath the skin. She watched their interplay as a slight tremor ran through the fingers, giving the lie to their marble look. He had always been thin, but he was even thinner now, as if his body has consumed its own flesh over these past few weeks, making him disappear from the inside. There were hollows around more than just the sunken cheeks and eyes. It hurt her to see him like this.

"Look at me, child. Do not avoid me. Look me in the face, at my eyes. I'm still the same person. Lift your head, girl," he said quietly, in almost a whisper. Traces of the old authority were still there, but tired, so tired.

Reluctantly Mahra raised her head, looking slowly up across his robe to the familiar yet unfamiliar face. His eyes watched beneath hooded lids within his hawk-like face, and they seemed even more accentuated by the wasting. Deep hollows marked the sharpness of his bones and made the face looked harder, sterner. They were the same eyes that have watched her over the years. Watched her play and watched her grow, but somehow no, they were truly different.

As she watched, his eyelids drifted shut again and his laboured breathing caught, hesitated, then started. For a moment, she thought he might have drifted into sleep, but then his eyes fluttered open, and he drew in a sharp breath, nostrils flaring, then exhaled with a shudder.

"My time is close, Mahra. It is very close. When it comes, do not have fear. Do not mourn, for there are things you have to do. I am only sad that it has come so soon — sooner than I had hoped. I wanted to be sure that you had already left to make your own path, but it is not to be. Soon you will be on your own. I have no fear for you in that regard. You are capable, an able student, but you should be careful. You are still young, and there are things afoot that you could not possibly imagine." There was a pause then. "Ah, Mahra, I only wish I could have been here to see you through these times to come." He sighed and coughed, then slowly shook his head.

She didn't really understand all he was telling her. She wanted to ask him to explain but couldn't. Too much emotion threatened to well up inside her. Hesitantly, she reached forward to touch his hand lying on the covers before her. She stroked the cool flesh, biting her lip, and trying to control the feelings that worked inside her. She didn't know what to say. She didn't know what to do. There were so many things she wanted to tell him, to ask him, to demand of him.

As she stood in confusion, he suddenly returned her touch, catching her hand in his and squeezing it as if to reassure.

"You know I love you, Mahra. Always know that. Though I should not say so, you above all others .... I have been hard with you at times, but that has always been to make you strong. It was for you, not against you — to help you grow. Forgive me that. You are special, child. You are strong. But are you strong enough? That I don't know." He paused before continuing. "You will need all of that strength and more in the times to come. For a time, you should stay here, succeed me in the work, take my place. But then ... ah, who can say what will come? Until then, you will know what you have to do ..."

His voice faded as he appeared to ponder what was ahead, then his attention wandered back, and he fixed her with his gaze.

"In the chest at the foot of the bed there, you will find some things. You will need them. Also, there, for you, a gift. Take it and use it well, Mahra. Think of me when you do."

She moved toward the chest, but he gripped her hand more strongly, holding her in her place.

"No, not now ... after ... the time. I only hope I have shown you enough." He frowned and gave a slight shake of his head. "The time is too short. Would that there were more. Enough to tell you all the things you need to know, for I fear you will know them whether I tell them or not. I'm too tired. I can do no more." He went quiet for a few moments, then spoke in a low voice. "Leave me now, child. Let me rest awhile."

"I love you, old man," Mahra murmured, feeling a patch of warm moisture trailing down her cheek.

"I love you too, child," he replies softly. "Now go."

She bowed her head in the gesture of respect and turned to make her way to the door. She barely heard the words he says.

"Farewell, Mahra my child, and may you go well."

Conceding to his wishes, she left the house. She walked out with heavy steps to the gentle, grass-covered hills rising away from the rear of their dwelling. Finding a spot at the top of a rise, she sat cross-legged, facing the mountains beyond. Deliberately, she placed herself with her back facing the place where she and the Old One had lived. She sat for several minutes, battling with herself until she could bear it no more and she gave way to the emotions welling within. The tears coursed down her face in silence, rolling one after the other to fall in the grass before her, as she gently rocked back and forth. For each of those tears, there was a memory.

After a time, she could weep no more. She stared off into the distance, focusing on nothing, face stained and eyes reddened, oblivious to the wind that whipped the strands of hair about her head.

Suddenly, she felt a deep wrench and she gasped. The pressure rose and something, something pulled with a feeling like thin strands were being torn from her mind. The threads wove and unwove, pulling more and more, feeling as if something was wresting at the very substance of her brain. The wind suspended the hair about her face, echoing the feeling in her mind. The pressure intensified then eased, then pulled afresh, stronger now, then weaker. It worked deeply at the fibres of her being. She threw back her head and tried to bring the strangeness under control. Her breath came in short gasps and her throat started to feel as if it was being constricted. Once more the sensation intensified and grew tighter, more tense, as if invisible strands were being stretched to their limit. Desperately, she sought the still place, reaching for calm, struggling against the pressure.

Then, abruptly, there was nothing. It was as if the strands had ripped free. Mahra felt a great emptiness wash down upon her. She seemed to hear the Old One's voice, far away.

"Farewell, Mahra my child. Fare you well."

She knew then with certainty what had happened, and a deep sense of loss flooded through her. The Old One was gone. For the first time in her young life, Mahra was truly and completely alone.

She realised then, that she was unaware of the complexity and level of the bond between herself and the old man. The intricate mapping of their brains and their continued proximity, day after day had forged something far more than a mere relationship. Suddenly, the loss ached within her anew. She stumbled to her feet, turning around and around, searching with blank eyes for something to fill that hollow within. There was nothing to be found —

nothing to make her whole again. What she had discovered, was already gone.

□

For the rest of the day and some of the night, she wandered aimlessly. She did not see where she walked, nor did she care. It was not until the early hours of the morning that she retraced her steps and found herself back at their dwelling. No, no longer the place they shared — no longer their dwelling; now it was hers alone.

She staggered inside and, brushing against walls, dragged herself numbly into the Old One's room. She swayed slightly, listening to the silence, and watching the motionless form that lay upon the bed. After a time of standing there, she moved to the side and slipping to her knees, rested her head beside him. She watched his immobile face for a time, unmoving, and then, tentatively, reached up and traced the coldness of his skin. There were no more tears. There was nothing more to do. Eventually, she drifted into sleep, oblivious to the discomfort of how she sat, or the body that lay beside her.

Mahra ached when she finally awoke. There was pain in her legs and in her neck. For a moment, she was confused, but then the realisation of where she was and how she came to be there found her, and the grief and the emptiness washed over her anew. Again, she wept, looking at the familiar yet unfamiliar face. She could see he was no longer there, that he was gone, but more importantly she could feel it. It was as if there are vast spaces inside her, empty and bare of life. Wiping her eyes and trying to marshal some self-control, she pushed herself to her feet and leaning forward, pressed her lips to his forehead.

She knew what she had to do now. The traditions were there for her to follow and the Old One had taught her well. She could call for assistance, but these last remaining things that she could do for him, she would do, alone. She would be his final witness; Mahra alone would put him to his final rest.

It took her the remainder of the day to do what was required. She was strong and fit, but it took all her energy and determination to move the body, to transport it to the hills and to lay him to rest in the specially prepared barrow within the hillside. He came into the world with nothing, and he would leave in the same way, clad only in his simple homespun robe. She placed him there with care and respect, having struggled to move him into place, and she murmured apologies for the rough handling necessitated by her lack of strength. It was only his empty shell, she knew, but his memory demanded her respect. This was her farewell to the one who had shaped what she was.

All that night she remained on the hillside and maintained vigil. Only with the first touch of dawn's light did she allow herself to sleep.

☐

The chest at the end of his bed, her bed now, awaited when she returned. Mahra didn't know what was inside, and she was afraid she didn't really want to know. She forced her fears away and hesitantly, with some trepidation, pushed back the lid to investigate the contents. There was his comp of course. She'd use it soon to inform the rest of The Cradle of the Old One's passing. There was time enough for that later. There was also a sheaf of notes, mainly written to himself. Flicking through them, she noted the occasional reference to herself, comments on her progress, about the stages of her training and other things of less significance — all in that familiar spidery hand. She only skimmed them. Although she was curious, she was reluctant to delve into what must have been his private observations and thoughts.

Samples of various plants and fungi sat in the bottom beneath the notes in clear bags with annotated tags and she pushed them aside. In the midst of the pile lay a plain, cloth-wrapped bundle. Gingerly she lifted it clear. It was heavier than she expected, and she lay it carefully on the bed, not wanting to drop it lest there was something fragile inside, though by its weight she doubted it. She stared at it for some moments trying to determine what it might contain. She shook her head and, pressing her lips tightly together, leaned forward to unwrap it.

Fold by fold, the cloth came away like the petals of a flower opening to its heart. The fine cloth was smooth, unlike any of the homespun materials she was familiar with. Inside, finally revealed, lay a bundle of leather straps. Mahra frowned slightly, confused, not knowing what it was before her. What use could the Old One possibly have seen for her in this?

One by one, she unravelled the straps to reveal what lay nestled in the protective web. Inside the hide cocoon was a finely tooled leather sheath, holding within it a blade — and what a blade. The handle was worked to a design subtly matching the contours of the hand. The mouldings were a little large for her still young fingers and palm, but she gripped it as best she could and slid the weapon free. The metal blade itself, if indeed it was metal, was like none she'd ever seen. It trapped the light, matte black and without shine.

This had to have been the Old One's personal blade, his mark of attainment, yet she had never seen him use any but her own during training. He had had the skills, but this — she could sense it was special.

Drawing out the gesture, deep in symbolism, she touched the flat blade to her forehead and mouthed silent thanks for so precious a gift. She'd keep it bound and wrapped to protect it from sight and only bring it out for practice sessions until she became accustomed to its weight and feel. Only then would she wear it, and she'd wear it with pride.

With this thought, she returned the dull black length to its sheath, wound the straps about it as she had found it, then carefully folded the cloth, corner by corner, forming a neat package. Tomorrow she'd return to the hills to the Old One and leave her own blade there beside him. A gift for a gift as was proper. She'd take one of the spares as her own until she was worthy of the new one.

Mahra reached into the chest and retrieved the comp. Now she had other duties to perform. She had to inform the other residents of what had transpired. There would be mourning, but she knew, as was proper, it would be mourning in silence. She keyed the sequence to access the network and invoked the bulletin area. There was nothing new there, nothing she had not seen. Taking care to enter the key strokes correctly she tapped out the message.

Marisian has passed. Mahra Kaitan takes his place. End.

The brief note would gradually filter through the rest of the community as individuals accessed their comps, one by one. They would note the passing and then move on with their lives. There was nothing special to be found in death.

Chapter Six

Mahra smiled to herself as she walked toward the battle pod. Who would have thought it? Here she was, surrounded by tech and for once actually enjoying it. Her early anti-tech training on The Cradle will have steered her right away from it. Aleyin would have been proud.

Chutzpah loved the battle pod and chattered excitedly as she headed up the corridor. Mahra was not quite sure what the attraction was. She supposed it was a combination of flashing displays and the feeling of boundlessness the pod provided. His natural habitat was, after all, one of open spaces.

She had taken to using the pod whenever she found the opportunity, and not merely as a courtesy to her small companion. It gave her much needed practice and also kept her out of Sind's way, for, despite Timon Pellis's assurances, the little man's demeanour had not improved. Whenever they ran into each other, something hard to avoid on a ship this size, his manner was unremittingly surly. He might be good at what he did, but as far as she was concerned, that didn't give him the right to treat her like a piece of hull scraping. Life in the cramped quarters on board a ship the size of *The Dark Falcon* was hard enough. So, she had found her own solution to the problem and taken to avoiding him wherever possible.

After one or another of their scattered encounters, she had tried to analyse the hostility. Sind and Pellis had been together for a few years now; that much as clear. She supposed she was merely an intrusion for Sind. Mahra was merely a short-hop sign on — a mercenary who suited their needs at the time. In that way, she supposed she could understand his lack of time for her.

Pellis himself had been charming throughout the few weeks she had been aboard *The Dark Falcon*, playful advances aside. She could think of worse places to be. She pulled her weight aboard ship, and he gave her recognition for that. True, all their engagements until now had been relatively trouble free and there hadn't been the opportunity for Pellis to see her full range of skills. But with some of their scheduled ports, she was sure it wouldn't be long before such a chance arose.

They were en route now, to one of the less reputable ports in the system, and she had a gut feeling that this one was not going to be an afternoon stroll. Up until now, she hadn't bothered to ask what they were carrying. To be honest, she really didn't want to know. Safer that way. Neither had the information been volunteered. It made her feel a little bit like excess baggage, but she could understand. Business was business. These two were partners, and she was a mere hired hand with no real need to know.

Regardless of all that, it was time for a spot of practice. She well understood the need of practice to hone her skills. Her years with the blade had taught her that much. Mahra pushed her hair back, gathering it behind with one hand, before donning the head set. She always had to go through this routine. The headset was designed with short-cropped navy types in mind and her long hair only got in the way.

Making sure the headset was sitting comfortably, she slipped each hand into a sensor-fitted glove. She clenched both fists to activate the mechanism and was immediately swept away by the sheer majesty of the spectacle that invaded her senses. No matter how many times she used the pod, she still felt that initial rush. The headset fed her images, sensations, and sounds, giving her the illusion that she was the centre of the ship itself, or rather that she was the ship winging through the darkened reaches. The pod ceased to exist, and she was left suspended in the blackness, surrounded only by the light of stars peppering the void. The display was so real that it needed to have safety mechanisms built into it. The light intensity was moderated according to her proximity to any body — it took account of the varying brightness in case she should suffer retinal damage.

If she concentrated, she could feel the seat beneath her and the controls at her hands, but it was so easy to forget them, to lose herself in the vision surrounding her.

She felt Chutzpah jump excitedly on her shoulder. If she didn't know better, she'd have thought he was party to the sights that swam in her vision. She allowed herself a few more moments to enjoy the spectacle.

Finally, she pressed down hard with her index finger to activate the controls and a ghostly image coalesced in front of her. The sequences and prompts were activated and controlled through the interplay of muscles in her hands and face, but manual override was always possible.

The pod was very good and very new. Pellis had spared no expense on the defences, and she revelled in the smooth interplay of vision and control and the instantaneous response it provided. Her ghost hands keyed the sequence to start a simulation and she threw herself into it as the images took shape.

Like the rest of the pod, the simulator was top of the range. Every new scenario was different and with each run she faced even greater challenges. Practice sessions in the pod were essential, not only because she needed to be familiar with the controls, but also because the pod needed to become familiar with her reactions. It learned about her from the way she moved. It built a store of information about how she responded and reacted with each new run. It used this accumulated data to face her with new simulations to probe her weaknesses and attempt to shore them up.

Over the past few weeks she had improved considerably, and she knew it. It gave her an extra level of confidence.

The pod provided sensory input over the entire surrounding sphere and her focus of attention within that orb was guided by the movements of her head, hands, and eyes. One of the hardest things to learn in the battle pod was to react to signals appearing in the periphery of her vision. She had got a lot better at that. Another danger was simulated physical incapacitation — then the level of control diminished. It was why full manual override was provided. Of course, manual control was not as effective or as fast, but if she got good enough it would do the job if it should come to it.

Now, to concentrate on the simulation. Sharpen her thoughts — achieve that focus.

The pod hit her with a multi-angled attack. The ships streaking toward her were unfamiliar, and very briefly, she wondered what new surprise they had in store for her. No time for thinking though; the ships were virtually upon her.

Warnings flashed up in front as the phantom ships swept in. There was no text. All the displays were in pictographs or colours. Learning to read and understand them was part of the process.

The pod had already identified the intruders as hostiles, and the pale glow of her shields suffused her vision as they snapped into place. An alarm sounded in her ear and a warning indicator flashed in front of her eyes. One hostile was approaching in close, out of her direct field of vision. Rapidly she spun about searching for it.

There it was, behind and below, taking advantage of her blind spot. It was a standard tactic in sudden attacks. Come up from behind and below. It was not normal for someone to have their full attention trained immediately beneath their backside. The capacity for all round concentration had to be trained, and she knew that many a raw weapons tech had been caught that way.

She sent a quick volley speeding toward the intruder, not even waiting to see the effect. She knew instinctively that she had met her mark. Instantly, her attention was back on the other three ships.

Two were grouped in formation to the front, providing support for each other. The third was fading off to one side, hoping to catch her off guard, slowly inching around behind, just out of range. It was not so different from hand to hand combat. She sent a salvo to the front, hoping to stall, or at least dissuade the paired ships from attacking her head on, and then just as quickly swung around to track the third. There was no third. Where had it gone? It couldn't just have disappeared.

There was no sign anywhere — nothing to suggest the other ship's presence. But wait. A slight flicker off to her left and above. Not one, but two.

Two ships. So where had the other came from? Too far yet. Concentrate on the first two. Focus on what mattered.

She swivelled to meet the more immediate threat and the screen flared red in front of her. Damn! She had taken a hit. She was too slow. Too much time spent thinking, not enough spent reacting. Faster — she had to be faster. She launched three quick volleys in succession at the pair in front of her, automatically compensating as the pod piloted the ship into a defensive roll against the return fire. She spun about to target the two ships to the side.

They were just pulling into the edge of her firing range. Perfect timing. Her finger was poised, ready to launch as she kept one eye on the images representing the ships approaching from her front, and noted with satisfaction that one was down. Her finger stayed poised, waiting for the moment. Not just yet ... now!

Two quick volleys shot out at the leftmost ship, and it blossomed into a ball of energy. The ship on the right did the same, then disappeared.

So that was it. One of the two ships had been a mere doppelganger, a defensive image projected to confuse and drew fire. She had just been lucky and picked the right one to fire on. No time to think about it though. She had the other ship to deal with. Once again, she turned to the front.

The simulator provided the illusion of *The Dark Falcon* sweeping down and in for the kill. She raised her finger with a sense of grim satisfaction, preparing to make the final shot. Suddenly Chutzpah scrabbled at her shoulder, dragging at her attention.

"Not now Chutz," she hissed at him.

A barrage of noise and light invaded her senses as her screens flared to white and then faded to black. The cacophony was replaced by a silence that roared in her ears.

She was dead. *The Dark Falcon* had been destroyed.

Mahra swore. But how? She had kept both sets of ships in her field of vision. She took out the ship to the side and was just about to deal with the one to the front. It fired and missed. She watched the shots streak past below her. So how had they managed to take her? She keyed the replay in frustration, pausing to wipe a trickle of perspiration from the back of her neck.

She saw it almost immediately. The first ship she had hit, the one that came at her from below, weathered the blast. It stayed in the background and waited until the height of the battle when she was otherwise occupied. Then it moved in for the kill. Somehow Chutzpah had known and tried to warn her.

She frowned. That was just not possible. It was only a simulation. The sounds and images fed directly to her and none other. She shook her head.

Pushing the mystery to one side for the moment, she concentrated on the remainder of the analysis. The rest of her performance was almost faultless, but once-again her overconfidence had led to her downfall. She should have made sure of the first ship and removed the threat while she still had the chance. If the scenario was played out in real life, she'd have lost all aboard *The Dark Falcon.* She berated herself for incompetence and hit the sequence for another run.

The only thing the pod couldn't simulate effectively was the interaction between pilot and weapons tech. The pilot also had weaponry, but it was secondary to the principle task of keeping the ship out of danger. The pilot's real job was to fly, not fight. When in the pod, in a live situation, she'd be patched directly to the pilot's com. She wondered how it would go in a live battle if it ever came to that. The combination of Pellis's impulsive nature and her own overconfidence could prove a dangerous recipe. At least she was becoming aware of that danger.

Chapter Seven

Valdor was near the end of his patience. He really had to get out. His frustration was gnawing at him as he paced his offices, chewing his lower lip, and gently massaging his left temple with one thumb. He had expected the Sirona to show by now and there had been no sign of them. And he was no closer to finding out anything more.

It wasn't Marina's fault that she'd come up with nothing. She had been an absolute gem throughout all of this, but Valdor felt crippled. He had to know. He stopped pacing for a moment and ran his fingers back through his hair before growling with frustration.

For the past three weeks, he had been tucked away, safe yet removed, as he kept a low profile — and that was the dilemma. He'd been in constant contact with his people throughout the intervening period and nothing at all untoward had happened. There had been not a single sign to suggest Sirona interest or involvement. His operations progressed, as close to normally as could be expected. In some respects, their momentum was self-perpetuating, but he was still not comfortable keeping himself away from the hub of it.

Milnus had drawn a complete blank as far as the Sirona intrusion and tampering were concerned. Even more frustrating. He had every faith in Milnus. If there was something to be found, Milnus would have found it.

Valdor was starting to have lingering doubts that anything had occurred. It was so surreal. The question was, what to do now? He could continue as if nothing had happened and take up where he left off. It would be that simple, but then again it would not. To be left harbouring that grain of doubt would be maddening. He needed some sort of resolution. He strode to the mantle, retrieved his com, and watched his stern reflection in the mirror as he keyed access.

"This is Valdor. Milnus — now."

His lips thinned with determination as he waited. The decision was made.

"Milnus? Yeah fine ... Good, have you come up with anything yet? ... Curse it man, what are you doing ...? No, never mind. I want to see you here ... yes, in about an hour."

He thumbed the connection and rested his chin on the back of his fist, still questioning the wisdom of the decision.

Milnus arrived on time and sat in front of the desk waiting for Valdor to acknowledge him. His Head of Security knew better than to speak to him before he was ready, and Milnus waited patiently, while Valdor prepared himself a drink and settled himself in the large wing-back. Valdor fixed Milnus with an expressionless stare, and toyed with his glass, deliberately drawing out the pause before he spoke.

"So, what have you got to tell me? Any progress?"

"None whatsoever I'm afraid, Mezzer Carr."

"Fire! What do I pay you for? I want results dammit!"

"I'm sorry, Sir," Milnus said calmly in response to the outburst, " — but nothing. There was no evidence of tampering. No sign of any untracked craft. Nothing."

The paused lengthened as Valdor thought, taking stock of the situation. At least Milnus had the good sense not to question his perceptions. He had been with him long enough to know better than that.

"All right, if you have nothing to tell me, then you have nothing to tell me. I've decided to continue operations as normal from here. I'm going to take up the slack. I don't think that I need to stress the requirement for extra vigilance. You are good at what you do, Milnus. Just make sure that you try to be a little better. If I've made myself clear, you can leave."

Valdor dismissed him with an arch of his eyebrows and backward tilt of his head before returning to slowly swirling the clear fluid in the cut glass supported in his hand.

He really had no choice now but to return to the way things were. Perhaps a little more care was in order, but apart from that.... One thing he had determined to do, was to find out as much as he could about the troublesome aliens. With the breadth of his information network, that shouldn't be too hard.

Valdor sent out his feelers and the results started to roll in rapidly. He occupied himself with his own bit of archival research as he waited for answers. For all their impact on various scattered worlds throughout the system, there seemed to be surprisingly little known about the Sirona, and that surprised him a little. They were definitely high tech and probably far in advance of anything Valdor was aware of. The trickle of technological trade with the Sirona in the past was enough to support that thought. It seemed the only things known for sure, were those pieces of information that the Sirona had provided themselves. All the rest was conjecture. There were various theories, of course.

One of the most interesting to Valdor was, that their social structure appeared very similar to that of an insect colony, rather than a sentient race. There seemed to be no way of telling any of them apart, and on the rare instances when groups were observed together, they all appeared to act in concert. Neither was there any visible communication between them. Each time a group was involved, there had always been only one, and one alone doing the communicating. The rest just appeared to be making up the numbers.

A few days later, his comp unearthed an obscure article by some academic, who claimed to have been aboard one of their ships. Within it, he claimed he observed more than one type of Sirona. He also asserted that the Sirona ships were basically organic in structure. Of course, he had no evidence to support his claims and the paper was taken as rank sensationalism designed to bolster an already obscure and flagging academic career. The scorn he garnered as a result of the publication had relegated him to the intellectual wasteland and he had retired to obscurity, what remained of his career in tatters. Valdor noted the information anyway and tucked it away for later reference. You could never tell when it might be useful.

For the next few weeks, things behaved fairly much as normal within Carr Holdings. The power base grew imperceptibly, and the income came in. Valdor set about removing a proportion of the dead wood within the structure. There was only little, because he ran the operation lean. By the time he had finished, it was almost skeletal. From time to time he had doubts, wondering perhaps if he was taking the paranoia too far, but he reconciled himself with the thought that anyone he had to carry, ultimately could not be trusted anyway. The process appeared to have a positive side-effect, for those who remained within the network showed that little bit more effort, as if trying to prove that their worth was real. Such dedication. Still, it was no less than he demanded.

The merger between Interworld Logic Systems and Germ Cells Incorporated progressed without hitch and he was faced with the further task of trimming the excess fat from the new corporate monolith. In this case he took a personal interest. Not only had the project always been his baby, but he wanted extra insurance. The Sirona had given him time to think after that initial meeting, but that was it. What were they playing at?

The corporate reorganisation provided him with many opportunities. True, the controlling interest in Interworld Logic and Germ Cells came back to Carr Holdings, but he wanted more than that. Along with the removal of those that did not, in his mind, deserve a place in the new structure, he made a few strategic placements of his own. Sometimes it was good to have a number who were on the payroll twice. It gave him a direct line to what was really going on, and not just through channels he already owned.

New Helvetica was conducive to power structures that rested on intrigue. The New Helvetian psyche had developed from a culture that survived on political subterfuge just like the economy. Valdor toyed for a while with the idea of placing Milnus within the organisation, but finally decided against it. Milnus was worth too much in Carr Holdings. Besides, he already had a few good people inside ILGC.

Naturally, the merger had repercussions; enforced redundancies, changes in contractual conditions. All did little to establish healthy employee relations. There was a series of rolling strike actions and industrial disputes. Valdor didn't care about these too much. It was the accompanying media attention that really annoyed him. Concessions and payoffs finally had to be made, and eventually, as was the nature of these things, the media lost interest. Some took their lump-sums and moved on, others accepted the new conditions and stayed. At the end of it, Valdor achieved the combination of resources and knowledge he was aiming for, and the resulting shock waves faded into insignificance.

A few troublesome wrinkles remained to be smoothed out in the strategic make-up at board level, but that was the heart of the organisation or what it did. They would be sorted out to his satisfaction in time.

At the core of ILGC, what the whole merger was about, was the strategic alliance of technical expertise that could produce the results that he wanted — the biocomp. The research effort took place in absolute secrecy. He made sure it provided a meeting of the finest minds from the two former companies, and he planned to be at the helm. Every researcher had been fully checked out and Valdor was sure there were no problems. Scientific careers could be made or broken here, and the participants were aware of what was at stake.

He also provided a little insurance. He had direct links with three of the individual researchers, and would be kept constantly apprised of any developments, as and when they took place. The research effort was to be shielded from the rest of ILGC, as the company went about its normal business, dealing in the diverse range of products it already produced.

Despite all this, Valdor was not content. He wanted to be sure that his hothouse was completely secure. He decided to take an extra safeguard and appoint Milnus's number two as Head of Security for the operation. In that way, he would have direct access, both inside and out. The time had come for the birth of a new idea and Valdor was to be its progenitor. He would worry about the Sirona if and when they showed up again.

Carr sat back to watch the seeds he had planted. If this came off, very little could stand in his way. Despite his low profile of the last few weeks, at last he was starting to feel as if he was back in control. The feeling was comfortable, and he sat back and finally allowed himself a smile.

Chapter Eight

Planetfall was in two days' time. Mahra felt a touch of excitement. She had never been in this sector of the system before. The world they were to visit had a reputation for tough conditions undercut by general lawlessness. She knew better than to appear curious, but she couldn't help wondering what dragged them to a world such as this.

For the last couple of days, the little she had seen of Sind had revealed him muttering to himself, and, if it was possible, surlier, and more withdrawn than usual. Pellis on the other hand was his normal effusive self, full of quips, striding about the ship as if he was on his way to a pleasure resort.

Half a day out, the mood changed, and he called them both in to discuss requirements for the visit. They gathered in the rec room over the obligatory mugs of hot, bitter kahveh. The room was silent, except for the ship's gentle hum about them. Sind alternated between sipping from his mug and shaking his head, muttering. Finally, he could contain himself no longer and he exploded into speech.

"Look Timon, I don't understand the purpose of this little exercise. You and I both know what we need to do. So why are we wasting valuable time?"

"Just bear with me would you, Jayeer? There is a reason for everything, you know," said Pellis. He glanced meaningfully at Mahra before continuing. "The reason I've called us here is to be one hundred per cent certain that we know what we'll be up against, and what we need to do down there."

Sind raised his eyes ceilingward.

"Well there is no need to make a theatrical production of it. For God's sake — such drama. You and I both know what we'll be up against down there, and all *she* is required to do is to follow our lead."

"Ah, Jay. You're right to a certain extent, but you know as well as I do that Belshore is not the most hospitable place. Better to be forewarned than step into it blind, is it not? Especially if Mahra here will be watching our backs."

Sind gave Mahra a sidelong glance then looked down at the swirling liquid in his mug.

"Granted," he said, grudgingly.

"Belshore indeed," Timon continued. "Now, that is a misnomer if ever I heard one. Still, it is business we're here for and it was business we'll do. So, Mahra, tell me, have you ever had cause to stop off there?"

Mahra shook her head. Pellis looked toward Sind briefly with a told-you-so expression, then continued speaking.

"So, Jay, my friend, it is just as well to have this little chat." He turned back to face Mahra and spent a moment or two gathering his thoughts. "All right then. What can I tell you? For a start, there is nobody on Belshore who doesn't have a damned good reason for being there — even if it is just that they're unwelcome anywhere else. One thing you don't want to do down there, is get in anybody's way. They'll not thank you for it. On that note, there may be one or two down there whose purpose runs more than a little contrary to our own. If that turns out to be the case, we could find ourselves running into the slightest bit of bother. For that reason, I really do hope you know what you're doing. Because if you don't .... "

Timon fixed her with a probing look from beneath darkened brow. It was the most serious she had yet seen him.

"For now, you're just going to have to trust that I do, aren't you?" she said to both, returning Pellis's gaze unflinchingly.

Sind raised his eyes from his mug and peered through his thick lenses with a speculative look. He pursed his lips and returned to toying with his brew.

"All right then," said Pellis. "Once we're down there, we go nowhere alone. We stick together at all times. Keep your eyes open and, most of all, take nobody at face value. Hopefully we should be in and out of the place quickly — a couple of days at most. I don't intend to spend any longer on Belshore than we have to. If we get separated at any time, for whatever reason, rendezvous will be back at *The Dark Falcon*. We won't be taking a hotel. Too risky. Is everything clear?" Mahra and Sind nodded. "Good. We dock in about three hours, so if you have any questions, ask them now."

"What exactly are we doing down there?" asked Mahra, her curiosity finally getting the better of her.

Timon fixed her with a level stare. "Even if I did know, which I do not right at the moment, I don't think I'm ready to tell you. You signed on to do a job. So far, you haven't had much chance to do that job. You're pulling your weight aboard ship, and you obviously know your way around, but that does *not* grant you a need to know. If you do need to know, then I'll tell you. Is that clear?"

Mahra nodded mutely, a little surprised by his tone. She wondered briefly what nerve she had apparently touched.

He watched her for a while longer, then stood and walked purposefully from the room. An awkward silence filled the air until Sind took one last swallow from his mug, pushed his glasses up his nose with one finger and stood.

"You'd better start getting ready," he said, with a faint smug smile playing at the corners of his mouth. He watched her for a moment longer, then also turned and left.

"Well Chutz, what do you think about that?" she asked the zimonette, absently stroking him beneath the chin, her eyes still fixed on the door.

This was a side of Pellis she hadn't seen — all stern efficiency. One thing she knew for certain, this visit was certainly not going to be any holiday. She wasn't sure she knew what to make of Sind's little smile either. All very curious. Still pondering, she cleaned the mugs then left the rec room to prepare.

Back in her quarters, Mahra changed her clothes, swapping them for a dark weave suit. She had found in the past that psychologically, the dark suit seemed to give her more authority. Sometimes it was better to bluff your way out of a tight situation using simple presence rather than escalate into direct confrontation. As she strapped on her blade, she bit her lip, feeling a pang of guilt. Perhaps she had been spending too much time in the simulator and not enough on her own exercises. Mind, body, and blade sharp. She'd even been ignoring the ritual care of her blade with the new toy. She could redress the balance over the next few days. One last check, and she was satisfied. Feeling slightly nervous, she left her cabin to take up her station in the pod.

Mahra had made it a habit to be in full battle rig for both take-off and landing. That way she could appreciate the full majesty of planetfall with her senses unhampered by the restraints of the ship. It also gave her direct access to the approach and departure conversations between Pellis, Sind and whatever control existed on the worlds they visited. In a way, she also felt it was her duty to be in that position — part of the job. Most trouble for a solo ship was likely to occur in close proximity to a world rather than in the deeper reaches. It was one of the reasons for the complex defence and monitoring systems that circled their based on New Helvetica. No such controls were in evidence about Belshore.

The only communication between *The Dark Falcon* and Belshore involved flight trajectories and docking instructions. There were no checks, no security clearances, or customs declarations. It was in keeping, she supposed, for a world where it was said you could get anything you wanted if the price was right. She felt excitement, but also trepidation as the darkened globe rushed toward her.

Traceries of light formed out of glowing clouds, then shaped into individual pinpricks, mapping out the surface contours. The major port was on the night side, making the landing all the more spectacular to her open senses. Two minor course adjustments on the way in and *The Dark Falcon* glided into a landing on a smooth open tract, delineated by rows of blue lights that marked the edges of the lengthened strip.

Mahra adjusted her perspective with difficulty. It was not easy to go from dealing with the vast image of planetfall to the narrowed viewpoint of her immediate surrounds. The set of green arrow lights trailed off in a huge curve to a point off to the side. They helped to focus her attention, and gradually she identified the regular shapes of low-slung buildings and the more rounded shapes of various parked craft. The normal configuration for a port would have the ships under cover. It was strange to see all these ships parked out in the open beside the large landing strip. Belshore had to have space to throw away if the designers could lay out a port such as this. From what she saw on the way in, the world was certainly large enough.

She unstrapped her harness after removing the helmet and gloves, stood, and bent her legs a few times to test her weight. No doubt about it, she felt marginally heavier — a touch of the heavies. She'd have to watch that when judging her reactions. Having skimped on her exercises wouldn't help. She was likely to became tired too quickly. Mahra cursed inwardly as she made her way down to join the others. It never did to take short cuts.

By the time she clambered down to join them, Sind and Pellis were already at the main lock. Sind was grumbling something about port charges and Pellis, as usual, was vainly trying to placate him.

She joined them in the lock just as the outer door slid open. Maintenance crews in coloured coveralls moved about their tasks, trading cracks with each other as they negotiated their way between the parking ships. Utility vehicles topped by flashing lights whirred along as they crossed from one area to another across the slick, smooth expanse. The atmosphere was heavy with the smell of fuels and lubricant. Traceries of white vapour curled up from grates scattered between the assorted dark shapes of ships at rest. The signs of activity made it no different from any port she had ever seen. Steps had already been wheeled into place and they descended, metal creaking beneath the weight of their feet.

A service tech met them at the bottom with a comp in one hand and the other stretched out toward them. The tech rolled his eyes as Sind fished about in his pocket, finally located his card, and dropped it into the outstretched palm. The tech peered at the card, then swiped it across his reader and stood waiting for the green verification light, before handing it back.

"Criminal," muttered Sind.

"Yeah, ain't it just?" The tech grinned from behind his beard. He gave a mock salute and flourish, then turning, wandered off, his interest in them at an end.

They followed Pellis's lead, out of the port buildings and up to a waiting line of trans-cabs. Moving up to the head of the line Pellis wandered over to the lead trans and knocked on the window. The driver peered at him and then each of them in turn before nodding his head. Only after he had received the nod, did Timon open the rear door and clamber in.

Timon obviously knew where they were going, because he gave the driver an address and detailed instructions about the route he wanted him to take to get them there. He politely added the suggestion that they didn't want a tour of the entire world in the process. Sind was still muttering about unnecessary expenses as they accelerated away from the port.

"There you go as usual, Jay. Couldn't you do something more useful than counting the creds? Such a waste of a mathematical mind," Pellis said. He rolled his eyes with mock despair. "Did you expect anything else?" he asked. "We're on Belshore. Supply and demand, Jay, supply and demand."

Sind snorted and turned his thick lenses to watch the passing streets. Peering through the plas into the darkness herself, Mahra tried to pick out the buildings and the sights as they raced by. The architecture echoed a grand style, overblown and opulent, but certainly not contemporary. Again, it was nothing like she had imagined it would be. The streets were clean and wide. Here and there she saw tracks of decay, but nothing to suggest the level of barbarity hinted at by Timon and Sind both. Perhaps it was just too dark to see the real signs.

The area was only sparsely populated. The odd pedestrian appeared from the gloom, rushing on his or her way, disappearing into the murk as the trans whisked past them. Their driver headed gradually away from the port environs, and the pattern changed. The number of people began to swell and with the increase came a general slowing of the frantic pace. The buildings grew more modern, and the streets narrow as they moved further in to a denser centre of habitation. Instead of the solitary individuals she had seen before, they all seemed to cluster together, moving as groups. After travelling a few more blocks, Mahra couldn't find a single inhabitant walking alone. She noticed something else as well. There were large well-built individuals who accompanied many of the pedestrians. Perhaps the place was not so secure after all.

As the byways became narrower and more congested, the trans-cab slowed, negotiating the growing traffic.

Suddenly, Mahra was thrown forward and found herself in a crumpled heap on the floor between Sind's knees. Quickly, she dragged herself back up to her seat. She was just in time to see the reason for their abrupt deceleration. Standing in the middle of the street, dead in front of the trans-cab, was a wild-eyed youth, hands outstretched toward them. In one hand was some form of projectile weapon. For a frozen instant, Mahra took in his wildly flowing hair, stained clothing, and grey pallor.

She locked gazes with him, sensing fear, and something else, something that merely bordered on the edges of sanity. She felt a question there, drawing the instant out as his weapon wavered from one side then to the other, then back again. His eyes locked with hers and, very slowly, he grinned. At that instant, Mahra knew exactly what he was going to do.

"Down!" she yelled, grabbing Pellis and Sind by their suits and dragging them both to the floor.

Mahra watched as her intuition was fulfilled, telescoping into slow motion. The youth's finger inexorably tightened on the trigger; a cloud of vapour escaped from the weapons' tubular end and a small metal projectile sped toward them with astonishing velocity. She barely heard the report that followed a fraction later. Her reflexes seemed to have slowed in comparison to the actions playing themselves out in front; actions with her as the focus.

She was just pulling her head down behind the protective moulding of the seat in front, when the projectile impacted the front screen right in line with her eyes. There was a sharp bang as it hit. The plas starred at the point of impact and the distorted metal slug dropped away, bounced on the front of the vehicle with a metallic clang, then disappeared out of sight to the street below.

Mahra stopped herself in the middle of the defensive crouch, eyes still fixed on the wild-eyed youth. A puzzled look crept over his face, then quickly disappeared. Still grinning, he broke eye contact, tossed his head back and gave a massive whoop before turning and sprinting down an alleyway, long tangled tresses and ragged coat trailing behind him. The crowd parted to let him through, one or two reaching protectively for their own weapons, but mostly just eager to get out of his way.

"Stupid fuckin' duster." complained the driver. "Now look what he done. Near put a hole in my screen. Just you look at that. I tell you, no stupid driver me. Put in special plas. Stupid fool. Damn near run him over I did."

Still shaking his head, he ran his finger over the inside of the screen surface to make sure the damage was only superficial. Finally satisfied, he slid back up his seat and started the trans-cab back on its way as if nothing unusual had happened. Pellis and Sind pulled themselves up off the floor and resumed their seats. They took a moment or two to straighten their clothing. Pellis was the first to say anything.

"Thanks, Mahra, quick thinking. It could have been worse."

"Yes, thank you," said Sind, obviously with some effort and without making eye contact.

"Yeah well, all part of the job," she answered flippantly. "So, tell me, what did he mean by 'duster'?"

Timon explained. "Cloud crystal. Crazy dust if you like. Crazy 'dust', hence the 'duster'. It's one of the newer designer recs. I've not seen it myself, but I'm not all that surprised to see it on Belshore. Looks like it is not one of the friendlier designers either." He turned to the driver. "Is there a lot of it about then?"

"The dust? Oh yeah man, there be plenty. Don't even have to go lookin' you know. Real bad it is. Soon it will go away. They all be dyin' or get killed soon enough. Then we get a new one, you know. Maybe the next one not be so fuckin' aggressive."

Pellis sat back in his seat and looked thoughtful.

"Aren't we going to do anything about that, Timon?" Mahra asked, a little surprised at the complacency being shown by her companions.

"No point at all," Pellis said and shrugged his shoulders. "This is Belshore," he continued, as if those three words explained everything.

Mahra sat back. She'd watch and see. Obviously, she was going to get nothing more from Pellis.

Belshore was covered with urban sprawl. Some of it lay in ruins, some nestled in verdant landscape or ranged to tall sky-scraping blocks. At one time, it was a rich and prosperous world, and she could see echoes of that bygone glory in the odd palatial edifice squatting between the haphazard plas and steel of modern growth. The port served as the hub of its scattered population. So those who curried their existence from the trade tended to cluster about that source. The population radiated out from the centre like a poisoning of the arterial blood that served it.

The remainder of their journey proved uneventful, but the incident had unsettled her, and she saw things through slightly different eyes.

The driver's calm, untroubled reaction and Pellis's response to her question told her this sort of occurrence was commonplace; part of normal day to day life on Belshore. If that was so, then she'd better take more notice of the warnings that were levelled at her by Timon and Sind before they left *The Dark Falcon.*

The trans-cab slowed and pulled to a curb side stop. Sind fished out his card and proffered it to the driver who swiped it across his reader. Mahra reached over to the door, intending to wait for the completion of the transaction outside. The door remained firmly locked. Pellis shook his head at her, indicating she should stay where she was. She frowned back at him, not understanding, and he offered her a quiet explanation.

"This is Belshore," he told her patiently. "Trust does not form a large part of the business dealings here, whether it be inside a trans or at the loading bay of a warehouse. We won't get out of here until payment is completed in full."

She sat back and waited as the reader gave the go-ahead and the driver handed back Sind's card. When she tried the door this time, it was unlocked. She stepped out of the trans, checking up and down the street as she did so. All appeared clear, so she allowed herself to relax. If you wandered around like a taut wire it took its toll, particularly in heavier grav.

The area was less populated, and the buildings were larger. It looked as if they've ended up in some sort of warehousing area. She curled her lip at the ripe smells lingering in the air, as Pellis and Sind clambered out of the trans to join her. They stood and waited, saying nothing until the trans-cab pulled away from the curb and faded off into the night, leaving them alone on the empty street.

"Right," said Pellis, "we have a bit of a walk, so we had best be going. Mahra, you stay behind us and above all, keep your eyes open."

She didn't really need the reminder, what with the events of the past half hour, but she held back her retort. She wondered why Pellis had chosen to walk from this point rather than be dropped off right at their destination, but again thought better of asking.

Pellis took off ahead, Sind a pace behind, and as she was instructed, Mahra brought up the rear. The streets in this area were empty and only sparsely lit. Pools of orange-yellow light made an occasional oasis in the darkened gloom of the evening haze. Their footsteps echoed from the walls of sheer-fronted windowless buildings. It heightened her feelings of exposure and vulnerability.

Pellis's 'bit of a walk' turned out to be a bit of an understatement. They traversed four blocks and there was still no sign of them reaching anything that looked remotely like their destination.

From time to time, as they travelled, Pellis looked over his shoulder and scanned the surrounding streets. He was clearly looking for something, but she wasn't sure what. They walked in silence, the only sound that of their footsteps, occasionally broken by the steady hum and whirr of an air-conditioning or refrigeration unit from the buildings they passed. She dared not ask how much further as Pellis strode purposefully forward. He obviously had a very clear idea of where they were headed.

Finally, when it appeared as if their trek could go on all night, Pellis turned down a side street and stopped. He looked up and down the stretch of roadway before stepping forward to speak to her. Sind, keeping an eye on the approaches from both directions leaned back against a wall, obviously feeling the strain of the concentrated burst of exercise in the slightly heavier gravity. A light sheen of perspiration glistened on his forehead, and he had to remove his lenses two or three times to wipe them clean as they fogged, obscuring his vision.

"It's about one and a half blocks from here," said Pellis. "One or two things you will need to know before we get there. When we do, just follow our lead. Say nothing and don't be surprised by what you see or hear. All may not be as it seems. Most of all, be very judicious about your actions. Restraint is the order of the day. Am I clear?"

"Yes, of course," answered Mahra, not really having any idea what he was talking about. For now, she was just sick of walking.

"All right then. Let's get going." He nodded and beckoned to Sind who pushed himself off the wall and followed. Mahra had to quicken her pace to catch up.

As they neared their destination, Chutzpah started to become agitated. His nose quivered and tail flicked up and down. Mahra sensed his tension and scanned the surrounding streets nervously. For an instant, she thought she saw a shadow flit across the intersection they had just left, but she couldn't be sure. It was probably just a trick of her imagination, helped along by the tension she was feeling from Chutzpah.

In front of a warehouse ahead, sat two long, dark vehicles parked strategically curb side in front of the long wide doorway. On the front of each nonchalantly lounged a figure; or so it seemed. At this distance, she couldn't tell whether they were male or female. The more distant of the two wore light intensifiers. As they neared, Mahra lifted her right hand and started to run her fingers through her hair, keeping them a mere hand's breadth away from her blade hilt. As if sensing what she was doing, Pellis looked over his shoulder at her, noted the position of her hand and narrowing his eyes, gave his head a slight shake. Taking his meaning immediately, Mahra dropped her hand back to her side, watching for further clues.

As they drew abreast of the vehicles, the man leaning against the nearest one stepped forward, deliberately blocking their path, all sense of nonchalance gone. The other stayed where she was, glasses trained on them, hand placed significantly at her belt. Pellis raised his hand and stood still. Sind and Mahra drew up behind him. The man who blocked their path looked them over one by one, all the time keeping his hand buried in the pockets of his long, grey synth-weave coat.

"A nice night to be out strolling," he said conversationally. "A funny place for it though, wouldn't you say?" He tilted his head to one side.

"Aye, a pleasant evening," said Pellis just as smoothly. "Now it is not so strange. Not, that is, if we are here to see Garavenah."

"So, Garavenah is it? I suppose that's supposed to mean something to me."

As he spoke, the woman slid off the vehicle behind him and stood, legs slightly spaced, both hands poised above her belt.

"Sure, it should. Just tell them it's Timon Pellis. She'll see me," he said without a trace of fluster. He punctuated the statement with an ingratiating smile.

The guard, for this was what Mahra presumed he had to be, looked Pellis over once more, then brought one of his hands into view holding a small com. He thumbed it on and spoke a few words; far too quietly for Mahra to make out. All the while, his eyes never left Timon. The woman in the background continued to stand at the ready. Mahra couldn't see where the woman was looking because of the light intensifiers covering her eyes and it made her nervous. She quelled the urge to reach for her own weapon, though she yearned at this moment for the security of having the grip held firmly in her hand.

They stood like that, for the space of more than a minute while the guard waited, listening for a reply.

At last it came, and he appeared satisfied. He withdrew his other hand from his pocket and motioned quickly behind him with his fingers. The woman relaxed, moved back to lean once more on the vehicle, and turned her attention back to scanning the street. The guard motioned with his chin toward the warehouse door and moved aside to let them pass. He continued watching them as they stepped toward the massive door.

A smaller door was cut into the main surface, and this swung open as they approach. A figure stepped out with weapon drawn, looked quickly up and down the street before motioning them inside, weapon pointing the way. One after the other, they stepped through, as the door banged shut with a metallic clang.

Inside, they were met by more people with their weapons drawn, who herded them down a long corridor of stacks of crates reaching from ceiling to floor. Cameras mounted on supports suspended from the ceiling tracked their progress along the full length of the artificial passageway. Not a word was spoken from one end to the other. They marched along with two guards in front and two behind until the passage opened into the wide expanse of the warehouse proper. Two more guards fell in beside them as they emerged, one from either side of the passageway. So, they were escorted to the centre of the open space.

Boxes, crates, pieces of machinery and all manner of detritus cluttered the floor. The brightness of the overhead lights made it all stand out in stark relief. Set a little back from the centre, a wide staircase climbed to another level. Standing at the top, a tall statuesque woman waited, her long blonde hair making a sharp contrast against the deep blue of her finely cut suit. She watched them imperiously as they moved to stand below her. The fine cast of her narrowly chiselled cheekbones only served to accentuate her regal presence.

"Timon Pellis. This is what you call yourself. What is it you want from me?"

Pellis looked up, observed the woman for a moment before placing his hands on his hips. He tossed his head back and roared with laughter. Mahra was totally confused.

"Well now. I could think of a thing or two," said Pellis, still chuckling. "But no, I don't think there's anything I *really* want from *you*. I don't think we've been introduced."

Just at that point, a short stocky woman stepped into view from behind the tall blonde. Her hair was cropped short and dark, shot through with grey. She wore drab grey coveralls and sported a large rifle slung over one shoulder.

"I'd recognise that laugh anywhere. Heh, same old Timon. Mind like a waste depot as usual." She grinned down at him. "Forgive the charade, but I have to be a little careful these days. This here's Roella. Jayeer, how are you? And a new face too. Well, just don't stand around down there all night. Come on up." She gestured for them to follow and disappeared from view, closely trailed by the woman she called Roella. After her first few words the guards at their sides faded away and they were left to mount the staircase unhindered.

Chapter Nine

The Cradle

Life progressed reasonably smoothly for Mahra over the next few months despite the Old One's loss. She settled into a routine, taking responsibility for the progression of her own training where the old man had involuntarily left her. She observed the rituals and the meditations, taking each component a step at a time, and moving herself to a point where she knew she was improving. At the same time, she read where and when she could, if the self-imposed rigors of her schedule permitted. The bulletins that appeared on her comp, from time to time, were her only real contact with the world outside.

Every day she rose at dawn and wandered out to the hillside performing the votives for the day before moving to her other tasks. As a part of this ritual, she cleansed herself, washing in the clear, icy stream finding its source in the snow-capped peaks that surrounded the sheltered valley.

Though dawn came early, it was some time before the sun crested the peaks and allowed warmth to caress the grassy hills. She felt the cold but didn't mind it. It made her feel fresh and alive as she plunged into those frigid waters. By the time she had performed her cleaning and rituals, the sun sent golden shafts of light through the gaps between the individual rocky outcrops, reflecting off their snowy faces and dispelling the mist rising from the damp ground in the stream's vicinity.

Her rituals over, she returned to the dwelling, drew forth the blade left to her by the old man, and walked outside to work her morning patterns. She had three patterns for the day: morning, noon, and evening. Each was slightly different from the others, working on different areas of her timing and on tautening and strengthening different muscle groups within her slim young frame. She was already near the end of her training when the Old One passed, but she still missed his guiding hand, or the word of reproach or approval to better hone her skills and forms. She tried her best to fulfil the promise the Old One saw in her.

At times, she could feel where she might be going wrong, but lacked the knowledge to correct those flaws and it frustrated her. Some were almost surely because she hadn't yet grown to a size where she could make proper use of the blade. She only hoped she wouldn't stop growing. At least not yet.

When she wasn't training, the remainder of her day was spent in several ways. The hills that surrounded her home were abundant with fauna and vegetation. One task the old man had set himself was to observe and catalogue as many as he could within the span of his life. He wanted to add to the data storehouse available to all who might inquire. In some ways, this was his life's work, and Mahra intended to carry on the tradition.

She wandered through the dappled groves, peering, and spying and note taking, gradually becoming more adept at spotting tracks or recognizing a plant. Several times she came across something she thought was new, only to find on her return that the old man had been and done that before her.

The secondary purpose of these excursions was practical. While on these exploratory journeys she stocked up on provisions, building up the contents of her larder and her medicine supplies. From time to time, she hunted.

The hunting stirred something strange in her. The adrenaline rush of the hunt and the kill was there, but it was as if when she became the huntress, and some creature became the prey, she became bonded by invisible threads to her victim. Sometimes she felt she could predict a creature's moves just as it was about to make them. She knew the way it was about to turn, or if it would attack if cornered. She could feel the heart pumping in the heaving chest and sense the blood coursing through the animal's veins. And she was linked to them as they breathed their last breath of life, feeling that rush of familiar emptiness. The chase was about survival and she had no moral problem with stalking and killing what she needed, if it was nothing more than that. She was not greedy, and she only took what was necessary. It was as if the land around her knew this and begrudged her little for what she took.

She became as one with the woodland creatures inhabiting the areas around her simple dwelling. They became so used to her that now they merely glanced up as she passed, as if she really belonged.

As the days passed, and the weeks became months, her strength improved. She could feel herself growing both in size and in skill. Mahra knew too that her knowledge was growing with the passage of time. Often, when she came across a particularly difficult concept, or something that made no sense to her at all, she visited the Old One and talked it through with him. She knew that he couldn't answer, nor could he hear her, but in some ways, it helped her sort things through. His body didn't disturb her. It suffered some deterioration, but the barrow's cold dry air made it more like a drying. She had seen many dead things before. It was a natural part of the life cycle. It was just as though being there brought her closer to his presence and his guiding influence in some way, wherever he might have gone.

On the odd occasion, deep in the night's darkening gloom, she imagined hearing his soft, firm voice whispering to her of things she should look for and those she had to do, but she dismissed these as imaginings brought on by her solitude and the dark.

Her routine was settled and went on without pause. Mahra became comfortable with it and felt herself growing to a point where she could desire nothing else. Not even being alone troubled her, for she foresaw each new day as a quest of discovery of herself and her world.

One afternoon, as usual, she stood outside to practice with the blade. They were her midday patterns and the sweat shone slick on her face. The sun was high, beating down upon her exertions and the yellow-brown hues that marked the summer season. Far off in the distance she could sense the brewing of an afternoon storm, the tension building in the air as if she could touch it, almost.

She finished as she had begun, legs slightly spaced, blade held out before her and with a practiced move, slid it back behind her shoulder and then returned inside. Carefully she unbuckled the straps, and, after removing the sheath from her back and laying it with respect upon the bed, rewrapped it, following the pattern she discovered on that first day. She never had any trouble remembering patterns and shapes. They seemed to come to her naturally and lay somewhere in her mind, waiting to be recalled without hesitation. The Old One had spent many hours concentrating on this part of her training, and now it was like second nature to her. She accepted this without a second thought. It was as natural as moving her legs one after the other when walking, and about as much effort.

Having wrapped the bundle carefully in its cloth, she was about to return it to its proper place within the chest at the foot of the bed, when she sensed a presence approaching.

For some reason, she thought better of replacing the blade, and she left the package on the bed, flipping open the wrappings to make sure it would be easy to reach should she had need of it. Mahra couldn't say exactly how she knew that there was someone approaching, but she knew it all the same. The presence moving toward her small dwelling was like a wave that disrupted the flow of harmony that surrounded the place and that was what made her cautious. In some way, it didn't quite fit the pattern of things.

She had not had a visitor in all the time since she had passed on the word of the Old One's passing. Leaving the blade, she made her way to the narrow doorway and looked out toward the slopes beyond. She still wasn't sure why she felt a need to leave the blade handy, but she did so all the same. They were all one people. None could be a threat.

At least some of her instincts were right. A solitary figure was just cresting the top of the nearest hill. Long dark robes fluttered about his frame as he strolled down the hillside toward the small dwelling. The figure was too far away yet to make out any features or to assign a gender, but she knew without doubt that the newcomer was male. She watched him without stirring from her position as he traversed the space between them.

Patiently, she leaned against the doorframe as he walked toward her. Now that he drew closer, she could see that her first impressions had not misled her. He was indeed male, but the dark robes and the feeling of tension flowing from him marked him as being something different. Mahra didn't know why, but it was clear that the newcomer was causing the disturbance. There was a sense of something uneasy about this one, something not quite right, as if he were at odds with his surroundings. She couldn't put a name to it, but if she was forced to describe it, she'd say that he gave off a prickly sensation. She knew intuitively that he presented no threat to her, but the odd feeling fed her disquiet.

He was almost on top of her, when he stopped abruptly and slowly raised his head. Dark eyes looked her up and down, deep shadows making them seemed set deeper than they really were in a slightly pasty face. An indulgent mouth pursed slightly, offsetting a permanent fleshy pout. Mahra waited, intent on letting the newcomer make the first move. This was her domain. She'd make sure that much was clear. After what seemed like an age, the visitor spoke.

"Where is he?" he asked. There was a deep, bored tiredness in his voice.

Mahra could barely conceal her look of incredulity. Firstly, this stranger arrived unannounced, not so unusual, but with his general demeanour, not exactly normal, and then, with neither explanation nor introduction he proceeded to demand information from her. Well, she'd see about that.

"Where is who?"

"Oh, don't play games with me," he replied with a slight shake of his head. "You know exactly who I mean. The Old One. I've came to pay my respects. Now, if you would just take me to where he lies, I'll do what I came for and be gone."

It was Mahra's turn to look him up and down. That a man such as this would have a link with the Old One seemed out of place. It certainly prompted questions. No, he should learn his place first.

"And what business of yours would the Old One be?" she asked.

She was uncomfortable with the severity that this newcomer seemed to invoke in her, of the harshness of her response. It was right that anybody from Cradle would wish to pay their respects invited or not, but there was something about this stranger that made her want to confront him. He narrowed his eyes and plucked at his lower lip before answering with a sigh.

"Yes, I forget myself. I've not been in the company of others for so long. Forgive me. I'm called Aleyin. I'm what you might call the Old One's great failure. I've been travelling since the news of his passing. Now please, would you show me where he is, so I might say my farewells?"

Mahra was still a little confused, but she couldn't help feeling sympathy for the hint of desperation that tinged his last question. It almost seemed as if he expected her to refuse. There was a feeling of something else etched deep beneath the tension and conflict that emanated from him. With a start, she realised what it was — a sense of great sadness and loss. She recognized the feeling within herself and for a moment, she felt a kinship with this man she knew nothing about. She could find out more about him later. For now, he had a need and she felt bound to satisfy it.

With the briefest of nods, she pushed herself from the doorway, and without looking back to see if he was following, walked purposefully off toward the barrow where lay the last remains of the old man that they both had lost.

When they reached the place, she sensed that this Aleyin wanted to be left alone, so she waited outside as he slipped inside to be with the Old One's body and pay his last respects.

It was funny, but she had never thought of the Old One having been with anyone else before her, and now that she was faced with it, she was not quite sure how she felt about it. It was even more of a surprise that she'd have been preceded by one such as Aleyin. There was clearly something in him that was outside and apart. One primary principle that the Old One tried to instil in her was a sense of balance and peace within herself. She was not sure, but it felt like it was just these things were a part of what was missing from Aleyin, as if he wasn't only at war within himself, but with all that was outside of him. And there was that strange thing that Aleyin said, that he was the Old One's greatest failure. What did that mean? There were things in the world yet that she needed to know and understand, she knew that, but that made no sense.

When Aleyin finally emerged from the barrow's dark recesses, it was to shield eyes red-rimmed with tears beneath his cowl. Mahra didn't know what private things passed between the Old One and Aleyin in the barrow depths, but clearly there was some unfinished business between the two. No matter how uncomfortable she felt with Aleyin, she couldn't help feeling some empathy. Still shielding his eyes within the depths of his hood, Aleyin looked up, scanning the now darkening sky before speaking to her.

"I've done what I came to do. Now I'll leave you in peace." He turned and started to walk up the hill toward the line of trees and the darkness beyond. Mahra pushed herself to her feet.

"Aleyin, wait. I ... " she called after him. It was as though he hadn't heard her.

"Aleyin, stop!"

He halted in mid-stride, not turning, just standing there.

"Wait, come back with me. The night is nearly here. You have travelled a long way. Come back with me to the house. Please. Besides, I want to talk with you."

Just for a moment, she thought he was going to reject her offer and continue. She could feel the moment of indecision and hesitation, but then, slowly he turned and made his way down the hill. Mahra waited for him and they walked together down the hillside to her small house in silence.

Once inside, Mahra bade him sit at the simple table in the kitchen, while she busied herself preparing something to eat and drink. He looked about him as she worked, drinking in the surroundings as if tasting them with his eyes. Not a word passed between them until together, they pushed their empty plates away, having eaten their fill. Mahra was the first to break the silence.

"So how did you know him, Aleyin? Oh, by the way, my name's Mahra."

"Yes, I know. I read your bulletin."

Of course, he had.

After a moment more, he continued.

"How? I don't know how. I don't know if I ever really did until it was far too late. But what would you know of such things?" he said, looking straight through her. He was making very little sense at all.

She frowned and waited for him to continue. Just when she thought he had said all he was going to, he started talking again.

"I also did my training here, within these very walls. It hasn't changed much, you know. Still the same. I was his student too. Probably one, no, more likely two before you. Only, well, things weren't quite the same for me. I found fear instead of harmony I suppose, and I left. I just walked away from him and I've been walking ever since. And now, now when it is far too late, I've walked back again."

Aleyin stared down at his hands resting on the table in front of him, turning them over once, closing his fingers, and then back again. Just for a moment he bunched them into tight fists, then let them relax to lie flat upon the wood.

Mahra was not sure how she should react. She could still sense the turmoil running through the man, and yet, despite the wrongness, she wanted to reach out and touch something within him. They did, after all, have a common link. Both had studied with the Old One. Both had felt his guiding hand upon their lives. That was something, but it did nothing to explain the discordance that was so out of character with the old man she knew.

"I don't expect you to understand," he said. "But the Old One couldn't give me the answers I wanted. That's where we differed. He didn't like things that questioned *his* way of doing things; The Cradle's way of doing things."

Aleyin lapsed into silence again and she studied him as he sat staring into his thoughts.

He was pale as if he rarely saw the sun. With his hood thrown back, the whiteness of his skin stood out. He carried a little too much weight for his frame making him plump in both face and hands. His pallid colouring served to accentuate the pasty doughy look of his features. The shadows around his eyes were dark and as he sat in silence, he narrowed those deep black eyes from time to time, as if random thoughts flowed through him, giving him pause before he moved on to the next. Mahra didn't know whether she'd like to spend too much time around someone like him, but she felt some sort of weird attraction to him all the same.

What was she to do with him? The night was wearing on and it didn't look like she'd get any meaningful conversation from him. Perhaps she'd do better in the morning.

She couldn't put him in the room where the old man slept. That would not seem right. That meant that she'd have to take that bed herself. The room had stayed empty since her mentor's passing and it didn't feel comfortable now that she planned to usurp his place. But there was no other real choice. By so doing, she supposed that finally she'd make the real acknowledgement that he had gone, something she knew consciously but had failed to admit deep within.

She cleared her throat to break the silence, and gestured for him to follow her.

He was amused at being given her bed. When she showed him his place, he looked around the room with a wry smile on his lips commenting on the lack of change. It made her feel further ill at ease knowing that he slept on the very same bed years before, that this was his room also. She tried to put those thoughts from her head as she bade him a good night.

She left him and returned to the Old One's room. Despite her efforts to relax, she spent a restless night, staring up at the ceiling for a long time before finally drifting to sleep.

The next morning was little different. Aleyin was moody and introspective, saying little as they shared the table over their light breakfast. Finally, Mahra could stand it no longer and decided to push the point. Here was an opportunity to find out more about the Old One, but from a different perspective. She also wanted to find out more about this Aleyin himself. He was so awkward and strange. She wondered what it was that brought him to be like that, so removed from the balance of the philosophies of The Cradle that had been instilled so firmly into herself.

"Aleyin, tell me if I cross into places where you would rather I didn't go, but, do you mind if I ask a few questions — about the Old One and the time you spent with him?" His only response was a slight shrug. "All right then ... you said something about being a failure for him. I'm sorry, but what exactly did you mean?"

There was a long pause before he answered. For a moment, Mahra feared she has been too direct too soon, but after a moment or two, Aleyin gave a deep sigh and started to talk. Once he had started, it was as if some great wall broke down and the words tumbled freely from his lips, following rapidly one after the other.

"Failure, yes, that was what I said, wasn't it? I don't know. We were so different he and I. He was so, well, balanced, and I was quite the opposite. He always wanted to see what was right with the world, whereas I would see other things. I wanted other things. I couldn't understand why so much was denied to us. I could see the signs and hints of civilisation all about us and yet we were not allowed to use it. Everything had to be so hard. The tools were there, yet we were not allowed to use them. Have you not ever felt that, Mahra Kaitan?" he asked, an almost pleading tone in his voice.

Now that he mentioned it, she supposed she had thought about it, but had never really questioned it. She gave a brief shake of her head and waited, as looking a little disappointed, he shrugged and continued.

"The Old One gave me explanations for my questions, but I was never satisfied with what he told me. What could I do? Everything for him was harmony and balance. Everything had its place and that was that. He used to frustrate me. Even down to that endless cataloguing and collecting and note taking that he always did. I couldn't see the point of it all ... all that order. I guess I wanted something more than that. Haven't you thought about it yourself, Mahra? There's all that tech out there, all these tools to help make our lives easier, and yet we are denied it. Well, not exactly denied it I suppose, but you have to go looking for it. Why should we have to be constrained to live like we do, when we obviously have the capacity for so much more? There are the signs everywhere; the comps, other things…."

"So, is that the problem, Aleyin?" asked Mahra.

She wanted a little time to think about the things he was raising but she didn't want to get into a debate about it all. Not just yet.

"In part I suppose it was, but I think it was more than that too. There was always some sort of friction between us, as if, I don't know, we didn't *fit* with each other. I could always tell when he was impatient with me — that was most of the time — and I resented the authority he tried to force upon me. He was always so dictatorial. I *would* do this and I *must* do that all the time. And of course, I fought against that."

The picture Aleyin painted of the Old One was of a man she didn't recognize. The doubt had to be clearly visible upon her face, because he noticed it and immediately attempted to counter it.

"Look, I've no doubt that things were very different for you, but you asked me what it was like for me, and I'm telling you. I'm convinced that each of us brings out something different in those we meet and deal with. It's almost as if there are relations of harmony and disharmony that flow between each and every one of us. With the Old One and me, we seemed to have the latter."

Mahra thought about this and in some way, it seemed to make sense. There was always a sense of rightness in her relationship with the old man. It was not only their relationship, but also in their proximity that there was that feeling of comfort. There were other people who came, but she had never really thought about the way people interacted before now. She remembered the strange prickly sensation she had felt when Aleyin had first approached.

"So, what do you do, Aleyin?"

"What do I do? Do you not mean, where do I fit in the scheme of things? What is my part in the great pattern?" That underlying sense of bitterness once again tinged his reply. He gave a brief laugh.

"Oh, I have my place. From time to time, they begrudge me a seat on the Council. They put up with me, more like. Most of the time I travel. I ask questions. I observe. In that way, funnily enough, I'm probably not too much different from the Old One himself. Wherever I can, I study the little tech we have access to and try to give it a place. Perhaps I'm classifying the wrongs and giving them a name. Who can say? All I know, Mahra, is that in this scheme of things, there is that which isn't right. There is more out there for us, and I'm trying to find it."

Mahra felt the conviction in his voice, but she wasn't sure that she understood what he meant. Everything you could need was there within reach.

"I can feel your questions without you having to voice them, Mahra. But let me ask you something. Don't you feel that you want more? What sense is there to the things that you do? Why are we kept away from those things that would take us away from ignorance and barbarism? I can tell you this much. If you were to ask those questions, you wouldn't get the answers. I know, because I've asked those questions and I continue to ask them. I believe there are answers, but I believe that those answers are kept to a very select few."

"I don't see where this is leading, Aleyin. What is the point?"

"Look, Mahra. I just want you to ask questions, that's all. Think about it. We see the evidence of tech about us. Who maintains it? Who kept it running? There must be those who keep the knowledge alive, and yet it is denied us. So where is the divide and why? Another thing ... these things in our heads, these implants ... why are they there? What purpose do they serve? That is a question I've asked many times."

"Implants? I..."

Of course, she knew about them; they were part of standard knowledge. It was never something they had had cause to discuss. Never something she had questioned.

"I could show you some things," Aleyin continued, "but there would be little point now. They are there for a reason, I just haven't quite found out what that reason is yet. I have my suspicions. I don't expect you to follow where I'm leading with a few words, but take the time to think about the things I've said. Perhaps, in time, we might have an opportunity to talk about them again."

Chapter Ten

The upper level was totally different from the warehouse floor. Offices and comfortable furnishings populated the deck. The tall blonde sat, reclining languorously on a wide couch. The shorter of the two, who Mahra presumed had to be Garavenah, had already unslung her weapon and stood waiting for them by a well-stocked bar.

"What's your pleasure Timon? I know your penchant for that evil brew you drink, but we don't run to the sort of standards that would suit your palate here. I know. I've got a nice bottle of Kalanian Green here. What about that?"

Pellis signified his assent and she took five tall glasses and placed them on the table before returning for the promised bottle. She re-joined them at the table and poured an even measure of green into each glass before sitting herself.

"Sit, sit," she ordered pushing a glass toward each. "So, who's your friend?" she asked, raising her eyebrows in Mahra's direction.

"Ah, forgive my rudeness, Gara," Pellis said then adopted a mock formality. "Garavenah, allow me to present Mahra Kaitan, most recent member of our happy little family. And her small companion there is Chutzpah."

Garavenah nodded in Mahra's direction and sipped at her wine.

"How much does she know Timon?"

Pellis paused for a long time before answering. "None of it, Gara. None of it." He looked down at his glass and placed it carefully back on the table.

"Fire, Timon! Then how could you — "

"No, hold on Gara. All in good time. You know we lost Polk. We needed someone and ... I don't know ... she felt right."

"But how could you bring her in without ... "

Mahra didn't like the way she was being discussed, as if she was sitting somewhere else, rather than at the table across from the both of them, but she remembered Pellis's warnings and held her tongue. What was developing was becoming increasingly more intriguing. Pellis had to have caught her mood from her expression and cut the line of conversation short.

"Enough, Gara. Trust me. We can talk about this later."

Garavenah held her hands up and grudgingly sighed her assent.

"There seems to be a lot of fresh faces about here," said Sind, his question lying pregnant in the casual statement.

"Yes, you're right," she said and sighed again. "Times are difficult right now. We've had a high attrition rate over the last few months. Lost some really good people too along the way."

"So, what's happening?" Pellis asked.

"I don't know. I don't know." She rubbed the back of her neck and Mahra could hear the weariness in her voice.

"There's a lot going on. The dusters haven't helped. There have been losses on all sides. We're not the only ones. We've had our suspicions for a while, but the big news is that we're getting hints of Sirona involvement. There's nothing solid, but it fits the pattern of what we know of them. We had reports of Sirona activity in Belshore space about two months ago. Then there were one or two reports of actual sightings planetside. About two weeks after that, the whole duster thing took off."

"Fire! But it's just what we need." Pellis slapped his leg. "Can you get nothing more?"

"By all we hold dear, we're trying. But you know the way Belshore works as well as I do."

"Ah, but wouldn't it be something to have some concrete pointers on those sly little buggers."

Mahra sat back and listened attentively as Pellis and Garavenah's conversation flowed back and forth with the occasional interjection or question from Sind. She sipped slowly at her glass, savouring the rich, almost sensual, taste of the Kalanian Green. During the course of the discussion, a pattern of subterfuge and hidden plans emerged that Mahra could barely have guessed at. Pellis had warned that all might not be as it seemed, but she had no idea of the extent of it. Now it seemed that she had become bound up in some skein of conspiracy. She wasn't sure she liked the idea or, for that matter, the fact that she was being kept firmly out of the picture. She might have expected that sort of treatment from Sind, but from Pellis it came as more of a surprise. She'd have a lot of questions for him when they finally got back to the ship, and this time she'd want some real answers.

Pellis and Garavenah talked for more than an hour. The subjects ranged widely across operations, losses, strategies, and contacts. More than once they mentioned the Sirona. Mahra didn't know much about the Sirona, but after what she heard, she was certainly going to set her mind to finding out more.

Finally, the conversation dwindled and drained away with the last of the Kalanian Green. Pellis slapped his hands on his thighs and sat up.

"Well, at least you're still in one piece. It sounds like things could be better for you, Gara. All I wish was that I could do more to help. Despite that, we've been here quite long enough and we should be making a move. Have you got what we came for?"

"Yes, of course. Roella, will you go and fetch the package for Timon please." Roella nodded and left.

She returned a few moments later with a small bundle and handed it to Garavenah. Garavenah hefted the package, then tossed it across to Pellis who caught it deftly in one hand.

"There are about two full weights of high-grade dust in there. Properly cut, street value about a mil. It should establish your cred well enough. Just try not to let it get into the wrong hands. And don't go using it yourself either. Now ... for the real package."

She pulled a card from her top pocket and slid it across the table. Pellis caught it at the edge and handed it across to Sind who, in turn, pocketed it.

"My full report is there," Garavenah said. "There'll be a few extras coming off Belshore in the next few months but they're all detailed in there. It's all encrypted and that's the only copy. Wipe it if you have to. It's all up here," she said with a tap at her forehead.

Pellis rose and moved across to where Garavenah sat. Leaning over he pulled her to her feet and, still bending down, threw his arms around her, hugged her close and planted a kiss on her forehead.

"You look after yourself, my girl," he murmured, then, picking up the package, turned and strode to the top of the stairs. Mahra and Sind both rose, nodded to Garavenah and Roella, and followed.

"Safe flight. Take care now," Garavenah said after Pellis, as she watched his retreating back.

The three were escorted back up the passage between the crates by only one guard. She unlocked the door for them, stepped back to let them slip through and closed it securely behind. They were left standing outside the main warehouse door, bathed in the yellow glow of the solitary street lamp across the road.

Mahra immediately sensed something was not right. At the same instant, Chutzpah began to claw at her shoulder. The two vehicles were in place in front of the door, but there was something missing. Then she realised; no sign of the two guards who screened them. Mahra scanned but nothing seemed out of place.

"All right Chutz, go!" she said quietly. In the same low tone of voice, she spoke to the other two. "Timon, Jayeer, be ready. We've got trouble."

Chutzpah leapt from her shoulder at the instant of her command, landing soundlessly on one vehicle as Mahra carefully drew her blade, her gaze flitting across the surrounding area, searching for any trace of movement. Pellis moved his hand to his belt, and pulled a small ugly-looking hand weapon free. At the same time as Mahra dropped into a defensive crouch, a figure stepped into sight from around the foremost vehicle.

Mahra experienced a moment of confusion. She knew the face. It seemed awfully familiar, and familiar from not too long ago. The stranger raised one hand and pointed a weapon toward her, a slow grin spreading across his face. At that instant, she knew him. It was the so-called duster who had stepped in front of their trans-cab, and this time, there was no special plas between them.

With the flash of comprehension, Mahra swung into action. She lunged forward into a roll, tumbling beneath his arc of fire, blade held out to one side. With the same movement, she brought her leg sideways and out, kicking out at his weapon arm. The gun went off as she made contact and she heard a grunt from behind her.

She continued the roll past and to one side and was on her feet in an eyeblink. Her blade was ready, but she wanted the youth in one piece for the moment. As he turned — so slowly now his movements came — she surveyed the situation. He still had his gun. Pellis was back, propped up against the wall. It looked like he had been hit.

Fire! she thought.

At that moment, another figure appeared from behind the rear vehicle, weapon poised, but as quickly as he appeared, he fell back with a cry of fear and pain. He clutched at a ball of grey-furred teeth and claws gouging at his face. Mahra took all this in as she spun, her boot edge connecting with the side of her opponent's head. He went down, crashing against the side of the trans and crumpled to the ground. She looked for the other, but there was no sign of him.

Chutzpah already sat back on the top of the vehicle, cleaning dark stains from his face and paws. A faint sound came from the vehicle's other side. Cautiously, she moved, flat against the black panelling and ducked her head round to investigate. The other assailant was there, lying spread out on the roadway, the remainder of his life ebbing out from what was left of his throat. Chutz was certainly efficient when he put his mind to it.

Lying propped against the side of the two vehicles were the two guards' bodies. Quickly checking up and down the street, she satisfied herself there were no other attackers.

Still watchful, she made her way round the vehicle's front, her attention now on seeing if Pellis was all right. If he was badly injured, things would be really difficult for them. He was still down, with the squat form of Sind crouched before him. As she passed the limp shape of her first assailant, she sensed, rather than heard, a sound.

Without a thought, her blade passed from her right hand to her left and she swung downward. She turned just in time to see those wild eyes take on a look of surprise, as the arc of her swing clove neatly through collarbone and chest. The youth slid slowly to the side and his weapon clattered to the ground.

Mahra cursed. She had wanted that one alive, or at least one of the pair. They had to have been good, both of them, to take out the two guarding the front door. It made her doubt that there were not more, but Chutzpah still sat cleaning his paws and face, obviously calm; enough to tell her that there were only the two. She probed her own senses, but everything felt right.

Now she needed help. Pellis was down and if any more did appear, they really would be vulnerable. Quickly she assessed the options. They had to get away from here or inside — anywhere out of a possible line of fire. She was sure banging on the warehouse door wouldn't bring the sort of response she wanted. There had to be some other alternative.

Stopping for a moment, just to make sure that Timon was not too badly hurt, she left Sind to attend to him and stepped round to the other side of the lead vehicle where the three bodies lay. Hurriedly, she reached down and searched the first guard's still form, unclipped the weapon from his belt, then reached in to his coat pocket to search for his com. He was still warm and blood ran from a neat hole in his temple, pooling on the road surface at her feet. The whole thing had to have happened moments before they stepped out the door. The guards couldn't have had a hint of warning. The com was still in the guard's pocket. She grabbed it, flicked it on and started speaking in low tones, without waiting for any response.

"Garavenah, Roella, anyone in there. We need help out here. Fast! You've got two down out here, and Timon is hit. Repeat, two down and Timon is hit. It seems clear for the moment, but we need assistance. No telling if there are any more."

A noise behind her cut her off. Whirling, she trained her newly acquired weapon on the source of the sound. She let out a breath as she worked out its origin. It was just the whirr and click of the still active light intensifiers adjusting as her shadow fell across them. And that was the other thing — the LI. They had to have been quick to get past the guard of somebody wearing an LI set.

A loud crash came from the vehicle's other side as the warehouse door slammed open. Mahra popped her head over the intervening roof to see the solid form of Garavenah herself storming through the door, weapon ready. She was followed by three crew from inside in rapid succession. Just as quickly as she emerged, Garavenah assessed the situation and started issuing commands.

"You two, get Timon inside. Jayeer, go with them now. You," she said pointing at one of the guards, "stay put until I can send someone else out. Mahra, are you all right?" she demanded in the same breath, barely waiting for Mahra's quick nod of confirmation. "Good. Any more?"

Her gaze flickered over the surrounding area as she spoke. She took in the wild-eyed youth's body at the side of the rear vehicle and pursed her lips then gave a slight nod of her head. Seemingly satisfied the immediate threat was dealt with, she moved round the vehicle to join Mahra, still keeping a watchful eye on the street. Looking at the bodies littering the ground, her face grew grim.

"Fire — another two. And they were two of my best. Here, give me that," she said, reaching for the com. "Garavenah. Yes. I want a couple more of you out here. Now! We've got some cleaning up to do. Yeah. Fizelle and Andi down." She flicked off the com and thrust it into her pocket shaking her head. "What happened to that one?" she asked, taking in the ruined throat and features of the other attacker. In answer Mahra tapped her shoulder.

"Chutz. Here."

As the zimonette leapt to perch on Mahra's shoulder, Garavenah's eyes widened with comprehension.

"All right. It looks like you two make a pretty good team. Now, better get inside before we get any more surprises. We'll get this lot cleaned up and see about getting you back to your ship as soon as we can. I don't think it's a clever idea to have you hanging around here any longer than we can help it. Come on," she said, and led the way back inside as more of her team emerged from within.

Pellis wasn't seriously hurt. The projectile had passed neatly through the fleshy part of his right thigh. It was messy however, and looked a lot uglier than it really was.

Of course, he made a great show of how much discomfort he was in. By the time Garavenah and Mahra joined them back inside, Roella was already attending to the dressing. Sind stood, arms folded, looking on with disapproval, as Pellis lay back on the couch basking in the attention.

It didn't take much prompting from Garavenah to get them moving again. It was obvious they weren't going to be travelling very far with Pellis in his current condition. Garavenah offered transportation in one of the vehicles outside.

"It will probably mark you out. Our vehicles are known, but I don't see that we've any choice."

"No, I agree," said Sind. "If you've finished enjoying yourself, Timon, I think we'd better move."

Timon looked pained, but raised himself to a standing position. Supporting him, one on either side, Sind and Mahra helped him down the stairs and out to the trans. When they emerged, there was barely a trace of what had just happened outside the fortified doors. The two guards had been replaced by two more, virtually indistinguishable from their predecessors.

Mahra was still annoyed that their first assailant had not survived to be questioned, but at the same time she realised that things could have been a lot worse. Perhaps it was too much of a coincidence meeting the same crazy twice in the one night; too convenient for it to have been simply a random hit. The way the guards were taken out, without so much as the hint of an alarm, alluded to something a lot more professional. If Garavenah was right, it was not what she'd expect from a simple duster.

Back at the ship, they set Timon to rest under a light sedation after cleaning his wound properly and sealing it with plas-skin. He made loud protestations but neither she nor Sind would have any of it. He had suffered a shock, and rest was the best thing for him. The plas-skin would aid the healing process, but it could not work effectively without the body's own recuperative powers, and that was best achieved when resting. There was no thought of even allowing him to attempt to take the ship up.

Seeing him finally settled, Sind stowed the package in Pellis's locker, and they repaired to the rec. Mahra sat across from him, staring at him thoughtfully. She felt a little drained, but wondered at the same time how she was going to broach the range of questions that she knew could no longer remain unasked. There was nothing else for it. The worst that could happen was he could refuse to answer her.

"Jayeer, I'm not quite sure what to ask you," she began hesitantly. "I have too many questions. Um, if you don't mind, do you want to start by telling me what the hell is going on?"

Sind paused for a long time before he slowly lifted his gaze and spoke.

"I suppose now you think you have a right to know?" He sighed deeply before continuing, a tone of resignation in his voice. "Well, I suppose you do. I suppose you do. All right then .... Where to start? I don't really know. I think you've probably worked one or two things out for yourself, but let me try to fill in the blanks, at least a little. You can stop me if I start to tell you things you already know. You handled yourself well out there, by the way."

Mahra didn't know whether she was more surprised by his agreement to talk or by his half-grudging tone of approval. Her surprise had to be evident, because he raised his hand to stifle any protest before continuing.

"Look, I *will* admit that I was against taking you on from the start, but I had my reasons, and believe me, they were very good reasons. Unfortunately, we were in a bit of a spot at the time. Our last little excursion before you came on board was — how shall I put it — a little less than fortunate. We lost a very good man as a result. It was essential that we were fully crewed and ready to go by the time we came into Belshore. You turned out to be the one. You represented a risk for us." He took off his lenses and wiped them thoroughly, before setting them carefully in place on the bridge of his nose and continuing. His last statement was so matter-of-fact, that Mahra could barely believe he had said it. "So, before I say anything more, tell me what you think you know."

Mahra thought for a few seconds turning events over in her mind before responding.

"There's just too much that doesn't seem to add up. There is the ship for a start. She's far too well equipped. Much too much to reflect the sort of income I would expect from someone trading out of New Helvetica. Not for a small operation such as yours anyway. You might do well at it, but I doubt that it would be *that* well. If I put that together with your ability to bring the conversation to a halt every time Timon starts to get into anything meaningful, well, then I start to get a little curious."

"All right ... go on."

"Secondly, there's the ease with which you seem to get in and out of systems, without once getting caught by a detailed check. That started me thinking as well. You know that I've been patched in every time we've made an approach or departure. There's lucky and then there's *too* lucky and somehow *The Dark Falcon* seems to fall into the latter category. I'll wager that we'll get back to New Helvetica with two weights of dust casually stowed in Timon's locker without so much as a second look."

"And, finally there's Belshore — Garavenah's operation. I'm not altogether sure what its real purpose is, but it's by no stretch of the imagination anything like it's trying to appear to be. It all seems to point to one thing. So, tell me ... who exactly are you working for, Jayeer?"

"You actually have more of the picture than I'd have thought. I'm impressed." His eyes were narrowed behind the thick lenses. "You're right of course. We're a covert operation, just as Garavenah's outfit is. It doesn't hurt to admit that much. You're already bound by what you know, you realise that? Should you want to leave now, it would be very difficult for all of us. Not a level of risk we could easily accommodate — you understand?"

"Yes, I think I do. In that case, Jayeer, you may as well tell me all of it. Just so I know exactly what I'm bound to. I think that's only fair, don't you? At least it gives me a chance to think about my options." Mahra spread her palms.

"I'm afraid, Mahra Kaitan, that you don't have any options any more. You're along for the ride." He paused, subjecting her to thoughtful scrutiny. "All right then. Be that as it may, I may as well paint the rest of the picture. Timon and I work for the Special Operations section of the Combined Council of Worlds, as does Garavenah."

Mahra's jaw dropped open. That, she had not suspected. Sind continued, oblivious to her stunned expression.

"Commander Pellis, um, Timon that is, has the dubious distinction of being head of this particular operation. I function as Chief Technical Officer. As you have noted, *The Dark Falcon* is well equipped. Very well equipped in fact. It's state of the art military, some of it still experimental. We have a secondary drive, for instance, that remains untested, but it's still there all the same. Just in case. You see? I'm sure you will have noticed Garavenah's mention of Sirona involvement..."

Mahra nodded, still trying to bring her surprise under control.

"Yes, well, I thought as much. When it comes down to it, they are our primary concern. For a long time, the CoCee has suspected Sirona interference in a number of areas. That's where we come in. If we can gather enough evidence, we should have the capacity to introduce sanctions across the board, or at least have them introduced in the right quarters. Sanctions against the Sirona trading monopoly would be a fine thing — a very fine thing indeed. To bring a halt to the destabilising influence and what we believe are their clandestine networks of ownership and control. That would be a very fine thing as well. It may itself, ultimately lead to a confrontation, but that's something we're prepared for, and have been preparing for, for a long time. We have long suspected that the Sirona employ Belshore as a testing ground and distribution point for some of the more insidious of their products. Often, after the spread of such things, like this, the most recent, the so-called 'dust', we find a timely Sirona intervention with a price that ultimately seems to have a great cost in social progress or stability. Their workings are very subtle. All that people are generally looking for at the time is a quick fix to their problems. They don't count the long-term cost. That's why it's all the more dangerous."

Mahra nodded. "So how does Garavenah's operation fit into the picture?" she asked as Sind took the time to sip at his mug of kahveh.

Sind nodded in turn, swallowed a large gulp, and replied. "It's very simple really. Her outfit has been set up along the same lines as any of the Belshorian syndicate families. It has taken a long time to build up to the position she holds now. Forget the morals, but they deal in the full range of vice and corruption found on Belshore, and that in turn, gives her access to the distribution and supply networks. More importantly, it gives her access to massive amounts of information. We visit her once every few months and pick up a report on whatever she might have unearthed. We arrive, leave and continue in the guise of freebooters, always picking up or delivering something that would legitimate our presence."

"But why in the world do you have to pick up the report, Jayeer? Why couldn't she just transmit it to wherever it has to go?"

"Fair question. We've found through bitter experience that we can't trust the com nets, regardless of any encryption. The only way we can guarantee the transmission's sanctity is to carry it ourselves. If at any stage *The Dark Falcon* came under serious threat, then such information would be quite simply disappeared and the interested parties would be none the wiser."

"Uh-huh, that makes sense. But if this operation is so sensitive, why not go through normal channels and second a replacement for the man you lost? Why hire me?"

"I had serious doubts myself, but I've already told you that. My thinking ran along those very lines, but the Commander calls the shots. There are only a few, a select few, who know what is going on. We can't trust 'normal channels' as they stand. We don't know how far the penetration goes. The problem we face, you see, is that even the Council is not secure, or at least we can't be guaranteed that it is. Your appearance was somewhat fortuitous. You seemed to have no specific ties, yet you possessed the sort of skills we needed. A useful combination. The simple truth was, you do not seem to fit anywhere, and whether you like it or not, you were expendable and that matched our specific needs. All of our checks came up that way before we sought you out."

"Before you…what?"

"As it turned out, the Commander's impulses, for once, seem to have worked out."

"I don't believe it, Jayeer. Is that a sound of approval?" She paused for a moment, as he snorted at her sarcasm. She thought for a moment before continuing. In essence, it hadn't been chance. It hadn't been a matter of right place, right time. They'd actually come looking for her.

"I still have questions though. What happens from here?"

"Well ... I suppose we go on as we have been, but a little more openly. Timon will have to be told of course. He will probably bite *my* head off for saying too much — for a change." He smiled. "Still, what is done is done. But I warn you now," he said sternly. "If I so much as suspect there's a chance that you might compromise the operation, I will have no qualms ... " He left the remainder unsaid.

"No need to rub it in Jayeer, I understand the implications," she said. She was already resigned to that much. "So again, where do we go from here?"

"Yes, well ... um, back to New Helvetica as soon as possible. It actually serves us as a sort of base. Timon should be in some sort of condition to fly come the morning, but I'll want to give him the once over first. We need to get the dust back to our labs for complete analysis as soon as possible. When we have a full understanding of how it works and what it is, we'll be able to work out some way to stop it working and detect its presence. Well, that's the theory anyway. If we can do that, it should help to limit the import and the supply. There are people on New Helvetica who can do all of that for us. It is such a convenient world New Helvetica, abundance of tech and the freedom to move. We could probably get away with such things on my own home world, but neither the tech nor the channels exist there."

"Hmm, I see. You're Andaran aren't you, Jayeer?" she asked. He nodded. "So, what about Timon, where's he from?"

"I don't really think it's my place to answer for Timon. He'll tell you what he wants to. What I will say though, is that he's a true spacer. Born and raised between worlds. If you want any further details you'll have to ask him."

Mahra accepted this and let him continue.

"Anyway, I think we've really had enough for one night. Don't you? I'm going to get some rest and I suggest you do the same. We don't know what we might run into on the way out. I don't think they'll try anything portside, but you never know. I'll set the security on auto before I turn in. Is there anything else you feel you ought to know before I leave you to it?"

Mahra shook her head.

"Well, in that case, rest well"

He nodded and stood, taking his mug to clean and stack before he left. As he reached the door Mahra called to stop him. "Jayeer."

"Yes?"

"Um ... thanks."

Sind gave a slight frown, looking vaguely puzzled, before he turned and walked off down the passageway.

She really should take his advice and get some rest, but her mind was ticking over too rapidly. She lifted Chutzpah from her shoulder, fished around and found a couple of nuts to keep him occupied, then wandered over to pour herself another mug of kahveh, running their conversation over in her mind.

Chapter Eleven

Valdor leaned back in his chair, fingers clasped behind his head and allowed himself the pleasure of putting his feet up on the desk. It felt good when something was working — really working, and finally the breakthrough had come. He'd pumped enough resources into the project and wrapped it in a security cloud. He had created a virtual think tank, if he thought about it. Well, now it had paid off. He had the biocomp.

He knew he was right about it. The biocomp was a beauty and he alone could lay claim to it. The fact that some of the keenest intellects in the system were unable to scale that pinnacle on their own, only added to his satisfaction.

One thing still troubled him — one small tarnish on the sheen of his success. His smile slowly faded as it came to mind. The Sirona. They still presented a threat, and so far, they had not played their hand. What the hell did the Sirona want with his little project? They could have no real interest in something that was probably, to them, just a piece of low-tech gadgetry. The story had to run deeper than that, but he was cursed if he could work out their reasoning. That failing troubled him all the more.

He liked to think of himself as reasonably astute when it came to the underlying motivations of others. Perhaps, after all, it was the sheer alien made-up of the Sirona thought processes that kept the answer from his grasp. He had to keep reminding himself that they weren't human. It was so easy to see them simply as short people with an accent, spawned in some edge of system backwater. But he couldn't allow himself to let it get to him. There had been no further sign since that initial brief encounter, and it suited him just fine. Carr Holdings could get along quite nicely without intervention, especially if that intervention was alien.

He had decided he needed to set up an insurance policy just in case they did decide to act. If he could get a few samples of the core gene plasm sets off world, it would act as a safety net for his interests in case anything did go dreadfully wrong. Always better to be safe. He was not about to let his designs be held hostage by a group of poisonous little gnomes, no matter how much power they thought they had.

Savouring the spiteful nature of his last thought, he dropped his feet to the floor and leaned across to establish com link with his erstwhile head of internal security. Carr had been right to place Milnus in the position of background control. It had paid dividends as he knew it would. There had been one or two dissenters when they closed off the research team from the outside world. During the project's life three more had created ripples because of their methods. One researcher was relocated; another two were victims of unfortunate incidents. Luckily those concerned weren't crucial to the ongoing success of the operation and Valdor was able to draft in replacements.

Milnus's number two was efficient enough at what he did, but when it came to a sensitive situation, Carr felt forced to place Milnus directly in control, time after time.

Dissent wasn't the greatest of concerns anyway. Exposure was, and Carr had given Milnus full authority to use all the means at his disposal to ensure it didn't occur. As a rule, scientific types were not high risk. They tended to be more bound up in their work and the vision of their own dissociated reality. They didn't usually get involved in the subterfuges and intrigues of corporate espionage. Valdor felt comfortable in the knowledge that everything was safe in Milnus's hands.

Now it was time to set his insurance in place. He flicked on the com.

"Milnus. Yes, Valdor. How are things, no further developments? No ... good. Look. I want you to arrange the transportation of some of the core sample offworld. Yes ... to my safe holdings on Kalany for the moment ... I don't know. Pick someone you can trust. There is someone isn't there? Hm-hm. I'll leave it in your hands. When you've seen to it, come over. I want a full report. In person."

Valdor severed the connection and sat back, running his fingers back through his hair and drumming on the desk top with his fingers.

Milnus sat pondering his options for several minutes after the connection was broken. He had one or two people he could use for this assignment, but he didn't want to leave himself too exposed. The task wasn't important enough to go himself, but if Valdor was being paranoid about the whole issue he had best be careful with it. If there was potential for an intercept, he wanted to safeguard the project's confidentiality and that limited his choices. A certain team member involved on the project would have been ideal, but he had a problem. He knew too much of the technical details. No, he could use Phildore for technical advice on how to achieve the transportation. He had someone else — the ideal candidate in fact — to perform the task.

Feeling pleased with his decision, he called Phildore in to set the first part in place. Having explained his requirements, he set about organising for the courier to be available.

Milnus liked the idea of Killara as the courier. She was a basic physical type. She was proficient at looking after both herself and those she was assigned to, and that suited the current need precisely. At the moment, she was assigned to routine bodyguard duty covering one of the organisation's corporate wheels who for the moment was slightly at risk. Killara looked after him and at the same time kept an eye on his activities, making sure everybody's interested were covered. She was good, but someone could easily take her place in that role. She was better suited to what he needed.

Having decided, Milnus put the procedures in place. He arranged for a replacement to take over from her, smoothly and seamlessly. He booked passage for her on an outgoing merchanter in six hours' time. That should give Phildore enough time to do what he needed to do. The passage was paid for out of Killara's own accounts and would be reimbursed later through another bank from virtually untraceable funds. She was easily the sort who would take passage on a merchant ship rather than a commercial transport vessel, so it was unlikely to arouse any suspicions. Because the merchanter was leaving in such a relatively short time, it would make it difficult for anyone to perform an intercept.

Satisfied that he had the necessary mechanisms in place, he contacted Killara and organised a rendezvous in a secure central office close to the dockside in four hours' time.

Milnus had risen far in Valdor's organisation for good reason. He was totally devoted to Valdor Carr and liked to watch the man's progress. Valdor's successes were his satisfaction. In many ways it was almost paternal, and Valdor lived the sort of existence that Milnus would have wanted had he the nerve for it. As Carr Holdings had grown, so had Milnus's importance. As time went on, Valdor's successes became Milnus's own, but they were achieved in subtle ways wherever possible. Often, he thought about how different it might have been had he been a younger man; how he himself might have risen to such heights. Now there was no longer that possibility, and he instead found satisfaction in his own role. He preferred to run things from the background and taste the successes in private.

Less than two hours later, Phildore arrived back with his solution. Milnus looked up as he entered the room.

"I think I have the answer," said the young man.

"Yes?"

"I won't go into too much detail, but we're trying to protect the sample from both detection and scanning, if I understand it correctly."

"Right."

"Well, you know the sample is biological." Milnus nodded. "What better way to conceal it than in something organic?"

"I don't think I understand .... "

"Think about it for a moment. You're sending the sample with a courier, the package is small enough to be concealed, and if we shield it in something organic, it won't show on scans or be detected."

"Ahh, I see," said Milnus and nodded.

Phildore, was clearly pleased with himself. "I've designed a little package from some of our organic waste materials. It is made in such a way as to protect the sample from the courier's body, and vice versa."

"So ... what? The courier will swallow this package?"

"No, no," said Phildore and smiled. "The courier will carry the package with them. If detection becomes likely, it's small enough that it should be able to be swallowed as a last resort. I had to provide for that eventuality. It won't show up on scans, and it would appear exactly like the remnants of the courier's last meal."

Milnus smiled slowly, struck by the beauty of the solution.

Phildore continued. "Of course, it's untested, but I believe it'll be safe." Phildore shrugged. "In the time available ... "

"Yes, yes," said Milnus and waved his hand "Well done. So, we'll be ready for the meeting."

The keenness of this young man's mind continually impressed Milnus. Phildore had a great future ahead of him if he played his cards right.

It would take about an hour to get to the dockside offices directly, so Milnus took the extra precaution of planning a roundabout route to add to their security. It also meant their arrival should coincide roughly with Killara's. Timing was often everything. Satisfied that everything was prepared, they left. Milnus felt confident that each party knew only as much as they needed to. The scientist's responsibility was only to provide a meant of effecting the end. Killara needed only to know how the mechanics worked and where she had to go. That was enough for each of them.

They reached the offices in good time and had several minutes to wait for Killara's arrival. With the remaining time, Milnus took the extra precaution of checking the office security systems. It gave him extra reassurance that his plans couldn't go awry. Considering Carr's experiences with the Sirona, it didn't hurt to be sure.

When Killara finally arrived, Phildore looked her up and down with an obvious expression of distaste. She strode into the offices like a piece of heavy machinery, short and squat and all compact muscle. She nodded to each briefly and stood in the room's centre waiting, without so much as a word. Milnus remembered now that she never had been one much for idle conversation. She was a good choice.

Milnus moved over to stand between them.

"Killara," he said. "Phildore." Killara grunted and Phildore nodded. "Well, Phildore, if you'd like to explain the procedure, we can get on with it.

Phildore lifted the small package for Killara to see.

"This is what you'll be carrying," he said. "What it contains is unimportant, but because of its sensitive nature, we've taken the extra precaution of making it so that you can swallow it if you need to."

Killara frowned and took a step backward.

"No, there's no need to be concerned," continued Phildore. "It is perfectly safe. We just need to be sure that it will pass any scans you might be subjected to. The material inside is biological, so it would pass naturally, but the coating surrounding it is biological as well, as an extra precaution. The coating is inert, and won't react with your own body's functions in any way. If necessary, those two things should make it pass any casual scan without being detected. I just don't want you to have any hesitation doing what is necessary if it comes to it."

Killara pursed her lips and looked sceptically from the package to Phildore's face and back again. Phildore seemed not to notice. Milnus was sure that Killara would not give up the package's location easily and would do what she had to do.

"Do you understand?" asked Phildore.

Killara looked over at Milnus, back at the package and nodded her head.

Phildore handed her the package and she shoved it deep inside her clothing. With Phildore's part completed, Milnus dismissed him, waiting for a minute or two after he left before explaining the task to Killara. She sat where Phildore left her, waiting.

"Right, Killara. You will proceed by merchanter to Kalany under the guise of a freelancer looking for work. There is money to be made on Kalany if you have the right skills, so it's a plausible cover. You'll be met on Kalany, you'll hand over the package and that will be the end of it." Killara had no questions, nor did Milnus expect any. "Passage has been arranged for you on board the trader *Catseye*. You should proceed straight to the docks now and board her. You only have a limited time window. As far as they're concerned, you are a paying passenger, nothing more. The financial side of things has already been taken care of. *Catseye* is berthed in dock F17. Your contact on the *Catseye* is a man named Strude. You'll be met on Kalany by one of our people, Palans. Don't look for him. He'll find you at the other end."

Killara nodded and, shouldering her pack, she strode out the door without another word.

The whole procedure had been straightforward and Milnus was mildly pleased with himself. The solution was clever and Valdor would have had his paranoia catered to. Certainly, it was better to be safe, but sometimes Milnus felt Valdor took things too far. In a few more hours it would all be over and they would be able to get back to the business at hand. He took a few minutes examining the options to see if there were any flaws. Satisfied that there were none, he reached across the desk and opened a channel to report to Carr.

☐

Killara knew what she had to do and she didn't have much time to do it. She had the name of the contact on the merchanter and the name of her contact on Kalany. First point to last point, end of job and then disappear for a while. All very simple. What she didn't understand was why she always got picked for jobs like this one? She knew she had to learn to control her natural resentment. It got her into too much trouble. She gritted her teeth and muttered to herself as she walked.

She was graced with a stocky figure, a particularly unattractive face with narrow squinting eyes, a huge jawline, and a very short temper. This meant she usually found herself in the sort of jobs nobody else really wanted, or with people that nobody really wanted to deal with. That was, of course, unless they had a serious psychosis. She didn't mind so much. It meant that life was occasionally very interesting, and from time to time, she had the added bonus of taking out her resentment on people she was allowed to hurt. Generally, it was a satisfactory life.

Every now and again she got one of these uncomplicated and potentially tedious assignments. These were the sorts of jobs she did not like. Right now, she'd like to hurt Milnus instead. And that tech type who had spoken to her like an idiot. That tech type would keep until later. She'd find her opportunity, eventually. Milnus, well he was a different matter. He was out of the game.

She could feel the tiny package inside her clothing and she curled her lip at the thought of having to swallow it. There had better not be anyone on board this ship who might get in her way. Underneath, she really hoped there was.

She reached the docks after a lengthy walk. Phildore said it would pass through her body within a few hours if she had to swallow it, but time meant very little to Killara and whether it caused her any discomfort or not, it didn't take away the indignity of having to retrieve it. Having to walk to the docks instead of catching the public trans or having some other private transport arranged was offensive as well, but orders were orders and she knew she had to follow them. It was just so much easier when she enjoyed what she had to do.

Killara knew she wasn't very good with numbers or reading, but she was very good at remembering. She had the name of the ship memorised and hoping that was enough, asked one of the dockhands for directions. He gave her a dock number and waved his hand vaguely over to the right. Why didn't she remember the number that Milnus gave her? It sounded like it was the same one, but she wasn't sure. She could tell already that this was not going to be a good day.

Three more times she asked directions wandering all over the dock trying to locate the ship. Finally, as luck would have it, she ran into a crew member of the very ship she was searching for. He wore stained coveralls, an unshaven face, lanky hair, and a distinct odour. He looked at her belligerently and asked what she wanted. His tone barely changed when she told him she was a paying passenger and gave him the contact name.

"Yeah, all right. That's me," he said and looked her up and down again.

Grudgingly he motioned her to follow and led the way, picking his way circuitously between the metal walls of other ships, stepping over pipes and machinery on the way. She was sure he had chosen the route deliberately to provide the maximum discomfort possible. Well, if that was the way he wanted it, that was the way he could have it. She'd find her opportunity. She was good at remembering. Finally, he drew to a halt and indicated a derelict vessel with a toss of his head.

The ship was a mess. If the crew member she was following had been made from metal and given drives he would probably look in better shape than the scow that sat before them. There were scars all over the hull's surface and distinct cracks within the outer insulating skin. There was a visible cant to it, as if someone had shoved it down with too much force on one of its landers. Killara had serious doubts about its capacity to make any voyage, let alone this one.

The scow's inside was little better. It had the added feature of that certain indefinable atmosphere that came from unwashed humanity and recycled air. She had seen and smelt worse, but not much. This was not going to be a good assignment. Without so much as a tour, the crewman led her to her quarters. She closed herself behind her cabin door, breathing in deeply of the sour recycled air. Even then it tasted sweeter than the odour she had to endure standing close to her guide. Killara was not overly concerned about bathing and being clean and other such social niceties herself, but even so, she'd be glad of a shower after this one.

☐

Up in the *Catseye's* front, its pilot sought clearance from dock control. As soon as he received it, he slapped the channel shut. He checked the settings then checked them one more time, sucked a large swallow from his bottle and spat to one side before initiating the ignition sequence. The deep throbbing whine of the drives grew in the ship's bowels, faltered, then sputtered and died, bringing a curse to his lips. Muttering under his breath, he spat once more and started the sequence again. This time the drives caught, and the ship rose ponderously, creaking, and popping, from the dock. Once more, they were under way and he leaned back and let out a breath of relief.

He nursed the dishevelled ship up from the pad as he had done many times before. Ever so gently, he eased her through the atmosphere. He knew how much his ship could take. They'd lived together for a long time. He would let it out a bit once they got out onto the open lanes, but he didn't want to come crashing back down to the dock just right now. Regardless of life and limb, the damage claims would be too high and insurance didn't come into the picture. Though come to think of it ...

□

Killara sat in her pungent, grease-stained cabin cursing her luck. With every creak and shudder of the claptrap ship she grimaced and held tighter to the bunk's sides, expecting immanent disaster. As she heard the noises lessen and finally fade into silence she knew they had reached the atmosphere's outer edges and she felt a small sense of relief. There were still creaks and groans as the ship travelled higher, but it sounded less as if it was going to break apart with every new noise. She wondered why they just didn't park her in orbit and take a shuttle down, if they even had a shuttle. They had to have their reasons, and besides, it was really none of her concern.

Dismissing the thoughts, she settled herself with her back leaning against an inner bulkhead and closed her eyes. The pressures of the take-off had not helped, but she'd cope. It was going to be a long voyage, that was for sure.

Vaguely she could hear noises of the crew moving about the ship doing whatever it was they did. She didn't have much interest in ship tech. If it got her where she wanted to go, that was all that mattered. She wouldn't trust a single one of the crew though — no more than she could throw them. Just let one of them try and come in here to chance their luck. It would certainly be in character. She'd seen their type before. They'd find out a thing or two if they did. Just like the last one who tried. A slight smile played across her lips at the thought. Maybe, if she was lucky, one of them would.

Chapter Twelve

The Cradle

After the dark robed figure had wandered off across the hillside, Mahra had felt the sense of pressure ease. She still felt uncomfortable with what he was, but there was something about him and the things that he said that had touched a chord within her. She was not a stranger to asking why, and there were things within the questions that Aleyin asked her to think about, that begged for answers. He had left her with a puzzle. She knew that there was no one to give her answers, so it sat with her, leaving her with a nagging doubt. For the days and weeks that followed, things were not quite the same. Nothing around her had changed, but it was as if Aleyin had cast a knot in the smooth path of her life. The sense of untroubled acceptance had gone. Somewhere, somehow, there might be someone or something playing with the shape and direction of her life without her knowledge, and she was less than happy with the thought.

One afternoon, something changed. She was kneeling at the end of the bed and had just opened the chest, when she noticed a small red light blinking insistently within the darkness. Placing the blade down, she reached forward and retrieved the comp. She flipped it open and keyed access. This was something new, and she thought, logically, something important. She waited for initialisation before accessing the bulletins. There was just one line spelled out in capitals across the screen. JOINT MEETING. CENTRAL COMMITTEE. STATUS: PRIORITY. The last word flashed on and off.

Mahra at once understood what she had to do and the thought filled her with excitement. At last, she'd have the chance to take her place among the senior members of Lantana. She was not sure if she was ready for it. She was still so young, especially compared to those such as the Old One. What could she possibly have to offer that body of collective wisdom with her mere fifteen years? But there was no point debating it. The summons had come.

Unwrapping the blade for the third time that day, she strapped on the sheath and made sure it rested firmly in position on her back, lying at a slight angle running down between her shoulder blades. Reaching up, she made sure there was no slippage of the straps or sheath. Such laxity could be costly, getting in the way of a smooth removal of the blade. When she first started wearing the blade, she had found it necessary to adjust the straps themselves, drilling holes further down the leather so they would fit snugly about her smaller frame. She'd grow into it in time, but for now, it was secure enough.

Wearing the blade was important. It served her as her identifier, marking her as one who belonged. It embodied all the aspects of her training. She remembered Aleyin, and that he didn't wear a blade. She wondered briefly if that was his choice, or whether he was denied it for some reason. That too was something else to file away for later reference. She scurried around collecting a few supplies, dropping them one by one into the woven carrier she'd take with her on the journey. Last to be included was the comp. This, she thought, was the only essential item in the bag. Although it would be a two-day journey to the collection point, she was perfectly self-sufficient and had no need to take anything else. But she didn't want to waste time having to forage for supplies along the way.

Despite her excitement, she took the time to scan each room to make sure she had forgotten nothing. Satisfied that she had all she needed, she retrieved the comp from the sack. She pressed an acknowledge, and watched with satisfaction as the red light stopped blinking, then she dropped it back into the sack. Finally, she walked out into the early afternoon glare, secure in the knowledge that all would be as she left it when she returned. There were no human predators on Lantana. The dwelling would be safe until her return, along with the little in it.

Striking out toward the northeast, she paused only long enough to make the appropriate gestures toward the great bowl that carried the ever-burning Flame of Life. Her thoughts went out to the Old One. Let her make him proud. Let her not make a fool of herself and let her actions show loyalty to his memory. Silently, she mouthed this as a prayer to whatever forces of continuity and life existed on this world. She knew that although he was gone, he continued within her with the mark of his hands upon what she was and what she may be destined to become.

The journey itself was uneventful. She took time from her march only to perform her daily exercises and to check on the comp's status, but there were no changes to the bulletins.

Not that she expected anyone to contact *her*.

She slept one night in the open, making her bed from leaves and moss gathered beneath the huge spreading trees that canopied the lesser reaches of the high slopes. Even though the days of this season had become warm, the nights were still chill, particularly at this altitude, for she was moving up the slopes before crossing the ridgeline to her destination. After a peaceful dreamless night, she woke with the dawn to continue her trek, the feeling of anticipation growing within her as she drew nearer to the call point.

Mahra crested the ridge that intersected her path around midday. Here she stopped, allowing herself the luxury of absorbing the vista that lay spread out before her.

145

The chill wind whipped about her on this exposed expanse of naked rock, but she ignored its bite, absorbed by the majesty. The skein of subtle colours was unmarred by the handiwork of human kind; not a road or blocky settlement to spoil the smooth contours of muted greens and browns. Those who lived on The Cradle were discreet in their interference, enough that it could almost be taken for a virgin world. Mahra's few minutes of absorption paid homage to the history of her people and their care to stay as one with this world that played host to them. Taking a deep breath, she shouldered her pack, settling the straps comfortably in place, and began to pick her way among the rocks that littered the path down to the plains spread out below.

She reached the call point late in the afternoon. The widely cleared circle of ground was marked at its boundaries with four upright bronzed poles. These were the key poles. The place was easily recognizable as she made her descent. The poles shone with the reflected sunlight, now low on the horizon. She could have located the place with the help of her comp, but her path was clear, and her sense of direction had never failed her. She had been here only once before, but that was enough to place its location firmly in her mind.

The grasslands stretched out in every direction from the rich, dark brown of the cleared circle floor. No vegetation grew within its boundaries. Some signal from the poles saw to that. She sensed rather than felt the low-pitched hum below the edge of her perceptions as she neared the edges. The patch of ground and the shiny untarnished poles were the only sign of a human presence as far as she could see. All about, the grasses waved slightly in the breeze, only broken by the crisscrossing paths of herd beasts. The continuing vibration stirred at the back of her senses making her feel a little unsettled, but she dampened the feeling and pulled the pack from her shoulders before fishing around in it for her comp.

Mahra placed it flat in her palm and crouching, rested its top edge at the pole base. Carefully she slid it upward, always keeping contact, along the entire length from bottom to top. Twice more she performed the sequence. The comp should now have keyed the call signal. There was nothing left to do but wait, so she settled herself cross-legged at the circle's edge to do just that. Sitting here, again she was reminded of the questions that Aleyin asked. She knew what the poles were for. She knew what her comp was for, but she had no idea how they really operated. She stared at the poles and wondered. Why would that knowledge be denied to her?

She didn't have long to wait, for less than an hour later, a shadow crossed the remaining light, stretching across the diameter of the circle and reaching to where she sat. Looking up, she tracked the oval shape as it passed across the setting sun's orange orb, growing larger by the minute. The flyer began its descent and Aleyin's questions were banished from her thoughts. Without a sound to disturb the tranquillity of the open savanna, the flyer soared gently to the ground.

The craft was an oval bubble with some sort of clear plas making up the upper half. The lower section was a uniform grey-black and sheenless like her blade. She sat staring at it for a minute or two, but nothing happened. The flyer sat, seemingly inert. All around, the grasses whispered in the breeze. Only the sound of her own breathing marred the natural silence.

Mahra's forehead creased. Picking up the comp, she pointed it at the flyer. When that produced no results, she slapped the comp on its side and shook it, before waving it again in the general direction of the craft. Still there was no response. She felt frustration beginning to well inside her, but with an effort, she took a deep breath and held it in check.

Hoisting her pack on one shoulder she moved toward the flyer one step at a time, comp brandished before her. Gingerly she circled the craft, caution foremost in her mind. Nothing was obvious on the surface, and the transparent dome appeared seamless. She took one more step, then jumped back with a start as a sudden noise broke the stillness. With the whirring noise of machinery, a section of the domed top slid back into a recess in the lower hull. Startled, she dropped the comp, then scrabbled to retrieve it, berating herself for stupidity. Of course, the mechanism was keyed to her proximity, and here now was her point of entry. She felt thankful that there was no one here to witness to her foolishness.

Inside, the flyer was as featureless as the outside, apart from a set of contoured seats and a small panel upon which a faintly glowing light winked on and off at regular intervals. All she had to do was work out how to operate it, for the panel was blank apart from the blinking light and a deep slot disappearing back from the smooth surface. There was no obvious sign of any control. Mahra clambered in and settled herself in the foremost seat, adjusting the blade between her shoulders so it didn't dig into her back.

Carefully, she scanned the panel and the interior, looking for something that resembled a set of controls. She pursed her lips and thought. Reaching forward, she tapped at the blinking light. Nothing happened. She pressed it firmly with her forefinger. Again, nothing happened. She tried pressing the flat of her palm to the panel, but again nothing. Perhaps, she thought, the flyer would activate by itself given enough time, so she sat and waited, feeling increasingly foolish as the time stretched on. After several minutes passed, she decided that there was nothing to be gained by sitting and waiting. Maybe the key was in her comp. It called the craft; perhaps it would start it as well. She held it forward and ran it across the surface of the panel. Then she saw it. The slot…might just….

Yes, it was a perfect fit. The comp slid neatly into the opening and she was immediately rewarded. The door panel slid smoothly closed and the previously dull grey control board blossomed with displays and lights. Mahra gripped the seat nervously, as the flyer rose silently and took to the air. Smoothly, it turned on its axis, and she was pressed back into the seat as it shot away from the open grassland into the setting sun.

Her eyes wide, Mahra took in the retreating patterns of the open countryside. The scenery whizzed past below and, despite the now fading light, she was afforded a perfect view of the passing landscape. Slowly she released her white-knuckled grip on the sides of the seat. Now, despite all she had learned, she was here, surrounded by tech, her own resources virtually useless and feeling excited and very confused. Increasingly she was starting to doubt the received wisdom she had taken so much for granted.

The flyer started to climb, the only sound that of the wind whistling past the outside the surrounding shield. She watched as a ridge of low peaks approached, whipped below, then receded into the distance, and she craned her neck to followed it. She turned to follow their passage behind, marvelling at the speed and the lines of cloud that formed streamers like banners trailing from the peaks. Everywhere below her lay sights she could only have dreamed of.

She faced front and gasped. A vast lake stretched from end to end of the horizon, edges purpling in the growing dusk. The water's depths smouldered with the reflected red and orange sunset. For a few moments, she was so absorbed with the spectacle that she didn't notice what should have captured her attention immediately. At last, she became aware of it. A tracery of lights spread in a web from a central point of oval darkness lying on one shore of the lake. As the ship grew closer, the dome's enormity registered and she brought one hand to her mouth in amazement.

The dome's shape became more defined with each moment of her approach. She craned forward in her seat. She had never seen a structure so large and she could barely believe that such a thing was physically possible. This was it, the great Place of the Assembly.

By now, many, probably most, of the great minds of The Cradle were gathered waiting for the last few stragglers such as she. How could she possibly be worthy to join and take part in such an assemblage, such a meeting of minds, let alone merely be here?

Orange and red flickered on the dome surface echoing the lake's sunset colours. The surface had to be constructed of some polished stone, made shiny to catch the setting sun's remaining colours and throw them back in intensified splendour. The colours grew brighter and soon they were even brighter than the setting sun. Blinking her eyes against the glare, she frowned. Then she saw what else lay before her, hanging above the lake. A huge silver shape was descending from the darkness above the dome. An arc of light lanced down from that shape playing across the curved structure. She narrowed her eyes, then she realised. The shape was a ship.

Almost at the very instant that she recognized the shape, the dome's surface erupted into flowers of force, blossoming fire as pieces of the structure fly skyward.

"No!" she cried out. "No!"

Her guts had gone cold. She slammed her fist against the clear plas in front of her.

"No!"

She knew instinctively what she had to do. Reaching forward, she wrenched the comp from its slot, still watching as the destruction played out before her. Open mouthed, she stared as the flyer descended, too stunned to move as her craft dropped rapidly to the gentle slopes below. The scenes of devastation continued, stretching out in slow motion as if time was oddly distorted. She shook her head to clear the images, but they stayed there, terrible with their power.

The flyer bumped to the ground and the door panel slid open. Mahra didn't understand, but she acted. She grabbed her comp in one hand and her pack in the other, then clambered and stumbled from the flyer. She sprawled face-first on the ground, catching her foot on the rim of her craft. She barely noticed the pain as she dragged herself to her feet and started to run up the hill away from the horror behind.

Mahra ran until she could run no more, and fell, wracked by sobs, to the ground.

Chapter Thirteen

Far beyond the slowly rising ship, the orbital platform continued with its duties. It registered the approach, identified the call signal, and catalogued it before flashing the displays on the main console. This time the display was blue. This ship had been recognised and was legally registered. Otherwise, the displays would have been in flashing yellow.

This was not a particularly busy time and the sole member of the watch crew on duty sat idly drumming on his thighs with his palms. He leaned back listening to music on his phones. There were times such as this where the job was pretty boring, but it had its advantages as well. Being able to sit and relax with a bit of head space was nice every now and again. Markin got through a lot of music that way. Of course, there were busy periods as well where there was no time to think and the work came thick and fast. Now, however, it was out of season and the traffic was slight.

Out of habit born of routine, Markin's gaze wandered from time to time over to the main console, checking for movement. He noticed the call sign flashing with its steady blue identifier and hissed between his teeth as he pulled off the phones with one hand. Work was never finished. There was always someone or something willing to interrupt a bit of peace.

He scanned the call sign and grunted his recognition. Markin knew this ship, one of the old beaten-up traders that occasionally frequented the system. It was legally registered but on an outward journey, so it had little to interest him. Once or twice he might have had caused to look the other way for this particular ship in exchange for the appropriate adjustment to his cred balance, but it was always on the inward journey. There was never anything to look for on the *Catseye* on its way out of system.

Markin tapped the sequence to bring her up on visual, letting his gaze wander over her as she approached. It amazed him sometimes how some of these traders got away with flying buckets like this one. They were a hazard to themselves as much as to other shipping, but that was of minor importance as far as he was concerned. It'd be nobody's loss if she were to break up. For a moment or two, he toyed with the idea of shaking her down just for the sheer hell of it to mark his disapproval, but then thought better of it. It would be a waste of energy and only give him a moment or two of satisfaction for all the effort. Then there'd be all the paperwork to fill out.

He shook his head and leaned forward to tap the sequence that started the ritual question and answer of the recognition drill. His finger paused above the pad, waiting for the next step. All of a sudden, the screens went crazy. First one, then the other flared brilliant yellow and flowered in reverse to darkness flecked with traceries of white. He had seen system downs before, but nothing like this one. Cursing he slapped his hand on the console. After a second or two, nothing changed and he rapidly tapped the sequences for re-initiation. Still nothing happened and he tried again. He slammed his fist down on the console.

"Come on, come on," he muttered between closed teeth.

Slapping both hands on the console, Markin pushed his chair back and shrugged off his harness. Now he had to go and check out the overrides. He hated the really technical stuff. He muttered to himself as he palmed the observation module's exit sequence and wandered down the corridor to locate the panel. Maybe he could work out what to do. He didn't hold much hope of being able to fix it, but he had to try. With any luck, it would clear itself. He really didn't want to call in the techs. If he did, that meant reports and reports meant work. He had enough reports to fill out as it was.

☐

    Slowly, above the blinded station, a shimmering haze distorted the images of the stars behind. Gradually at first, and then more rapidly, the wavering form acquired substance as if collecting matter about itself. The stars behind it dimmed and the blackness became lighter. The shape became steadily more defined until the backdrop could no longer be seen behind the large silvery ovoid that now hung in its place. Its smooth surface was unblemished. Nothing protruded from the curving shell and not a single marking distinguished the outer skin. The vast ship hung for a moment, suspended, then with a speed seemingly contradicted by the immensity of its bulk, slid forward to position itself between the platform and the approaching scow.

    The tramp ship grew inexorably closer. A glowing beam of light stabbed out from the front of the great orb. For an instant, the two ships hung connected by a bridge of light, then the smaller ship shuddered and a moment later, simply ceased to be. Not a trace of debris remained to mark the scow's position. The luminous spear winked out of existence at the same moment. The great orb glowed faintly, a slight shimmer grew around it, then just as rapidly, it was no longer there. The space around the orbiting platform was empty.

☐

The navy watchman returned to his post still muttering and cursing to himself, ready to summon the techs to see to the problem. Markin knew he wouldn't be able to fix the damned thing. He was pleasantly relieved to see that the screens were back to their normal steady state. He was just settling back into his seat ready to don his phones, when he realised there was something odd. He'd forgotten about the *Catseye*. The call sign for the tramp trader ship no longer showed.

"That's not right," he said.

He had not been away long enough for the ship to get past the platform, and there was absolutely nothing else in the area at the time.

He frowned for a moment then flipped the controls for search. He keyed in the call sign and began both an automatic and visual scan of the surrounding field. After a few minutes, the search came up negative. Perhaps the old rust bucket had finally met its fate after all. With that thought, he strapped himself into his chair and, cueing visual, began to search the surrounding area for debris, or at least some sign of the missing trader.

After several more minutes of scanning, the fields were as empty as before. This time Markin cursed. It looked like something really had happened to the *Catseye* and he was going to have to file a damned report anyway.

▯

News of the tragic loss of the trader *Catseye* made Valdor curse out loud when he saw it. Having been briefed in full by Milnus, Carr knew what he was looking for. During his ritual scan of the nets he was paying particular attention to the shipping movements. As a result, the report caught his eye a lot sooner than it normally might have. The ship was missing, presumed broken up just off New

Helvetica. A search was underway for survivors, but little hope was held for any success.

He read the report three times over to make sure before slamming his fist down on the desk and spinning his large chair to face the wall behind. Anger and frustration seethed. He stared at the wall through narrowed eyes, his lips tightly pursed, his hands held under his chin as one by one he cracked his knuckles. It was so unlike Milnus to get things wrong. Why hadn't he at least chosen a decent ship? He was going to have words about this one. His thoughts of retribution were brought abruptly to a halt by a voice coming from behind the obscuring back of the chair. It was a voice that had haunted Valdor in his dreams and had done so for weeks.

"Well Vald' Carr. As I tell — to you. We speak again."

Valdor slowly turned the chair to face the smug alien voice. He narrowed his eyes even more as he looked at the Sirona's diminutive frame and oversized head. As in the last visit, there had been no sign or sound of entry. The Sirona was simply there in his innermost sanctum having passed all the security measures — without so much as a whisper from the alarms. He couldn't be sure if this was the same one, Tarn, but he assumed it probably was.

"What do you want now?" he demanded. "Did I ask to see you?"

"No, Vald' Carr. I believe that this is the problem."

"What do you mean?" he said evenly, fighting the temptation to spit the words at his unwelcome visitor.

"Since we talked, you — and the Sirona. The Sirona have been watching Vald' Carr. Vald' Carr has shown nothing to tell the Sirona that he — recognised any of what the Sirona said. Vald' Carr has taken measures working — against the Sirona. This much we know. Vald' Carr has displeased us. So, the Sirona have taken measures. Does Vald' Carr know what the Sirona are telling him?" The Sirona tilted its head to one side as if listening.

"I don't know what you're talking about, Tarn, if you are Tarn, or whatever you want to call yourself," he said slowly, deciding to bluff it out and see where this was leading. "Why don't I just have you thrown out of here?"

"We are afraid this is not possible, even if — you wished it. Besides, the Sirona know that you are aware of our — displeasure. It was an unfortunate incident with your ship. It was — a shame? — that your person was on the ship. Very sad — this loss of life. Do you agree, Vald' Carr?"

So, this was the confirmation. The Sirona really were behind the trader's loss. The pieces started clicking into place.

Valdor's mind raced over the options. They obviously had some sort of access to the innermost workings of his organisation and its personnel. There was very little he could do about it at this stage, but there had to be some means to extricate himself from what now appeared to be a tightening web. If he could bargain with the creature for position ... it might buy him time to get out and away from here, hopefully out of their reach. Meanwhile, he could put mechanisms in place to ensure his plan's survival. His thoughts were ticking over rapidly. Perhaps there might be a way ....

"All right, Tarn. What is to stop me informing the proper authorities about what's happening?"

"This you could do. The Sirona would not stop you." The creature gave a toothed smile. "But, when they ask — where is your evidence, you would show them — what? Also, the Sirona ask Vald' Carr how much of Vald' Carr's organisation does he wish to show? The Sirona think — Vald' Carr is not stupid."

Valdor weighed up the response, and on balance, he had to admit the Sirona was right. The question wasn't serious, anyway. It was just a meant of buying more time for him to think.

He still had every intention of getting a gene set sample offworld, but there had to be another way to achieve it. But he just couldn't understand the Sirona's interest in what he was doing. Certainly, it would provide them with an avenue to exploit what was bound to be a highly successful commercial venture, but there had to be more to it than that. He saw no reason why that alone could interest them. They obviously had enough success with their own ventures and it seemed as though they were not interested in true commercial success as Valdor understood it.

"So, Tarn, let's talk then. What is it you want of me?"

"This is — a wise decision, Vald' Carr," said the Sirona nodding slightly. "The work your companies do now — the Sirona would like to stop. You have moved — faster — than the Sirona expected. The Sirona want — to watch Vald' Carr's business with co-operation."

"I don't quite understand," Valdor said slowly. He was genuinely puzzled.

"The Sirona would like all of this work — to stop. All records must be removed. All — minds — have to be reassigned. The Sirona will supervise this process. It would be easy for the Sirona to — terminate your operation, but that would — create attention? With Vald' Carr's assistance, this is a more — elegant solution for the Sirona."

"Uh-huh," Valdor replied, chewing thoughtfully at the end of his thumb. "I see. What the hell would you want to do that for?"

The Sirona simply stared. Valdor clearly wasn't going to get an answer, so he continued. "But if I go along with this, what do I get out of it? I'm likely to suffer a substantial loss as a result, and I don't just mean financial. You couldn't really expect me to give up this opportunity just because the Sirona want it."

"Of course, the Sirona do not — expect this. Vald' Carr is a business man — a trader. The Sirona know this. The Sirona are traders. You would be assured — of compensation. There are many further opportunities for

Vald' Carr that the Sirona could — provide. All would be taken care of."

Valdor knew better than to start talking terms with the alien at this stage. That was not the way to play it. He had to show a little interest, but not too much, and then reel them in under his own terms. That may be difficult, because right at this moment, they seemed to have the advantage. So, let him play as if he were going ahead. It might give him a few more options if his plans should go awry over the next few days. Suddenly this was more familiar ground, and Valdor was warming to the task.

"I still don't understand, Tarn, why the Sirona are so interested in this operation; why you want this work to stop."

"That is not of interest, Vald' Carr. It is what the Sirona desire. That can be the only interest."

"All right. I suppose I'm in a little bit of a no-win situation here. I need some time to think about it though ... say a week? If I'm going to do this I need to put some things in place, you understand, and I want to think about how I might go about that. Give me a week or two to sort things out, to put things in place, then we can decide whether this arrangement is to our mutual advantage. Depending on what decision I arrive at, we can discuss my terms. Is that agreed?"

"Yes — one week, but no more. We shall talk again — after one week. Then we shall discuss the Sirona terms — not the terms — of Vald' Carr. Vald' Carr has already had much time. Be sure to make the right decision, Vald' Carr. Think well," said the Sirona.

Tarn got down from the chair, turned and walked silently to the door, not even looking back at Carr as it closed the panel behind it.

Valdor drummed on the desk. He had no intention of acceding to the Sirona demands. Obviously this biocomp thing was worth a lot more to them than they were going to admit and that made him convinced that he wanted to run with it. He was in a difficult position, but no circumstance was too difficult to negotiate to an advantage. Besides, Valdor was fundamentally stubborn. The sure arrogance of the Sirona, despite their alienness, and their interference in his operations made him more determined to go ahead with his original plans and damn the consequences. He would beat them at their own game, damned if he wouldn't.

It would take same clever manoeuvring. The idea had still to be to get a sample of the gene sets off world to a safe holding and that was clearly going to be a little more difficult than it had been before. It seemed the Sirona had links, or at least access, to the inner mechanisms of his organisation. He was convinced of that now. He knew he could trust Milnus but he didn't know what other leaks there might be. He'd have to use other meant to achieve his ends.

There was no choice left to him. He had to organise the whole thing himself. Who he could choose to assist him remained the only question. He couldn't transport the samples himself. He'd already seen the fate of one courier, and he valued his own skin too much to take that risk. A week wasn't going to be all that long to get the right things in place.

He sat toying with options for a number of minutes. Not only would he get the sample off world by whatever meant it might take to do it, but he would get himself off world as well. He could leave the basic workings of the organisation to Milnus while he was away, but if he was not around himself, it made him less of a target. The first thing to do was to get himself out of circulation. Probably time to pay Marina a visit. Marina's was well enough out of the way to keep him from the Sirona for the time being and let him act without their interference. The Sirona probably had access to his net too, so despite the loss of information while he was out of the picture, he decided to shut it down for the duration.

He would contact Milnus from Marina's and get him to deliver a sample at some secure location. The only information he would give Milnus was that his Head of Security was to supervise the running of the operation for a few days. That should be enough to keep things ticking over while he was gone.

Valdor reached across and keyed the shutdown sequence into the console set into his desk, then wrapping his cloak about him, made for the private elevator. His decision made, all that remained for him to work out were the finer details of exactly what he was going to do.

Chapter Fourteen

The Cradle

At first, she scrambled through the scant undergrowth, searching for some refuge from the nightmare below. Her body was running on automatic. The Cradle was a place of sanctity and peace, not somewhere torn apart by disharmony and destruction. She knew with an awful certainty that it was true, and yet it lay beyond her grasp. It was just so alien to everything she knew. She ran and ran, trying to leave it behind her.

She spent the rest of the night huddled beneath a clump of bushes, trembling and cold. She dozed fitfully, waking now and again with a start. Each time, she slowly came to awareness of the reality through the sleep haze, and she shivered with the stark chill of shock. Eventually, she reached some sort of control over her emotions, pushed back the disbelief, and realised that she had to do something.

The morning light further revealed the destruction worked the previous evening. She ventured a quick look from her concealment and it was enough to tell her that where she sat was not a good place to be. Egg-like shards stuck from the ground at the lakeshore — all that remained of the vast structure that had previously stood there. Large blocks of what had once been walls lay scattered about the surrounding plane and deep black trenches scored the ground. But there was activity down there.

The large ship was nowhere to be seen, but it had left behind a score of smaller craft flitting and hovering above the landscape. Though tiny, she could see organized groups picking their way among the pieces of wreckage. It looked as if they were searching, and she got the impression that their activity was being directed by the flyers hovering above. It didn't take her long to work out that they were searching for survivors. These people, if people they were, didn't belong to The Cradle. She knew that without even having to think about it.

If whoever it was down there was searching for survivors, it would not be too long before they widened the area of their search. Mahra was too close by far. She needed to put some distance between herself and those ships quickly. Keeping low and as close to any cover she could find, she struck off up the hillside toward the mountains that beckoned in the distance. There she'd find shelter and refuge, and perhaps some space to work out what she was going to do next. She could survive for weeks in the mountain forests if she needed to.

Her instincts were right. It was late morning by the time she heard the first flyer's sound pass overhead. Quickly she ducked beneath a group of bushes and crouched while the craft whined overhead. She could see the silvery hull glide past through the leaves above her and she stayed very still until the whirring drive sound faded away through the branches. The craft was moving in a zigzag pattern, obviously searching for something. They couldn't know about her, or at least she thought they couldn't, so it should give her some space to get away.

Several times during the course of the day she was forced to duck for cover, as one or more craft passed over her. She was oblivious to the cuts and scratches she sustained. All she could think about was to get away. She had no idea if they were searching for her. All she could feel was her breath catch in her throat and a sense of urgency driving her onward toward the distant crags as her heart pounded in her chest.

Mahra paused to catch her breath, panting with the exertion. Nestled beneath the shadows of a large leafy tree, she rested her back against its trunk. Still breathing heavily, she looked down at her hands, and saw the comp clutched firmly in her grasp. She had been gripping it tightly since the moment of her flight. Painfully she relaxed the grip.

She allowed herself a few moments to work back the feeling in her fingers. Once the numbness had passed, she tried to activate the comp, but the device was dead. She shook it once, twice, then tried again, but it remained an inert lump. She was well and truly on her own. She tossed the small box in frustration to the carpet of drying leaves at her feet. She stared at it thinking about what Aleyin had said.

Suddenly there was something wrapped around her face. It covered her nose and mouth and pressed her back against the tree. Mahra struggled against it, tried to shake herself free, the panic welling up inside her.

And then there was someone crouched in front of her. He was garbed all in black and her eyes widened in recognition. Slowly he took his hand away from her mouth.

"Aleyin!" she said.

"Shhh," he said, raising his hand to his lips. "I don't know how close they are. Can you tell?"

"How did you get here?"

"No time for that now. We have to get away."

The Old One's former student looked ruffled and full of fear. His gaze flitted nervously round the surrounding trees. Mahra could see his robes were torn and there was dirt on his face.

"Who are they? Why have they done this?" asked Mahra. Aleyin shook his head, still throwing nervous glances about him.

"I don't know. I don't know," he said. He dragged at her arm. "Come, we have to get away from here."

Mahra nodded. He was right. She got to her feet and beckoned him to follow.

"Aleyin, this way. If we can get to the mountains, we should be able to make it hard for them to find us. We'll be all right if we can get there. They'll never find us."

Aleyin swallowed and nodded. He looked completely lost. She urged him to follow and struck out through the trees. Aleyin seemed to be moving with some difficulty and she slowed her pace.

"Did you see it?" she asked him. "Were you there?"

He stopped and a look of horror washed over his face. "Yes. I was close — very close. A few minutes more ... "

"Did anyone else get away?" she asked.

He seemed to shake himself and then realize what she was asking. "N-no, I didn't see. I just knew I had to get away. I was on my own."

Mahra still felt afraid herself, but she knew she couldn't give into it. She had to get them as far away as possible. That was the first thing. She could think about contacting the others later. She urged Aleyin to follow and headed off toward the distant peaks. She had to think. Mind sharp.

Then she remembered — her comp. How could she contact anyone if she didn't have it? It might not be any use, but she had to take that chance. She quickly looked back at Aleyin, but he carried nothing with him apart from his dishevelled robes.

"Aleyin, wait," she said. "Wait here. I have to go back. I dropped my comp back there."

"Are you sure that's a good—?"

Mahra stilled him with a motion of her hand and a quick shake of her head.

She headed quickly back down the trail they had just come up. She found the clearing again without any difficulty and spotted the comp nestled there to one side among the fallen leaves.

Then, suddenly, she heard movement through the undergrowth behind her. There was not much cover in the clearing apart from a small clump of bushes off to one side and the sounds of approach were growing steadily. Quickly she made a break for the tangle of shrubs and vines, dragging her pack behind her beneath the mass of leaves. The clear sound of feet tramping through the undergrowth was punctuated by voices, indistinct as yet, but without doubt, coming her way. She barely dared breathe as she made herself as small and as still as possible.

Three tall figures burst into the clearing. The three men stopped at the small wooded glade's centre, scanning the vegetation about them for signs of movement. Mahra's heart pounded in her ears as she lay frozen watching the dark unkempt figures standing before her. It seemed so loud, she wondered that they didn't hear it as well.

The three were dressed in dark padded leathers, belts crisscrossing their jackets. Long straggly hair flowed freely about their swarthy features. Very slowly, they turned their heads, listening. One looked in her direction. His head turned slightly to one side and she caught her breath. He seemed to be listening to something coming from a device set in his ear, because he lifted his hand to reposition whatever lay there.

"Yah, about here?" he said in a rough, accented voice, holding something to his throat as he spoke. He turned slowly studying the area again. "You sure that thing's not telling you lies again? No sign of a runner here."

Mahra felt the pit of her stomach go chill as she remembered the comp she so carelessly tossed to the ground. Her eyes widened as she saw it, half buried beneath the boot of the man who spoke.

"What do they want, miracles?" He muttered to his companions. "I don't know what we're going to find. Nothing to get a bloody trace on." He looked clearly disgusted and spat to one side. "What sort of job is this, rounding up savages?"

This elicited grunts of agreement from his companions. He swung whatever he was carrying lazily in one hand, up to his shoulder. It had to be a weapon of some sort. All three carried a similar device.

Mahra started to inch her way slowly backward, carefully limiting her movements so as not to attract attention or make any noise. At that moment, the one who spoke shifted his stance. His boot slipped on the comp's smooth surface, he looked down, rapidly crouched, retrieving the small box, and a slow smile spread across his face. His eyes narrowed and he swung his head around to scan the surrounding area.

"Well, mates, still warm. Looks like we've got ourselves a runner after all." he said as he tossed the comp to one of his companions. He lowered his weapon to a horizontal position so that it was pointing out toward the trees that circled their position, slowly tracking it in an arc as he spoke into the device at his throat.

"Yah, we have contact. Starting sweep now."

He motioned to the two with him and they split off, one on either side, each holding their weapon the same way, slowly tracking from side to side as they started to walk toward opposite edges of the clearing. It was time for her to get out of here, and quickly.

Very, very carefully, she edged backward, deeper through the tangled undergrowth. She moved a fraction at a time, her heart pounding ever louder in her ears. Twigs and branches caught at her hair and clothes. The other two were moving away from her. The one who had spoken had disappeared into the trees off to one side, and if she planned it right, she should be able to get out of their view and be able to make a run for it. She was certain she could outdistance any one of them in the forest. She eased herself through the leaf litter, worming backward on her stomach.

Then her foot encountered resistance. She turned her head to see what was blocking her path and froze, her mind gone chill. Her foot rested hard against a solid black boot.

She looked upward and gasped as she saw the grinning face of the boot's owner looking down at her. He reached down and grabbing her ankle, effortlessly lifted her skyward.

"So, what have we here?" He laughed. "Hey mates, I've got our runner. It's a mere child. A girl."

Mahra swung helplessly in his grasp. She heard the crashing of his companions through the undergrowth. The pounding in her ears grew louder as the blood rushed to her head and she waved from side to side, suspended in his one-handed grip. The other two emerged from the trees and let their weapons drop as amused expressions covered their faces.

"Not bad," said one of the newcomers.

Mahra didn't like the way his expression changed as he looked at her, scanning her body.

"We could have ourselves a bit of fun here."

"Time enough for that later," snapped the one holding her. "The day's not over yet. Now, you're coming with me, my pretty," he said to her as he bundled her unceremoniously across his shoulder and strode off into the trees.

She still had her blade. They either hadn't noticed it, or didn't care. Her comp and pack were gone; all she had now were her wits. She only hoped Aleyin had sense enough to get away.

Too much was happening too quickly. The sour smell of the one carrying her washed over her as she was bumped along on his shoulder. The combination of the smell and the jolting motion of their passage made her feel queasy. She worked hard to keep the bile from rising in her throat. There was another smell about this man, something very different and unfamiliar. It was a smell that didn't fit here, that didn't belong.

The indignity of her passage was short lived. The trees gradually thinned to reveal a broad grassed clearing upon which sat a craft of the type that passed over her position earlier. She craned around the man's torso to see. This craft was a very different design from the one that she rode in from the call point. It was broad, squat, and ugly. The exterior was metallic with none of the clear plas that afforded the all-around view in her flyer. There were dents and score marks on the outside of the hull. It suited the appearance of her captors — probably functional, but not very pleasant to look at.

Her view was rapidly obscured as she was bundled through a large open door on the craft's side and her captors clambered in behind her. Roughly she was shoved to the rear of the large open space and motioned to sat on the hard metal floor as the three took up seats and strapped themselves in, after stowing their weapons beside them. The one who made the remarks about her glanced at her from time to time, and she didn't think she liked the look on his face.

She had little time to consider what was in store for her, because her original captor yelled something and banged on the bulkhead beside him with a closed fist. The large metal door swung shut and there was a definite chunk as a locking mechanism slid home. The floor beneath her began to vibrate and a deep whine grew somewhere beneath her, gradually building in intensity as the craft rose from its position and lifted into the air, before turning and shooting forward. She huddled at the back, reconciled to wait, and see what was in store, though if the glances she was getting were any indication, she didn't much like what it might be.

The three men talked among themselves, almost shouting to make themselves heard above the drive noise that filled the vessel. The insistent whine made their conversation incomprehensible and rattled her bones.

Mahra didn't know how long they travelled. The day's events had proved too much and despite the noise and the vessel's vibrations, she dozed. She was shaken from her light sleep as the craft bumped to a stop with a deep, resonant metallic tone. The three rapidly unstrapped themselves and got to their feet, grabbing their weapons, and waiting for the large side door to open. One casually wandered back and dragged Mahra to her feet and forward to join them. The metal panel swung slowly upward into empty space.

This place was like nothing Mahra had ever imagined. It was an expanse of metal and oil and machinery. There were several vessels of the same type as had brought her here parked across the bay, and between them walked small groups of men, with similar looks and attire to her captors. All around, the noise of metal upon metal struck at her senses and everywhere was a smell of steel and oil.

She looked upward and could barely make out the vault of a roof above their heads. The metal floor stretched out in both directions as far as she could see. She had little time for observation though, for she was grabbed roughly from behind and propelled forward with a shove between her shoulders. She slowed for a moment and she was rewarded with another shove, pushing her stumbling forward again.

All the people in this place were the same. They were dressed in long black boots and dark coloured padded leathers. Most wore their hair long and mostly it was matted and knotted about their heads. Not all carried weapons, but many did, either held loosely by their sides or slung across one shoulder with a strap. Her passage attracted one or two curious glances, but for the most part, it was as if she was beneath their attention

Finally, they reached one end of the vast parking area and she was shoved roughly again toward a doorway. There was a legend painted against the door in an unfamiliar script. Her original captor grabbed her by the shoulder, signalling her to wait. He turned, slapped palms with his companions who each departed, going their separate ways. He then played with a control to the side and leaned forward to speak something into a small recess above the panel. Immediately the door slid open and she was ushered forward into a long corridor stretching off into the distance.

As soon as they stepped inside, the door ground shut again sealing firmly behind them. Plucking up her courage as they walked, she finally found the strength to speak.

"Where are you taking me?" she asked, trying to sound defiant, but keeping her eyes fixed in front of her so as not to lose her resolve.

"Oh ho. So, it speaks as well as squeaks. You'll find out soon enough."

"But why — "

"Enough talk." He cut her off and shoved her forward again for emphasis. Biting her lip, Mahra lapsed into silence.

They reached their destination soon enough. Her escort stopped at another doorway and pulled her roughly back to stand beside him. There was nothing to distinguish this doorway from any other. Again, he leaned forward, manipulated the small panel sitting beside the door, and spoke into the recess. Again, the door slid open in response, this time revealing a small room. Lounging in a chair just behind the doorway was another man. He looked up as the door slid open and nodded to her captor. She was handed over without a word. Another door was opened and Mahra was pushed unceremoniously inside. The door hissed shut behind her.

This new room was large and it lacked furnishing, but as she stood in the doorway, she saw several people huddled disconsolately against the walls. One or two bore the marks of fresh injuries and mostly they were men. She recognized none of the faces, but she didn't need to look twice to know that all were from The Cradle. She could feel their rightness, so different from those outside. Mahra stood looking from face to face, not venturing to ask how they came to be here, receiving a brief nod from one or two, but mostly blankness.

Suddenly, Mahra was awash with despair. What could she do if those who were so much older and wiser than herself had come to this? She wanted to collapse in a heap on the floor and giving way to her feelings. She was on the verge of doing just that when she spotted a figure sitting a little apart from the rest, deep in the shadows of one corner. The solitary figure was dressed in robes of black.

Quickly she strode across and crouched in front of him. It couldn't be anyone else.

"Hello, Aleyin," she said quietly.

"Hello, Mahra," he said just as quietly, barely raising his head to look at her. "I had hoped you got away. Welcome to the exalted company of survivors."

"Where are we Aleyin? What is this place?"

"Sit," he said patting the floor beside him. He waited until she was seated beside him before continuing.

"We're on board a ship, Mahra — their ship. Bound for I don't know where. That is if we're bound for anywhere. See what has become of the great dreams of The Cradle? Where is their perfect society now?" He lapsed into silence, tracing patterns on the cold floor between his feet with the tip of one finger.

"What do you mean?"

"Well look at us, this fine collection. It is not much left of a world, is it? I doubt there'll be many more. Most will have been at the Dome. It's my guess that we few are all there is. Can't you feel the *emptiness*?" he asked. Sadness tinged his voice.

Mahra realised he was right. There was something missing and she could feel the lack. She hadn't noticed it before now. There was a space there as if something that belonged had been moved, something that she didn't notice directly except by its absence. She was reminded of the Old One's passing, and it made her even sadder.

"Why has this happened? Why would anyone want to do this to us?"

"Oh, Mahra, I don't know why. No, I don't know why, and I don't know who. But I do know how. It has something to do with what I talked to you about that day when we met, about the differences I had with the Old One. We were vulnerable, always, to that which was denied us. Can you not see now? If we knew about these things, these machines, and these weapons, then we might have been prepared. We might have been able to deal with it," he said, stabbing at the floor with his last few words. Mahra bit her lip. He looked up at her, a humourless smile on his face. "And now, here we all are." He sighed.

A few others had turned to watch them, drawn by the passion of Aleyin's words. One or two shook their heads and looked away, but a stern-faced, greying woman continued looking. Finally, she narrowed her eyes and spoke.

"So, you're still trying to fill other's heads with your nonsense, Aleyin Amarr. Even now. Even in the face of all this. Leave the child be."

"And what nonsense would that be, Lilliath Graydan? Things that you could not face," Aleyin answered angrily. "Look where your precious creed has got us."

"Enough from both of you!" snapped an older voice from the side near the door. "What good does it do now?"

Both Aleyin and the woman called Lilliath glared at each other across the intervening space then dropped their gaze, grudgingly acceding to the authority of the old man's voice.

All thought of further talk was quickly put to rest as a deep humming grew in the walls and floor. Moments later, the vast bulk around them slowly started to move and she could feel herself being pressed down against the floor and back against the metal of the wall behind her.

☐

It was some time before the noise about them subsided to a level where conversation was possible. Until that time, they were forced to bear the noise and the sensations of their movement in silence. Mahra felt the despair that surrounded the group of captives huddled against the walls and corners of their holding area, pressed against the cold metal with eyes full of fear. At last, the noise subsided to a dull rumble, low enough to allow conversation. She took a moment to distract Aleyin from his thoughts. He dragged his gaze reluctantly from the floor somewhere in front of his feet.

"Aleyin, where are they taking us?"

"I don't know, Mahra," he answered with a sigh. "I don't know. If we were given access to a little more knowledge about what lies beyond The Cradle, I might have some idea. I'm afraid that I have as many questions as you do. I doubt either of us will get the answers until we reach wherever it was we're going."

"But who are they, and why did they want to do what they have done to us?"

"Another question that will remain unanswered for the time being, I'm afraid. Somebody obviously has some idea about who these people are and the fact that something was going to happen on The Cradle though," he said. He narrowed his eyes pointedly in the direction of the grey-headed woman who spoke earlier. "They just didn't feel fit to tell anyone."

"Why? What makes you say that?" Mahra asked, following his glance.

"Well, it is fairly obvious isn't it, if you think about it? The message. The gathering. Why do you think it was so urgent? There hasn't been a gathering like that since, well, I don't know. There was definitely something going on, and for something to have been going on, somebody had to know something. There was knowledge behind that meeting."

Both lapsed into silence. Mahra didn't really know enough to speculate about the broader scheme of those who shaped what happened on The Cradle. She wondered what the Old One would have done in this situation, but she was dragged from her thoughts by the voice of one of the older members of their ragged group.

"Please, can I have your attention?"

He was a tall thin man with snow-white hair and he rose to his feet with obvious difficulty. His robe was dirt-smeared and an ugly purpling bruise marred his jawline.

"We do know something about our captors, but only that they are employed by another. They are merely mercenaries working for someone else. We already know from experience that we should expect little sympathy from them. Now, despite what we do know, I can't tell you where we are being taken. We do know that whatever, we must not offer them the sort of resistance that would provoke further violence. The knowledge we have among us is too valuable to risk."

There were nods of assent from among the older members of the group.

"For this reason, we must survive. Each of you must take every step to ensure that you survive to carry our knowledge beyond what has happened here. If that means a sacrifice of principles, then so be it. Do I have your agreement?"

He scanned the bleak faces that lined the walls waiting until each slowly nodded assent.

Mahra didn't understand what the old man was talking about. She frowned a query to Aleyin who merely shook his head. The old man looked satisfied beneath his obvious pain and carefully eased himself back to sit before leaning his head back and closing his eyes.

They sat again in silence for some time, then Aleyin gripped her hand and spoke in a low whisper.

"Mahra, I've been thinking. I want to show you something. It's just a little trick, but I want you to know it in case we get separated. It might help you. Remember I said I could show you things? Well this is one of them. I don't know how long we've got, so I want to show it to you now."

Mahra gave him a puzzled look but waited to see what he might offer. Aleyin continued in the same low whisper.

"I don't want the others to see that I'm showing you this, but circumstances prevent me doing it any other way. Now, I want you to concentrate on my eyes. Keep holding my hand. That's it. Right, now in a moment I want you to close your eyes. Not now. When I tell you. When you close your eyes, I want you to concentrate on my face. Call up an image of me in your mind, but at the same time try to keep your thoughts as free as possible from anything else. Do you think you can do that? Good. Close your eyes now."

Mahra closed her eyes and tried to form an image of Aleyin's face. She found it difficult to concentrate and her thoughts flitted backward and forward, becoming cluttered with unwanted images. After a few moments, she gave up and opened her eyes.

"No Mahra, keep trying. This is important."

She tried again, closing her eyes, and attempting to calm her skittish thoughts. Finally, she could draw a picture of Aleyin's pale face in her head. She concentrated on filling in the detail, making the image clearer and clearer. She held the image tightly, concentrating on nothing else. It was difficult to hold the image and keep her mind clear of the other thoughts that constantly threatened to intrude.

A moment later, she noticed a new sensation inside her head. It was like a buzzing, but it was broken up, fuzzy but regular. She tried to keep her attention focused on the image of Aleyin's face but the more she tried, the more the buzzing grew. It became regular and repetitive, following the same cadences over and over again. Slowly it became more distinct. Then, suddenly, it was as if she could make out words in the regular pattern of sounds.

Mahra, can you hear me? Mahra, can you hear me?

Her eyes flew open with shock. Aleyin was peering intently at her face.

"B-but ... " she managed to stammer.

"No," he whispered quietly, holding a finger to his lips. "Now, try it again. Don't say anything. Just close your eyes and try it again."

Doing as she was told, she closed her eyes and tried to draw up the image of Aleyin's face. It was more difficult this time, her head filled with thoughts of what just happened. With some effort, she could frame Aleyin's face in her mind's eye. The buzzing grew in the back of her head and started to take shape.

Mahra. Mahra. You can hear me now. Nod your head once slowly to show me. That's it. Now it's your turn. Start with my name. When I have it, I'll squeeze your hand. Concentrate. Direct the words at my image.

The words in her head became clearer with each passing second. She found it difficult to control her excitement and concentrate on what she was supposed to do, but with a little effort, she managed. Focusing on the image of Aleyin's face, she directed one strong, clear thought at it — his name. Almost immediately she felt him squeeze her hand and she opened her eyes.

"You are very quick, Mahra," Aleyin whispered. "No wonder the Old One held so much store in you. I can see how the two of you must have been very close with a talent like that. Do you think you could do it again?"

Mahra immediately closed her eyes and framed Aleyin's face. Clearly, she directed her thoughts toward the image.

Aleyin, you know I can. His squeeze of her hand was immediate and strong.

"Good enough," he whispered, causing her to open her eyes and look at him again. "Remember it. And if ever you need me, you know what to do."

She nodded, watching his face, and fixing it clearly in her mind as he dropped his gaze back to the floor between his feet and relaxed his grip on her hand.

During the next few hours, the refugees were separated and led off one by one. The old man who spoke was the first to go. The door slid open and a swarthy, leather-clad soldier entered, looking around the room. As he looked in Mahra's direction, he paused for a moment as if considering something. Mahra's insides went cold as he fixed her with that calculating look. The process was repeated several times. Without warning, the door hissed open and a mercenary stepped in before making a selection and leading one of their number away. More than once, she found herself the subject of a lingering glance. Mahra started to guess what those looks contained.

Only a small number of those who were taken away returned. The old man who was first was among them. Generally, it seemed that the older members were the ones who didn't come back. Mahra watched the faces of those who were led back in. She could sense rather than see the wildness haunting their eyes when they were led back in and it filled her with dread.

Then it was her turn. The soldier entered the room as before, but this time he walked straight over to the corner where she and Aleyin sat, a little apart from the rest. This time the look was more than a lingering glance. The mercenary ran his gaze with deliberate slowness up and down her body, an unmistakable leer plastered over his face. He barely glanced at Aleyin.

Mahra felt the panic rising inside her but she returned the look with her face devoid of emotion. A moment or two longer and she'd lose control, but he allowed her no time for that. In one deft moved his hand swept down, grabbed her by the wrist and dragged her to her feet. Aleyin stared fixedly ahead, failing to meet her eyes. Almost, she saw him give a brief shake of his head, but by then it was too late. She was dragged by her arm toward the door.

That sour smell she noticed before was with her again as he dragged her down the corridor. He seemed to be in a rush to get her wherever she was being taken, for no matter how hard she tried to keep pace he dragged her on by the arm, wrenching her shoulder forward. She bit her lip against the pain and tried to keep herself from stumbling. He finally stopped before a door and gripping her strongly with one hand, used his other to manipulate the mechanism that opened it. As the door hissed open, he dragged her forward and through, quickly turning to seal it after them, closing them both into semi-darkness.

The mercenary had brought them to some sort of small living quarters. It was lit only dimly by a panel on one wall. A crude bunk and a cupboard were the only other pieces to break up the drab greenness of the small space. Roughly he lifted her with both hands and tossed her onto the bunk. Mahra felt a sense of horror growing inside her along with the fear. Suddenly she knew what was about to happen and she scrabbled backward on the bunk pressing herself tightly against the corner. The soldier seemed to find this amusing and he grinned at her in the darkness as he tossed the long matted strands of hair back from his face and started to fumble at the fastenings of his leathers. For some reason, they had allowed her to keep her blade. Up until now, she had not even thought of using it, but right then she remembered it and started to reach up. A resounding slap across her face made her head ring, and stunned her into inactivity.

Chapter Fifteen

The Dark Falcon sat in orbit for several hours while
Mahra and Sind waited for some sign of recovery from
Pellis. It turned out to be a long night and Mahra had a lot to
consider. The last thing she'd have picked the pair of them
for was establishment. What with Pellis's flamboyance and
that of *The Dark Falcon* itself, it was little wonder she
found it slightly hard to accept. Chutzpah expressed his
annoyance with her for ignoring him by chattering sternly in
her left ear.

"Oh, sorry Chutz," she said with a preoccupied crease
of her brow. "Lot to think about."

She absent-mindedly scratched him under the chin as
she mulled over the new circumstances. This seemed to
placate him and he clambered down from her shoulder to
position himself in her lap. Very soon, his soft insistent
purring grew and started to have its usual soothing effect,
allowing her to think more easily.

With any luck Timon would be in better form when
he woke and they'll be able to leave the environs of this
inhospitable world. It couldn't be soon enough for her
liking.

Mahra gently lifted the protesting zimonette from her
lap and headed to see how Timon was getting on.

Sind met her at the entrance to Pellis's cabin. He
obviously had the same concerns and was eager to depart.

He graced her with a little half-smile as they paused at the doorway before entering. He gave a slight upward movement of his eyebrows, palmed the door open, and gestured for her to enter in front of him.

Pellis was just barely awake. His eyes had that half-asleep narrowed look that was a combination of sleep and sedative. Making a visible effort, he gave them each a wry smile.

"Now, what are the both of you doing here? Isn't it enough that you already treat me like a big child without having to come and check whether I'm tucked in properly? Come on, enough you two. Let's get out of here. Time's a-wasting and I'd rather not be around Belshore much longer if I can help it."

"Our thoughts exactly, Timon," answered Sind. "We were both thinking you'd had quite enough of the easy life lying around here in your bed and that it was high time you got up and did something useful."

"Oh yes. Listen to him now would you, Mahra. A man lies dying in his bed and not a thought from his hard heart." He grinned, a little more easily this time.

"Seriously Timon, how are you feeling?" asked Mahra.

"Oh, I'll be right enough I suppose." He shrugged. "Give me a few hours and I'll be as good as new." Dismissing the subject entirely, his tone became crisper. "I suggest that both of you stop wasting time with this idle chit-chat and get to your stations anyway. I want to get us moving as soon as possible."

He dismissed them with a wave of his hand and pulled himself upright. An expression of discomfort passed across his face.

"Go on the both of you, to work. I'll join you shortly, after I've attended to nature's necessities. Come on. What are you waiting for? Can't you give a man a little privacy?"

Mahra and Sind acceded, palming the door shut behind them. Mahra gave Sind an inquiring glance as they stood outside the door, but he shrugged in response. He was obviously satisfied with what he had seen and made his way forward along the corridor, leaving Mahra to make her own way to her station. She only stopped to collect Chutzpah on the way. If she left him out of a session in the pod, she'd hear about it for days.

Mahra strapped herself into position, listening patiently for the signs that Timon was on line. They had lain at orbit too long for her liking, but they had to be sure that Timon was fit before they took off. She could have piloted the ship, but it was far better to trust that task to one who was totally familiar with it, particularly with a ship as well equipped as *The Dark Falcon.* No, she felt far more at home in her place in the pod. At last, Timon's voice came over the com and they got under way.

There was a slim belt of circling debris on the outer perimeter of Belshore's space that required some tricky navigation. For those unfamiliar with the territory it would have presented a distinct hazard, but Timon and Sind had been this way many times before. As they neared the sphere of spinning junk, Chutzpah became agitated and hopped up and down on her shoulder. Mahra couldn't tell whether he was vocalising as well. The com covered her hearing with the noise of ongoing banter between Timon, Sind and Belshore approach control. She had used Chutzpah's senses as an indicator too many times before though, not to pay attention, so she scanned the surrounding fields carefully, as the tricky manoeuvres began.

She saw the first ship even before the tell-tale indicator appeared on the holo overlaying her view.

"Timon, company. Two seventy up."

"Yes, I see it. Hold on Mahra, we're going," came Pellis's warning as *The Dark Falcon* swung into a tight arc away from the approaching ship.

Timon reacted immediately not even waiting for any identification of the newcomer. Being in proximity to Belshore was enough. *The Dark Falcon* was built to take movement such as this, and the ship slid into the turn smoothly, accelerating. Pellis's presumptions proved to be founded because the other ship responded immediately with a new burst of speed.

"Looks like it's on, Mahra," came Timon's voice over the com just as another indicator winked into existence flashing red, up and behind them, shortly followed by yet another.

"Yep. Right, Timon. Three's a crowd. Up and behind."

"Got them. All right then. Let's go."

Pellis threw *The Dark Falcon* into a tight upward arc in an attempt to shake the first ship and get over and behind the newcomers.

A narrow beam of light pierced the darkness of their wake as he executed the move. As far as Mahra was concerned it was clearly no overture of friendly intention and her finger hovered over the fire pads waiting for an opportunity to respond in kind. The voices of Sind and Pellis filled her com, reeling off figures and trajectories and she tried to shut them out, concentrating on the markers in her view, now targets for her poised attention.

Pellis rolled *The Dark Falcon*, taking her round to complete the arc, pointing the ship back in the direction they had just come from. As he did, a cloud of small metallic particles spewed from the rear to fill the void behind them. Mahra's finger hung poised, straining for the instant when the two ships behind would turn to follow. She almost fired as they turned — almost — but she knew the shots would be wasted. Each attacking ship split off and away in opposite directions, turning, one on each side to face her, well out of effective range.

"Very clever, mates," she muttered to the two pursuers. "Timon, hard turn, back through the dust."

"Got you," Pellis responded immediately, banking *The Dark Falcon* about to pass through the particle cloud he had released moments before. The two ships off to their side swept in to catch them in the interlocking pattern of their aims.

Mahra found what she expected as they emerged from the dust. The first ship approached the area warily, its weapons person waiting for the moment when he or she might distinguish the signature of *The Dark Falcon* from the blur of images left by the metal haze sitting in her wake. The ship was almost upon them when they emerged and Mahra was ready. Her fingers stabbed down in rapid sequence, sending shot after shot volleying out to meet their foe before it had time to react. Most found their mark. Mahra was shocked as her shots were joined by other fire that lanced from the area behind them. The other two ships had fired regardless of their companion!

They had ignored the cloud's obscuring shadow and fired anyway, hoping to meet their quarry regardless of the safety of the other ship in front. Mahra had only an instant to see her target rupture in a tumour of light and go spinning toward the waiting world of Belshore. Further impacts met *The Dark Falcon* and she was tossed heavily to the side with the force.

"Down Timon, now!" she yelled into the com, knowing that they could not sustain such firepower for long and remain in one piece.

Pellis obliged instantly, dropping the ship down and away from their obscuring cloud. The area glowed with incandescence as the small metal particles were caught in the beams playing across them.

"Watch the back," Timon snapped as he thrust *The Dark Falcon* forward with a burst of acceleration.

It took less than a second for the other two ships to realise that their quarry had left the camouflage and to leap forward in pursuit, one above and one below. They continued firing as they came, the occasional beam rocking *The Dark Falcon* as they tried to make good their escape. Mahra sent fire back toward them but with limited success. They were two and she was just one. She could not hope to match their combined firepower. Both ships were larger and more powerful than *The Dark Falcon* and each could easily take more damage than she could deliver by splitting her fire. As she assessed the odds, she continued her fire, looking for a solution.

If she concentrated her fire on one of the pursuing ships, it would leave them open to the attention of the other. If she continued to split her fire, she had little hope of scoring enough damage on either to have any effect. She started to panic as she was jolted to one side and a large gouge splashed across the outer skin by another beam finding its mark.

"Hold Mahra, and be ready to front," came Timon's voice, snapping her away from the growing desperation in her mind.

Mahra felt the ship begin to turn upward, bringing them closer to the higher ship's range, but away from the arc of fire of that below them. Timon was about to make them a sitting target. There was no way *The Dark Falcon* could survive through a sustained barrage from the rear, and her heart lurched as the impact of another shot caught them on the tail.

Suddenly, *The Dark Falcon* came to a virtual stop in mid-space. As their velocity died, the ships tailing them shot past above and below. Just as rapidly, Timon accelerated. Mahra was ready and as they drew up behind the leading ship, it sat, perfectly framed, in her line of fire. At that moment, she understood what Timon had done and she let loose. The ship in front glowed and then erupted as Mahra's beams found their mark. One down — one to go.

Seemingly oblivious to the fate of its two companions, the remaining ship turned and began inching toward them. Timon turned nose down to face the lingering threat. Rapidly, the two ships accelerated toward each other, each blazing with the fury of their active weaponry. *The Dark Falcon* was by far the more agile of the two and Timon used it to great advantage. Mahra continued to pour fire at their opponent as Timon, letting out one long whoop over the com, started a dive that seemed destined to take them on a path to suicide, nose down into a maelstrom of searing fire.

Mahra's fingers pounded the pads sending forth all that *The Dark Falcon* could muster. She felt the ship shudder as it sustained hit after hit, but Timon was good at what he did, and he ducked and wove as if *The Dark Falcon* was an extension of himself, mapping a path through the lancing beams.

Mahra concentrated her efforts on one small section of the approaching ship, targeting a point on the aggressor's hull just above where the drives should lie. It was total concentration for her as *The Dark Falcon* bobbed in and out of the threatening beams. Her perspective changed from instant to instant. The buffeting they were receiving threw her aim off.

Timon had set his course straight for the nose of their opponent, only moving from it to take subtle evasive action. Mahra's eyes grew wider as the ships sped toward each other, convinced that at any instant *The Dark Falcon* would fall to the opposing weaponry.   Finally, just as it seemed as if they were about to collide, her efforts bore fruit. *The Dark Falcon's* weaponry speared through the other ship's drive section and it blossomed into a ball of fire and debris.

They swept through the growing cloud, the ship shaken by the force of the blast, as huge chunks of twisted metal spun past them trailed by streamers of burning gas.

Mahra was unconvinced that it was finished. She scanned her displays over and over, checking for any remaining signs of craft, but her field of view was clear. She remained poised for action, the adrenaline still coursing through her system.

"Good shooting, Mez Kaitan. Well done."

"Timon Pellis, you are a complete madman," Mahra responded in disbelief. "What was that last little run meant to prove?"

"Ah well, you know. Sometimes you just have to grab the situation with both hands. I think that's enough for one day though. Let's get the hell out of here."

She rubbed the back of her neck and shook her head as she felt *The Dark Falcon* pull away from the now-dead ships' fragments. Keeping one eye on the displays, she listened in as Timon and Sind ran through the damage checks. She still couldn't quite believe how close it had been. They had been big ships, all three, and they packed quite a bit of weaponry. Somebody wanted them out of the picture pretty badly. On balance, they should not have been able to get past two ships of that size let alone three, but they had, and that was good enough for her.

She remained strapped in her couch and scanned the surrounding displays until they were well out of Belshore space. As she did so, she thought about how Chutzpah had prompted her; how he'd done so more than once, and she began to wonder how.

Chapter Sixteen

Mahra met them in the rec room when she was finally satisfied that they were out of further danger. Timon and Sind seemed content that *The Dark Falcon* was going to make it without emergency repairs, even though the ship had taken a fair beating during their encounter.

They assembled with the customary mugs of kahveh, looking a little sheepish, a raised eyebrow from Pellis being the only comment for several minutes. Finally, Timon cleared his throat.

"Well, just a little warm, wouldn't you say? Some damned fine piloting though, even if I do say so myself." He grinned.

"Humph," answered Sind. "And if it hadn't been for the suggestion of Mahra here, where would we have been then?"

"Point granted, Jay my friend. Credit where credit is due. That was a fine tactical display there, Mahra. Good shooting too. Got us out of a sticky situation even if it took my skill to put it into place, eh?"

Mahra dipped her head in acknowledgement and Timon smiled at her.

"Well, one thing's for sure now. They're on to us on Belshore. We seem to have drawn attention to ourselves. We'll need to keep a low profile for the next couple of months. A pity really, just when it seemed we were getting so close."

"So, what now?" asked Jayeer.

"First things first, Jay. Back to New Helvetica. Get rid of our suspect load and then .... " Timon shrugged. "Play it by ear a little bit, I suppose. We have to get ourselves out of the picture for a while. I don't know where yet, but something will come along. It can't be New Helvetica. Too close to the centre of operations, and if our little reception party was anything to go by, we may as well light a marker beacon for the opposition."

Mahra didn't think she could offer anything constructive, so as Timon and Sind sat and thought, she occupied herself with an analysis of events.

"Timon, that deceleration of yours was a pretty smart little move. Do you want to tell me about it?" she asked.

"What? Oh that. Sometimes I forget about the capabilities of *The Dark Falcon*. I just fly her, you know. Jayeer here is probably better equipped to fill you in on the details. Jay?"

"Yes ... I suppose ... " Jayeer began hesitantly. Pellis nodded and Sind continued. "*The Dark Falcon* has more than a little bit in advance of your normal ship's rigging. I'm sure you've noticed by now. From your position, the weaponry is fairly standard, but the battle pod itself gives you more speed, warning, and accuracy. She has not been designed for offence, but for speed and agility. But sometimes, in a tight situation, she has to be able to look after herself. The reverse drive, when you talk about that deceleration, is another of those features. It's just a little more than your normal manoeuvring drives. There are a few more non-standard features as well."

"Such as?"

"Well as you saw, we have some reasonable defensive countermeasures installed. The metallic dust cloud is just one such. Confuses the hell out of tracking and range guidance systems. These days, that one has become more standard. There are some additional ones though. I suppose the main one is the backup drive, for all the good it does us. I've already mentioned that drive to you before."

"So, what do you mean, 'for all the good it does us,' Jayeer?"

"Well, the thing is, anybody who has used it except for one or two, has been unable to report back on the results. It's a jump drive."

"But I thought — "

"Yes, I know," he interrupted, holding up one hand to stop her protest. "Totally the province of the Sirona. Research in that area has not been particularly public. There would probably be an outcry if it were. In theory, there should be no problem with the drive principles and we really do believe it works. The problem is, that in the testing phases, unless we were extremely lucky, the ship made the jump without any problem, we just didn't know where it jumped *to*. We lost a few ships and a few good people that way. A couple of times we were lucky enough to have the jump's end-point appeared in known territory. That gave us enough confidence that the drive actually worked. And, put that together with the fact that the Sirona seem to have been doing it for years ... " He shrugged.

"You sound like you're talking from first-hand experience, Jayeer."

"Well, yes, I had some personal involvement in the early programs, as did Timon, but that was as far as it went. They've come a long way since those times. So, we have the drive but, and it's a big but, we're not quite sure if we can use it."

"I see." Mahra nodded thoughtfully. "Anything else?"

"One or two things. The external skin for instance. That is a special alloy. It's blast and beam resistant and makes the ship exceedingly difficult to track. I'm sure there are more, but I suspect they will come out in time if the situation arises."

"Uh-huh. So, all this is Council funded?"

"Of course. Even without knowing what you know, do we look like we have the kind of resources to put even a small part of that in place?"

"No, I guess not."

"No, you guess right," said Pellis and laughed.
"That'd be the day. Well, if you two have finished your
technical discussions we can get on with things." He waited
for Mahra to nod. "I've been doing some thinking and I
think I know how we're going to handle this when we get
back to New Helvetica."

"So, what is the plan, Timon?" she asked.

"All in good time. All in good time. In the meantime,
we have to lie low for a while and I think we can do that by
using a few of your skills. Whatever we come up with, it
has to be non-CoCee. The risks are too great right now. The
way we first met has given me an idea. And it just might
work at that. I don't think we'll leave it to the off chance of
hanging around bars though. When we get into port we're
going to register *The Dark Falcon* for hire. That way we'll
have more of a choice. I think New Helvetica is as good a
place as any for the sort of thing we're after. With a bit of
luck, we'll find something in the couple of days it takes to
get *The Dark Falcon* back in shape and for Jay and myself
to do what needs doing with the Belshore stuff. I'll get
clearance for what I'm planning at the same time."

Chapter Seventeen

The Sirona visit had managed to upset him, but no, at last, Valdor was ready to act. His original plan had failed and failure didn't sit easily with him. This time, he was determined, failure was not on the agenda. He had a week to play with; not very long in the scheme of things, but it might be enough to accomplish what he needed. He knew he could pretend to play along with them for only so long, so he had to be sure he had the backup he needed. The major problem was how he was going to get the core sets offworld without Sirona intervention.

He could always send a number of couriers in the hope that one or two would get through, but he needed to keep the operation low profile and that wasn't the way to do it. No, the best way was to find a single guaranteed method and hope that Sirona attention was elsewhere when he set it in place. He might have bought himself enough room to move with the last meeting but, after that week was up ....

If he wanted to get something offworld, then the clearest point to start was the portside region of New Helvetica. He couldn't trust any of his own couriers. He had no idea how many the Sirona had already tagged. What he needed was new blood. Any number of freebooter types looking for employment populated the portside bars. Most didn't really care what side of the authorities their work took them, as long as it paid, and that suited Valdor just fine. It virtually guaranteed the required discretion. With his contacts, finding someone shouldn't be too hard. Marina's would make the ideal base to work from.

He made ready and left his place, informing Milnus before he left that he could be contacted on his private com.

He arrived at Marina's and breezed past the girl on reception. She made to stop him, but then recognised him from last time, gave a slight sneer and returned to her reading. Marina answered the door almost immediately. She looked at the bag he carried and ushered him inside.

"So, what is it, lover? Why the bag?"

"I need to ask you another favour, Marina," he told her. "It's a little bigger than last time. Things have taken a turn and I need to stay out of the picture for a while. You know what's happening and I didn't think you'd mind. I thought of you immediately."

"Come on, sit down and tell me what's happened. Of course, you can stay here. You have no real need to ask, lover. Do you think it will be for long?"

Valdor dumped his bag, sat, and ran his fingers back through his hair. "Not too long, I hope," he said with a sigh. "It should be no more than a week."

"Fine, fine," she said, taking a seat opposite him. "You know that. Everything you see is at your disposal." She waved her hand dismissively. Now, lover, fill me in on what's been going on."

Valdor told her about the second Sirona visit and that he was involved in a business deal that they had interest in. He neglected to fill in the details, merely indicating that he needed a secure base of operations until he had completed his side of the deal. She seemed to accept it, and he sat back feeling a little more relaxed. He knew he could rely on Marina to keep things quiet. Milnus knew where to contact him if anything came up, so he could get on with what he needed to do in relative confidence.

The next evening Valdor made ready to start cruising the bars. It wasn't too far from Marina's place and that made it all the easier. The first thing he did was tone down his image. He knew the clothes he wore and the manner in which he carried himself didn't typify the usual customers frequenting many of the watering holes he planned to visit, so he made do with plain black coveralls and a pair of eyeshades. He dispensed with the cloak and his boots, and substituted a pair of ordinary canvas utility shoes for the latter. When he was done, he surveyed himself in the mirror.

The whole ensemble made him appear regular enough. He should be reasonably at home in any one of the dockhand crowds, blending in, but not identifying himself as attached to a particular service. As an afterthought, he tied back his hair. Dockworkers never wore theirs out. It was too dangerous. There was always something it could get caught in.

He had been careful to maintain contacts among the portside bar staff over the years. From time to time they had their uses. Never sever a relationship that could turn a profit — Valdor had learnt that one long ago. He got in touch with those that he thought he could trust most out of an untrustworthy lot and had them spread the word that there was a contract on offer. Simple job, paid well, but had to be discreet. Having set the wheels in motion, he left to find a convenient location.

Valdor sat back in one of the more relaxed establishments for the bait to drew them in. The information network portside was undeniably good and he didn't have long to wait for initial contact.

The first prospect that approached him he rejected almost immediately. The man smelled and it was not only the liquor that made him sway on his feet and slur his words. Valdor wanted discretion and steadiness, neither of which the man would have provided.

The second appeared somewhat better. He was basically a mercenary and had tracked Valdor down through directions given by another of his contacts. The first had been directed over by the barman, but this one asked for no directions, just walked straight up, and sat down. He was sharp.

Valdor talked to him for a number of minutes and was impressed by the man's self-confidence. He seemed to know what he was about and was probably the sort that he could use for the job. Though he seemed competent enough, he finally turned out to be far too inquisitive. He wanted to know where and who and what for and Valdor was having none of it. He sent him on his way and the next hour was spent idly watching the crowds as he waited.

At last his patience was rewarded by the appearance of another potential candidate. The woman seemed capable and didn't ask too many questions. She was the rough and ready type and seemed as if she could look after herself. He was almost on the verge of giving her a try when the barman caught his eye with a slight toss of his head and a meaningful lift of the eyebrow. Very subtly his man behind the bar shook his head deliberately from side to side. That was enough for Valdor. It was one reason he had chosen this particular bar for his interviewing. The landlord not only had many contacts, but he knew a lot more about most of the local inhabitants than they realised. Valdor felt he could trust the barman's judgement without question. So, the third joined the first two and went on her way.

After she left, Valdor caught the barman's eye and gave him a querying frown and slight shake of his head. The man simply pursed his lips, shook his head, and shrugged. Well, there were clearly reasons. He really didn't need any further explanation, but he was curious all the same.

The crowds came and went, and so did the potential applicants. By the end of the first night Valdor still hadn't found anyone suitable. He was conscious that he now had less than a week and he felt the sense of urgency begin to grow.

The second afternoon began as the previous night ended. The applicants were fewer, and he rejected more than one by dint of a simple gut feeling or a spurious look from his ally behind the bar. More than one was Council and that was not a good sign. Either that, or they had links to certain parts of the dockside organisations that he wanted no involvement in for the moment, so the field was narrowing steadily. He was beginning to wonder if he was going to have any luck at all. It looked like he was going to have to explore other avenues.

He did have other contacts but in the time remaining he had less of a choice. He'd been out of touch with the right channels for too long. There was another lesson to be learnt here. Always keep his own hand in; never do everything by proxy.

Sighing and getting to his feet, he cast a glance of appreciation toward the barman, shrugged his shoulders and made his way outside into the night air.

He chewed over his options as he wandered through the neon- slicked streets. The hour was rapidly approaching where he had to make the decision that he'd been avoiding. Inside he had been denying it, but he knew he would have to use Marina's contacts again. He just hoped that this time she was in a position to help. He could use the nets, but they were too open and so ceased to be an option. His experiences with the Sirona had taught him that much. He was going to end up owing Marina, and owing her big. He was sure he could trust her, but it still made him uncomfortable. He wandered through the corridors of glowing holos barely registering his surrounds, lost in thoughts of what he needed to do.

Before he knew it, he was in the narrow side street, the red of Marina's sign flashing like an alarm above his problems. Shoving his way through the chime bead curtain he walked past the desk, ignoring the girl who sat behind it. She paid him just as little attention, his gaunt figure having become a familiar sight over the last couple of days. He took the stairs two at a time, strode up the corridor and palmed the door to Marina's apartments. She had keyed the lock to respond to his palm as well as hers on the first night he arrived.

Valdor saw with relief that Marina was already there, reclining, surrounded by a diaphanous gown, and sipping delicately at a long, tall glass. She peered over the rim as he strode through the door.

"Welcome home, lover. You look a little flustered. Where have you been — anywhere interesting?" she asked sweetly.

"Not enough time to go into that, Marina," Valdor said and sighed in reply. "You're right though. Things aren't working out exactly as they should be."

"Now, Valdor dear, just tell Marina and she'll see what we can do. Hmm?"

Sometimes Marina had the skill of making him feel like a small child without really trying. He moved over and sank into the couch as she patted the space beside her, rings catching the light with the movement of her hand.

"Well Marina, you know the spot of difficulty I've been having?" he asked, waiting until she nodded in reply. "I'm afraid it's a little more complex than I'd led you to believe."

"Hmm, I see," she answered, thoughtfully. "I might have guessed as much. Perhaps you should fill me in with all of the gory details."

She flicked back the tresses of her hair with one hand before fixing him with a clear gaze and waiting for him to explain.

"I don't know. I've got myself tied up in this business with the Sirona. They want something from me that is the result of one of my latest ventures and, well, I don't exactly want to give it to them. Well, no, that's not quite true. I want to look as if I'm giving it to them, but I want to do so without *actually* giving it to them."

"Valdor, lover, I think you'd better slow down. You're not making a lot of sense. What exactly is it that they want?"

"Yes, all right," he said with just a hint of reluctance. "This latest company venture of mine has come up with a certain product. It doesn't matter what it is for the moment. That is unimportant and it doesn't influence the position in any way. Let's just say that I believe it's going to be very significant. I have no idea just how significant yet, but for the Sirona to be interested .... The thing is, I don't exactly know why. Anyway, they have an interest in the operation. To the extent that they want me to stop production. Put the operation away for good. I've worked too long and hard on this one, Marina, and I'm damned if I'm going to concede just like that to those poisonous little dwarves."

"All right then, so what's the problem? You have what they want. You don't want to give it to them. Then don't."

"I know. It all sounds so easy, but I'm afraid it's not as simple as all that. They've second-guessed every move I've made since I first had contact with them. They are inside my network, Marina, and I don't know where and I don't know how. I used to think I had one of the most secure operations around, but they've managed to side-step everything that is there. By itself, that's worrying enough, but I'm just not sure how far they're prepared to go. So, anyway, I set up a bit of insurance for myself. I've arranged to get a sample of the product offworld to somewhere I can be assured it will be safe for a time. If they managed to close me down on New Helvetica, I'd be able to move the operation and take it up again. As it stands, they know far too much, and I don't know enough about them to have the confidence to leave myself unprotected. You can see the sense in that, can't you?"

"Well so far, my dear, it all sounds as if you could handle it with your eyes shut."

"Yes well ... that was what I thought. That was until they took out my courier, Marina. I issued the instructions direct to Milnus and got him to organise it. They knew what was going on and they still took out the courier. Not a hint of how they did it. I don't know how they knew, but they did. And I can be damned sure it was *not* through Milnus. The only option I have left, is to arrange it myself. That was what I've been trying to do. The thing is, I just don't know the ropes anymore. I've been out of touch for too long, always relying on someone else to do the detailed work for me. I've a few contacts left, but for the last couple of years Milnus has been handling most of the things at that level."

"So, lover, what you need was someone to get your package off New Helvetica discretely without involving anyone in your own network. Am I right?"

"Yes, basically. The rest of the details I can sort out later. That's not a problem. I have some ideas but I'd just like to have the feeling that I've covered my back if any of it goes wrong."

"Well, why don't you sit back and let Marina sort something out for you, Valdor my dear. You really are a bad boy you know — not letting me know all of this sooner," she said and patted him on the cheek.

She placed her drink on the small table beside the sofa then stood and with her hands on her hips looked down at him, shaking her head.

"I don't know, Valdor Carr. You've always needed to do things on your own, haven't you? Well for once in your life you're going to have to swallow that pride of yours and let someone else take a hand. Now, you just sit there and relax while I go and see what I can come up with. We'll think of this as a favour owed, shall we?"

Tossing back her hair she turned and walked out of the room still shaking her head but smiling as she left.

Valdor sat where he was, as Marina instructed. He had a lot to mull over as he waited and he spent the time toying with options. Carr Holdings had interests in a lot of areas that he didn't really want to make public and in that respect, he was vulnerable. The Sirona knew far too much about what he was doing and what he was involved in. On the face of it, they probably had enough inside information to shut him down publicly and that was not good. Of course, he could come out with a public accusation of interference, but he was sure quite a few of his own dealings would became casualties as a result. He doubted that escalation to the level of the Council would do much to further his cause. He was, after all, not the CoCee's most favourite son.

The other thing that was clear was that he didn't want to become involved in a war of attrition with the Sirona. They had resources at their disposal that would made things very difficult, if not outright dangerous for Carr Holdings and for him personally. The best option was to hedge his bets, play both sides of the game. If, on the surface, he seemed to be playing along with them, he could make out of it. Meanwhile, if he could use Marina to get the sample offworld, and carefully, arrange for some of the technical expertise to follow it, he had places where he could keep the operation going fairly quietly. That way, he *should* be able to benefit from both sides of the deal. When the time was right he could sweep those little aliens off the board. The question was how. He had to think. He was chewing his lip thoughtfully when Marina reappeared.

"Well, my dear, I've been considering a few options. I've just been checking out the port list. There are some ships in, registered as free, seeking cargo. Most are chain owned, and I'm not sure that is exactly what we want. Too many procedures. Now, one or two possibilities present themselves among the rest. A couple I know. I'm not sure whether I'd be confidant about their ability to get a job done. But...."

She let the last word hang, clearly waiting for him to bite.

"But what, Marina?" he asked obligingly.

"Well, it might be a long shot, but there is one particular ship there that might fit the bill. It's owned by someone I used to know a long time ago. I think it might just be worthwhile renewing old acquaintances. What do you think? Mind you, the man was never a fool, Valdor. He'd have to be approached very carefully."

"So, tell me what you think. What's your gut feeling?"

"I think he may be worth a try, lover. And ... it would be good to see the old reprobate again," she said.

The tone in her voice told Valdor there may have been a little more than mere acquaintance there. He was surprised to feel just a slight twinge of jealousy.

"Fine. I'll trust your judgement, Marina. Set it up," he said.

Chapter Eighteen

Timon registered them as soon as was practical after landing. There were matters to attend to with the ship beforehand, but as soon as they were out of the way he got *The Dark Falcon* on the boards. The ship had been sitting in port merely a day when the message came in. Neither Timon nor Jayeer had expected a response so rapidly.

Several ships were in port at the moment, and many far more likely to attract a decent sized cargo. The registration was merely to cover their options while they looked around. There was always someone on New Helvetica looking for a small fast ship to take someone or something offworld and out of the system in a hurry. Knowing the course of their luck up to now, it was just as likely to offer them an assignment back to Belshore.

Timon scanned the contents as it scribed across the com, read it, and re-read it, shaking his head as he stroked his moustache.

"Who would have thought it?" he said to no one in particular. "Marina Samaris. Now there's a name from the past. I wonder what she wants with old Timon."

The message was a personal invitation to dinner at one of the more celebrated eating houses on New Helvetica.

"Well, Mez Samaris is certainly moving in interesting circles these days by the look of things. You never know, this may be exactly what we're looking for. Marina was never one to came right out and ask for what she wanted. I think it's just too much of a coincidence that she should invite me after so long, just when we happen to be for hire. Time to revisit the past I think," he said thoughtfully, and rapidly keyed a response. "Now, I hope you two can amuse yourselves this evening. It could turn out to be a long night."

Mahra and Jayeer looked at each other bemusedly as Timon graced them with a foolish grin.

Pellis spent longer than normal preparing himself for the scheduled rendezvous. He appeared several times in the rec seeking approval from both before he was finally satisfied. Mahra found herself wondering about this Marina Samaris and how exactly she slotted into Timon's past, especially with the amount of trouble he was taking. This amount of preparatory preening had to mean something. His final promenade saw him decked in a formal, matte-black, one-piece suit buttoning across the shoulder, offset by a deep-red, drop cape. He had even neatly curled the ends of his moustache. Mahra raised an eyebrow as he stalked from the rec and out. She couldn't help being amused. The red boots had stayed.

☐

Timon made his way out of the dock humming to himself. The wound he had sustained on Belshore was almost healed and gave him only the occasional twinge as he strode confidently through the clusters of idle ships. It was quite a distance to his destination, but he felt like walking. He had come out making sure he was armed, but there was little worry of running into anything untoward here — not in his home territory. He had a real fondness for New Helvetica and always felt that little bit more at ease when he was here. He knew all sides of it, the well to do and the darker aspects it concealed.

Trouble could be found on New Helvetica if one was not careful, but only in particular areas. The sterile surrounds of the well-to-do classes who frequented this world also brought security and safety. The underbelly only touched their lives when they wanted it to and then, only if it suited their devious machinations. Some would never encounter it knowingly and would likely avert their eyes if they did. He liked it when it was a matter of choice. It was so much more pleasant than the circumstance that came with Belshore. On Belshore one just didn't have that choice.

The Barast Skewer nestled high in the old section of the city. This quarter was definitely non-commercial and it abounded with high-walled residences covered with vines and surrounded by extensive gardens. The restaurant was fronted by a gravelled courtyard filled with neatly parked trans from the market's lux end. As he crunched up the drive he smiled at the surprised look of the liveried doorman who stood at the top of a set of wide stone steps flanked by burning torches. The doorman was obviously not accustomed to greeting people arriving by foot.

Making a show of ignoring him, Timon climbed the wide stairs to the tall glass front and walked right past him. He was intercepted as soon as he stepped inside, by a cadaverous individual who looked him up and down with an air of disdain.

"Excuse me, Mezzer, but have you a pre-booking?" he asked with a sniff. "I fear that we are extremely full tonight. Perhaps Mezzer would like directions to another establishment that could accommodate him?" The tone dripped superiority. It was obvious that Timon was not the type for *The Barast Skewer*.

"No. I'll be fine right here, thank you. I'm meeting a Mez Samaris" he answered cheerfully.

The transformation was astounding. "But of course, Mezzer. Please forgive me. Mez Samaris is expecting you. Please. Please. This way."

At the mention of Marina's name, the supercilious tone had disappeared from maître d's voice and been replaced by one of almost fawning respect. Timon was impressed despite himself. Marina had certainly come a long way.

He was ushered to a table in one of the better positions of the house. It afforded a clear view over the length of the New Helvetian cityscape. It was also far enough away from the kitchen and the toilets to have prestige. Timon noticed immediately that it was obvious enough to be seen and to see from, without suffering intrusion by other patrons. He took a moment or two to admire the view, both of them. The snow-capped peaks in the distance appeared as light shadows against the evening sky's darkness. Marina sat resplendent in evening dress, her hands clasped beneath her chin as she looked him over in return. Her lips were somewhere between a pout and a smile as he seated himself opposite, unclipping the cape and letting it drop to the back of his chair.

"Late, Timon, but not too late," she scolded as he settled himself comfortably.

"Marina," he answered, reaching over, and taking one of her jewel-studded hands in his. "It's been a long time. Fire, but you're as radiant as ever."

"You're not doing too badly yourself, Timon my love," she said approvingly. "I'm glad you could make it."

They were interrupted momentarily by a waiter who took their drink orders then discretely left them to peruse the menus. Timon noted immediately that there was not a price to be seen anywhere.

What was the old adage? he thought to himself. *If you had to ask the price, you couldn't afford it.* Marina seemed to be doing quite well for herself.

They passed the next two hours in idle conversation, catching up on old times and what had happened to each in the intervening period. The food and wine that passed between their conversations were exquisite.

When Timon finally sat back, hand toying with the handle of a small cup of syrupy dark kahveh he felt overwhelmed by a sense of satisfaction. He savoured the feeling for a moment or two longer before he could bring himself to speak.

"Marina, this is all very pleasant, but you've not asked me here for the sake of old times, have you? We've had a wonderful meal. It has been a joy to see you again. But don't you think it's time to tell me the real reason? You've softened me up for something, and now you can tell me what it is."

"Ah, Timon my dear, I'm not that transparent, am I?" she said tilting her head a little to one side and fluttering her eyelashes at him. Adopting a more serious tone she continued. "No, lover, you're right of course. I have a little problem. Well, not exactly me, but a close friend of mine. He has something he wants transported offworld discretely. It just so happens that I noticed you had *The Dark Falcon* registered for hire and, well ... here we are."

"Mm-hmm. It has got to be a little more complex than that, Marina, for all this. What's so hard about getting something off New Helvetica anyway. Is it something I should know about?"

"Well, yes, it *is* a little more complex than simple transportation. The problem is not so much what it is, but there's another party interested in it."

"How do you mean?"

"The package itself is harmless enough as far as I'm aware. It's just that the other party are, well ... " Marina leaned forward and lowered her voice. "We'd just rather not have them involved."

Timon frowned. What mysterious party could it be on New Helvetica that he didn't know about? Here he was running away from something that spoke of Sirona involvement only to be offered something that bore the signature of some mysterious group or organisation that clearly offered some sort of threat. He thought about it for a moment or two and slowly a suspicion began to form in his mind, one that caused an almost imperceptible narrowing of his eyes as he asked his next question.

"That's quite interesting Marina. But why me? Why *The Dark Falcon*? Out of all the ships in dock at the moment, why mine?"

"Why, Timon dear. I don't think the answer to that is very hard. I know you. I know you're reliable and I think I can trust you. I also know you can look after yourself in a tight spot. There's nothing particularly strange about that is there?" She narrowed her eyes in turn and studied him. "What exactly is going on in your head, my love?"

"Oh nothing, Marina. It's just funny how things happen sometimes. That's all," he said, his suspicions a little allayed. Perhaps he was just being paranoid. "Why a tight spot? Do you expect trouble?"

"I'm afraid so, Timon. It's not as simple as it sounds. The exercise has been tried once already. The people involved are, you might say, no longer with us." She paused to let this information sink in before continuing. "So, even with knowing that, are you interested?"

Timon leaned back and considered. He took one final sip of his kahveh, rolling the bitter liquid round his mouth before answering.

"Aye, Marina. I think I am. I think I am."

"Good. That's settled then. I thought I could rely on you. I think my friend will be in agreement, but we have to go through the motions. You know where my place is?" Timon nodded; he remembered it well. "Good. I'll expect you there before noon tomorrow."

She signalled with a raised eyebrow and the waiter appeared in a moment at her side. "Could you arrange a trans for the gentleman please and bring me the bill while you're at it." She waited until he had disappeared before continuing. "You know, just being with you, Timon Pellis, has brought back some good memories. It's good to see you."

Timon stood and fastened his cape back around his shoulders, understanding the evening's session was at a close. Leaning across the table he stooped to kiss her lightly on the cheek. "It has been good seeing you too, Marina. Sure. it's been far too long." He held her hand for a moment longer before placing it back gently on the table. "Until tomorrow then."

"Uh, Timon, tomorrow, it would help if you don't let on how much I've told you. Just that there is a job to do ... if that's all right."

Timon shrugged, not really understanding the reason for the request but willing to go along with it anyway. He bowed his head to her and walked calmly out the door, ignoring the staff who now fussed around him.

The trans was already waiting for him as he stepped through the door into the chill night air, his breath fogging in front of him. He had a lot to consider on the short journey back and a lot to discuss when he arrived.

☐

Valdor was a little bemused the next morning when Marina ushered in the tall figure of Timon Pellis. This flamboyant character was not exactly what he had expected when she'd told him that she had a potential candidate. The tall man with the red boots sat down at the table opposite and thrust forward a large hand.

"Timon, Timon Pellis. How do you do? I hear from Marina that you're looking for someone to do a small job for you."

Valdor flicked a look toward their host, who simply nodded and shrugged. All right, so the first hurdle had been crossed.

"You've heard right, uh, Timon is it?"

"Aye, Timon, Timon Pellis." The man grinned under his large moustache.

"So, tell me Timon, have you got a ship?"

"Ah, that I have. She's a beauty she is, that is if you discount the few scuffmarks on her body at the moment. They won't stay long though."

So far so good. Valdor couldn't quite place Pellis's accent and that bothered him just a little. It was a sort of unidentifiable mix and he suspected the man used it to advantageous effect.

"Is this ship of yours up to a long haul ... say to the Rim?"

"Now I'm sure she'd make that trip without much strain. The Rim you say? Now then, this sounds even more like the sort of thing I'm looking for. Where on the Rim are you talking about?"

"No. Not so fast, Pellis. Why are you so interested in a small job like this for a start? By the look of you, someone like you might be able to find a thing or two in a better league than what I'm offering. Why are you interested in what I have to offer?"

"Oh, no doubt I could find something a bit more glamorous. But you see I have a vested interest in being out of the immediate vicinity in the near future."

"Hm-hmm. And why would that be?" Valdor asked with genuine interest.

"Well ... we ran into what you might call a slight bit of bother just off Belshore. As a result, there are one or two people we don't exactly want to run into in the coming short future. If you know what I mean?"

Valdor mulled over this last piece of information. Anybody who was mixing it up on Belshore could certainly looked after themselves. If Pellis had run into trouble off that world, then the odds were that the ship was built to take it too. He had a potential candidate that was certainly worth considering a little further. Unfortunately, Valdor didn't have that much time to waste. Besides, he already had Marina's seal of approval. Normally that would be good enough on its own, but in the current circumstances, things were less certain.

"So, Mezzer Timon Pellis, is it?" Valdor waited for a nod of confirmation. "Do you have a crew that goes with this ship? Actually, more to the point, can you trust them?"

"Now that would be a positive to both."

"All right then, can I meet them, and if so, when?"

"Well, I'd say there was no time like the present, would you? That is if you haven't got any other plans ..."

"No. Agreed. Just keep in mind that this doesn't mean that you've been accepted for the job."

"Fine, understood. Nor does it necessarily mean that we've accepted it. Now if you'd like to come with me, my companions are waiting in a bar a few blocks down. Before we set off though, have you a name? I can't refer to you simply as The Gentleman, now can I?" Pellis asked with a hint of a smile.

Valdor thought for a moment before responding. "No, fair point. You can call me Milnus."

He shot a glance at Marina as he gave the name but her face remained impassive.

"Aye. That will do," Timon responded in a tone that had Valdor wondering just how much he might know, or at least suspect. "Let us be off then Mezzer, um, *Milnus*," Pellis added as he stood and made his way toward the door.

Valdor watched him from behind as he followed. This Timon Pellis was a big man and carried himself with a deal of self-assurance that he appreciated. So far, his gut instinct was ringing no alarm bells and that augured well for what he had in mind. Added to Marina's seal of approval, it was almost enough to make him feel comfortable — at least for the moment.

Pellis attempted to probe him with questions as they walked the few blocks to the bar, but Valdor simply responded with half-framed non-committal answered until the man gave up. When they reached the front of the establishment, Pellis halted for a moment and held up his hand for Valdor to stop.

"Listen, Mezzer Milnus, if you wouldn't mind giving me a couple of minutes alone with them before we talk. I think it would work out better." He fixed Valdor with a steady look.

"Whatever you think, Pellis" Valdor answered, liking the man's directness.

They headed inside and Valdor found himself a spot at the bar and ordered a drink. He sipped as he watched Pellis in animated discussion with his two crew members. One, the woman, sported some kind of animal on her shoulder, the other was short and fat and seemed to be the one doing most of the talking. They were an interesting trio. If they turned out to be to his liking, he supposed he'd have to check the ship as well, just to make sure.

After more discussions and much hand waving the trio seemed to reach some sort of agreement, because Pellis stood and beckoned him over to their table with a smile. Nodding, Valdor strolled over to join them.

"Mezzer Milnus, these are my crew, Jayeer Sind and Mahra Kaitan," Pellis said indicating each in turn.

Valdor gave both a quick assessment as he nodded to them. The one called Jayeer wore thick lenses and a patina of sweat. The woman was obviously fit and her gaze roamed the room, constantly on the alert. An idea was beginning to form in Valdor's mind. The pet she carried was somewhat out of the ordinary and it probably attracted attention to her, but she was the sort who attracted attention anyway. Then again, the same could be said for the man Pellis. The good feeling he was having was growing steadily by the minute. After some more probing, Valdor decided to outline what he wanted them to do. He sketched the road brushstrokes of the task without filling in the details.

Having told them what he felt was enough, Valdor moved back to the bar to give them a few minutes to discuss it among themselves. He was quickly called back over to join the huddled group. They agreed to meet back at their ship later the same evening. Pellis explained to him that it was likely to be one or two days before they could leave, subject to successful completion of repairs to the ship. That suited Valdor fine. It would give him time to have the gene set prepared. Armed with directions for the rendezvous, Valdor left to pick up the sample and to make his own plans. The later meeting also gave him the opportunity to do some research and satisfy himself about the ship itself. While he was waiting for them to be ready, he could get his own network to find out everything they could about this Timon Pellis. He was all right by Marina, but Valdor wouldn't be comfortable until he could verify things for himself.

As he walked, he wondered to himself if he had given them too much information to start with, though the name Kalany was not much for them to go on. He quickly put his doubts to rest. He had learned long ago to trust what he felt and there was nothing yet that made him feel anything but satisfied.

Milnus had briefed him on Phildore's innovation and the idea that had been forming in Valdor's head started to take more shape. He wanted to be very certain this time that the package would not be detected. Perhaps, just perhaps, he could use Phildore's idea to his advantage. What better way to conceal something organic, than to conceal it *in* something organic? That was what the man Phildore had said. He would have to talk to Milnus and see if it was possible, but if it was ... The only remaining question was who would be the one to carry it.

☐

After Valdor left, the conversation among the three crew members continued.

"Well," said Timon, "that seemed to go quite adequately. Things seem to be working out. Kalany is far enough out of the way to suit our purposes, wouldn't you say?" He looked at Jayeer who nodded.

"Sorry, Timon," said Mahra. "I'm not familiar with it."

"Primarily agricultural. Staple crop, the wonderful kahveh. They have the best strains in the system. It's pretty much off the main travel routes, so it should keep us conveniently out of the way."

Mahra still had some doubts, but considering the risks they had already taken in the last few days, she decided it was relatively minor.

"Now," said Timon. "This whole thing, and what Marina hinted at, has given me a suspicion about what's going on here. What powerful clandestine group could there be on New Helvetica that we know nothing about?

Jayeer narrowed his eyes. "Do you mean ...?"

"Well, think about it, Jay," said Pellis. "Who do you think it might be? It certainly isn't us."

"Hmm," said Jayeer looking thoughtful. "It just could be possible at that."

"If it is, keeping the Sirona wondering would give me a great deal of satisfaction," said Timon, and smiled. "I'm a bit concerned about this Milnus. He's just too secretive about the whole thing. There is something else going on there. Whether it concerns us or not remains to be seen. He appears to have the resources, though. Did you notice his clothes? They were understated, but I wouldn't mind betting that they cost a few creds."

"Whatever is going on," said Jayeer. "If we can frustrate our little friends, then I'm for it."

"Yes, me too," said Timon. "Though I wouldn't mind knowing what he's doing in Marina's company." He shrugged. "Well, regardless, it looks like it's what we want. Mahra?"

Mahra nodded to Timon and then to Jayeer. As far as she was concerned, getting out from under Sirona scrutiny suited her. She was a little worried about what they were getting in to, but decided it couldn't be any worse than the position they were now in. She had faced worse things and survived.

"Good," said Timon. "Then we're settled."

They finished their drinks and made their way back to the docks to prepare for their meeting with their new employer.

Chapter Nineteen

Valdor found very little information about the man Pellis, and his ship. The standard registration details were there. Pellis was listed as a trader, nothing more. The name was known, but there was nothing significant to report. In truth, Carr will have liked a little more, but in the current circumstances he recognised he would have to do without.

He was feeling relatively pleased with himself as he headed to the dock area. His plans were falling neatly in to place, almost of their own accord.

When he reached the berth holding *The Dark Falcon*, he was suitably impressed. She looked like a good ship. Pellis's talk of running in to a spot of bother off Belshore would appear to have been slightly more than that, for the outer hull bore marks of a heavy battle. Work was proceeding to remove those scars, but from what he could see it must have been some firefight. Deep gouges marked the surface in several places and he doubted whether they could be patched effectively without a complete overhaul. He suspected the ship would bear the traces of the conflict for some time to come. Despite the apparent damage, it still looked up to making the journey he intended for it.

Valdor announced himself at the lock, banging sharply on the inner metal wall. Pellis appeared in the doorway a few moments later and ushered him inside. Valdor was impressed by what he found inside too, as he was given a brief guided tour. It was definitely non-standard, but it showed superior design. He had no doubt it was adequately crewed by three people and had been planned with that in mind.

As they entered the rec room Valdor's nostrils filled with the strong aroma of freshly brewed kahveh. The other two crew members were sitting around the central table with mugs in front and their faces lifted as he entered behind Pellis. Both nodded and he returned the perfunctory greeting. There was an extra mug sitting half-finished on the table, obviously belonging to Pellis. The tall man followed Valdor's glance.

"Can I offer you a mug, Mezzer Milnus, before we get down to business, as they say?" he asked.

Valdor shook his head in response. "No, thanks all the same. I think it'd be better to get straight on to what we have to talk about."

"All right then. Grab yourself a seat," Timon said, outstretched hand indicating a place opposite the other two crew members.

Valdor took the proffered place making a mental note of the lack of ceremony and waited until Pellis sat at the end of the table before speaking. As he did so, he reached into his coat and pulled out the package which he placed on the table in front of him.

"Now, this is what I want you to carry. It's not very large, but it has quite a bit of significance for me. There's a problem, in that I want this to remain hidden at all costs. The way I plan for this to be transported, is to have it implanted."

"What do you mean, implanted?" said Pellis, frowning at him. "If you meant what I think you mean — "

Valdor held up his hands. "No wait. Hear me out. It's perfectly safe. My technical people have assured me of that. It is essential that this is not discovered. For that reason, I want it inserted into the body of one of you three. Possibly a large muscle, say in the thigh. Because it's totally organic, it will escape scanning, and somebody would have to know exactly where they were looking to find it. I think that's doubtful, don't you?" He looked around their faces before continuing.

"I've been thinking about which one of you should carry it, and I have decided that it should be Mez Kaitan."

"Wait just a minute. Why her?" said Pellis.

"Well it's obvious, isn't it? It's clear to me what function she performs as a member of your crew. She looks like she can look after herself. And people are going to think twice about searching her. On top of that, it would not be unusual for someone in her line of work to have a fresh cut or wound on her body somewhere."

Pellis still looked doubtful and Mahra, though not having said anything was sitting with a frown etched across her brow.

"Now I realise you may need to have some form of cover story in the event that you were intercepted en route. For that reason, I will arrange to have a light cargo of art works delivered to your ship. Overtly they would be the reason for the voyage. You will be shipping them to my private estates on Kalany."

Pellis raised his eyebrows and glanced at his companions. Not an unexpected reaction. Valdor should had phrased that last better.

"Are there any problems with the concept so far?" he asked, and turned to look at each in turn. Sind merely shrugged and Mahra gave a brief shake of her head. He was about to continue when Pellis interrupted.

"Would you mind telling us the nature of this package?"

"Um, I'd prefer not to go in to exact details," answered Valdor. "You don't really need to know that at this point."

"So you say, Mezzer Milnus. But if one of my crew is going to be carrying it, especially within, rather than on her person, I'd feel a lot more comfortable knowing what it is."

Valdor turned to Mahra as he framed his response. "As I think you're the appropriate person to do the carrying, let me assure you there is absolutely no risk to you personally. The package is sealed in a carefully designed coating that will protect your body from it, and, at the same time, it from your body. It will be virtually indistinguishable from your own tissue in the event of a scan."

"So, you say there's no risk involved. If it's organic, how can I be sure of that?" asked Mahra.

"Yes, I can see your point. I can give you no guarantee of that, nothing that can prove it to you here and now. In that respect, I guess you'll just have to trust what I'm telling you. You can rest assured that I'm confident that what I'm telling you is the truth. Besides, in the event you were to experience any ill-effects — that won't happen — but if you do, you'll know the implant's location and you could take steps to have it removed."

Mahra considered his response, then asked him to proceed.

"Now just to be sure of that, is there any one of you with med training?" Valdor asked.

"Aye," said Timon. "Jayeer here has his fair share of skills in that area."

"Good. I thought as much. It would be unusual for at least one person on a crew not to have the skills, but I thought I'd better make sure. If we're agreed then, we can get this exercise under way," Valdor said, pausing for any negative responses before continuing. "I noticed on the way in, that you had quite a bit of work going on. Repairs and the like. How long do you think before the ship will be in a fit state to leave?"

"Oh, no more than a two day," Timon answered thoughtfully. "She could leave right now, but it would not be pretty travelling with all those unsightly marks, if you know what I mean. I'd prefer to have her in a state that has some semblance of her normal pristine self. I'm sure you appreciate that the sort of wear and tear she's showing at the moment would only drew attention to her and make people inquisitive."

"No, that's fine. I was only concerned that it shouldn't be any longer than that. In fact, as far as I'm concerned that is almost perfect timing. It gives me time to arrange for the consignment I mentioned and to have it delivered. It also should allow the implant to be just about fully healed."

Valdor held up his hand placatingly as the woman humphed dubiously at the last statement and looked away.

"If you're sure you're in agreement, we can proceed," he said, looking questioningly in Mahra's direction prompting, after a pause, a grudging nod of assent. "Good. I'll arrange for the appropriate cross-transfers to be made and for the delivery. You should expect that two days hence. If everything is in order we may as well get this started."

Chapter Twenty

The time came too quickly for Mahra's liking and she made sure Chutzpah was securely locked away in their cabin before the proceedings began. She didn't want him to get the wrong idea about what was happening to her and react accordingly. She had visions of him leaping to her defence without really understanding and causing quite a bit of damage before they could stop him. It wouldn't do to have him upset the process at this stage.

Jayeer used his med training to good advantage as the implant was set in place. The operation was painful, but not more than she could stand. The upper area of her right leg was numbed with anaesthetic spray and a quick incision made just below the muscle in her thigh. Blood flow was minimal, not only because of the speed of the exercise, but also because they had chilled the relevant area in preparation. The suitably sterilised package was slipped into the small wound and pushed into place. The cut was then sealed with a healthy layer of plas-skin. The entire exercise took less than three minutes and their employer looked on with approval as Jayeer's fingers deftly did what was required.

Mahra was still disturbed about what she was doing. She was not sure she liked the idea of being a human container, but she supposed she could live with it. The anaesthesia was enough to keep most of the discomfort at bay. At the moment, her leg merely felt warm where they had placed the implant. The plas-skin would see to the healing process and it also contained a fair share of numbing chemicals. She knew, however, that it would took a full two days at least to regain proper use of her leg.

For now, there was very little for *The Dark Falcon's* crew to do except wait. The mysterious Milnus left them with his stated expectation that they were to have no further contact with him. The consignment of artwork would be delivered at the proper time and he would arrange for them to be met separately when they reached their destination. As far as their shadowy employer was concerned, his part of the arrangement was at an end.

Mahra settled herself for sleep. During the night, she hoped that nature would take its course and speed the healing process. She decided before turning in, that she'd skip her ritual exercises. There was no point in putting unnecessary strain on her newly opened leg, and missing one night of the routine wouldn't do too much harm.

When they were in port, they slept on board as a matter of course. There was no need, after all, to hand over good creds for accommodation when they had their own. She was used to the narrow quarters and she doubted whether she'd feel comfortable in the open spaces provided by a hotel room. Chutzpah had also made himself at home. When he wasn't perched on her shoulder, he claimed a spot on the shelf above her bunk as his own. Any attempt to move him results in angry protestations. At night, he would jump down from his chosen roost and burrow about in the bedding until he had found a warm spot to nestle in close to her body. That routine was unchanged as she prepared for sleep. She had to push him gently away from her leg as he pressed against it and gave her a twinge of pain.

Next morning, she woke and breakfasted as normal. It was late in the morning by the time they all rose to the din of the workman attending to the ongoing repairs. If the work kept up at the current pace, *The Dark Falcon* would be ready well within their budgeted deadline. Again, there was little to do until their shipment arrived, and they didn't expect it until the following day, so Mahra spent the day wandering the local streets. She reasoned that a bit of exercise wouldn't hurt the healing process and would also prevent the wound from stiffening up. She had learnt from experience that stiffening of the limb was likely if she left a deep gash without movement during its healing process. When that happened, she had to expend double the effort to bring herself up to peak form.

By late afternoon she was bored and restless. New Helvetica was not really that interesting as an attraction, and as a port city it was the same as any other. She felt she could do with a bit of recreation. There didn't seemed to be much to warrant her keeping her senses about her and perhaps a good session was long overdue.

When finally she reached the ship, the other two didn't take much convincing. They grabbed something quick and horrible to eat at one of the local diners just so they might have something in their stomachs before they started. Then, shortly after dark, they hit their first bar.

Two drinks later, they headed to the next one, and after two more, the one after that. By the time they reached the fifth, the evening was beginning to wear on, the crowds were becoming more boisterous and the atmosphere full of noise and recreational haze. They were all starting to feel a little fuzzy.

The fifth establishment was obviously one of the less reputable houses in the area and the patrons were a mixed and seedy lot. The three were beyond the point of caring at this stage and headed into the bar regardless. They ignored the belligerent looks and slight shoving they experienced on the way to make their order. All they cared about was continuing what they'd started.

Mahra stood behind the other two at the bar as they tried to signal for drinks through the press of bodies clustered around the serving area. She felt herself being jostled but couldn't be bothered raising a protest. It was not until she felt the hand groping her from behind that she turned and swung. She did so by reflex. Nobody touched her like that without her permission.

Her fist connected smack in the middle of a rough-hewn face, turning the look from intended lechery to immediate surprise. The navy type staggered back, blood starting to stream from his nose. Immediately a hush fell over the surrounding customers. Slowly her assailant raised a hand to his face and inspected it as it came away covered in blood. Equally as slowly, his gaze rose from the hand to rest on Mahra's face. His eyes widened and then narrowed in fury. The crowd around them stepped back a pace in anticipation.

"Now, friend," came Timon's voice from over Mahra's shoulder. "I think that my crewmate here has expressed her displeasure and that should be an end to it."

Pellis stepped forward from behind her, placing himself, hands squarely on his hips, just to one side. The navy type with the bloody nose looked from one to the other, eyes still narrowed and his mouth started to curl in a sneer that was accentuated by the trail of blood from his nose. At the same time, another burly crewman stepped up beside him, crossed his arms over his chest and grinned at the pair. Mahra assessed the situation and slowly, she let her arm creep backward toward her blade.

"Why don't you just forget about it, mate?" she asked. "We can all have a drink and cool down a bit."

"Naah. I don't think that's going to happen, girlie," the second of the two said still grinning. "I think you're going to provide us with a little entertainment. Hey mates?" he said, addressing the watching crowd as he took a step forward.

Mahra knew that look and she felt the anger burn within her as she quickly drew her blade. "I don't think that's such a good idea, friend," she said, calmly fixing him with a steady gaze. "Do you?"

She backed toward the bar, stopping as she felt the comfort of its solid surface protecting her from behind. She willed herself to calm. The man facing her paused for only an instant at the sight of her blade, losing his grin for just the briefest instant. She could feel Chutzpah tensing on her shoulder.

Then, everything happened at once. The navy type she was facing off reached for his belt and in one fluid motion unclipped a sliver. The one facing Pellis moved forward swinging and Pellis strode forward catching him a ringing blow on his already damaged nose.

The crewman Timon hit fell back swearing into the crowd behind him and they promptly pushed him forward again. Mahra wove her blade in the air in front of her as the other crewman circled warily.

There was a sudden pain in her right leg and Mahra looked down to see a hand holding a small knife. She cried out and fell forward to one knee. The blade had gone in almost exactly on the spot where the package was inserted, digging painfully into the half-healed wound. At that very moment Chutzpah leapt, launching himself at the navy man holding the upraised sliver.

She was just about to regain her feet when she saw the man shoot. She couldn't see where he was aiming. She didn't think it was her way, and yet, the next instant, with an enormous wrench and a rushing sound in her ears, everything faded to black.

☐

Mahra slowly struggled toward consciousness. Blearily she opened her eyes vaguely focusing on the concerned faces of Pellis and Sind bending over her. She recognised, at least, that she was lying on her bunk in *The Dark Falcon,* but of anything else she was unsure. Her head throbbed, and there was something else that didn't seem right. With a massive effort, she tried to bring her eyes to focus properly, but their faces kept skipping backward into lines and tangents that flickered off around their heads.

She remembered that they had arranged a cargo haul and were relaxing in a portside bar. Then after that ....

The last thing she remembered was seeing the knife stuck in her leg, then the man pulling the trigger, then ... nothing. Everything blanked out. Maybe he had shot her, but she didn't feel like she had any other wounds. She had to have been hit from behind. Carefully, she lifted her hand and felt her skull, gingerly applying pressure. There didn't seemed to be any bruising. So, what exactly had happened to bring her down like that?

"Welcome back, Mahra. How are you feeling?" It was Pellis's voice, but try as she might she still couldn't bring his image into focus.

"How long have I been out?" she mumbled still trying to clear her head.

"About a day and a half," Sind replied, the concern evident in his voice.

"That long ... Fire! ... What happened?"

It was Pellis who responded this time. "We're not really sure. You took that knife in the leg, you were getting up again, and then, well, you just went down. It didn't look like anybody touched you."

She tried desperately to clear some of the fog and shook her head. That turned out to be a bad move. The images of everything in front of her distorted vision spiralled off in all directions. She closed her eyes. Painstakingly, she tried to reconstruct the events of that evening in the bar. She seemed to recall everything right up to the point where she lost consciousness, so what was she missing?

A strange hollowness nestled beneath her thoughts as if there was something gone from inside her. She had felt that feeling before and it was something she had not felt for many years, so she struggled to recognise it. Then, with a start, she realised what it was and that something was terribly, terribly wrong.

"Where's Chutz?" she asked, her alarm growing.

The other two looked at each other for what seemed like an eternity before they turned back to look at her. Sympathy was evident on their faces. Finally, Timon spoke.

"You don't know then, Mahra?" he asked gently.

Mahra felt panic well within her. "Where is he? Is he all right?"

"No Mahra, I'm afraid he's not."

"What do you mean? Where is he? Timon? Jayeer?"

"I'm afraid he is pretty badly off, Mahra," Timon answered gently. "Took a sliver to the head. One that was meant for you, I'm sure. It just glanced off him but it seems he cracked his skull on the bar coming down. I'm not sure what happened, but you went down at the same time, almost as if you took it rather than him."

Mahra couldn't believe what she was hearing. She frowned. "So where is he, Timon? Where is he now?"

She started to push herself up from the bunk but fell back again, bells of pain tolling in her head. She had to see him, to know that he was all right. Somehow, inside her, she knew that what Timon was telling her was true. There was no other explanation for that sense of hollowness inside her. So much time had passed since she had felt anything like it, but it was the same sort of feeling, though different. She had known her link with Chutz was strong, but to leave her like this .... The fear and concern welled up to fill that empty space. Chutz was a part of her and if he was hurt, so was she. It didn't feel right not having him near. She started to cry despite herself.

It was much later before she felt composed and well enough to join both in the rec area. The occasional lurch still ran through her chest in waves, but mostly she was in control. She took the time to splash water over her tear-stained face before stumbling out into the corridor. Her leg was hurting again. It throbbed in time to her pulse.

Something was still not quite right about her perceptions. Everything she looked at lanced backward into infinity, trailing afterimages if she moved her head too suddenly. It was as if the edges of solid objects wavered and rippled in the periphery of her vision. It was as if she had lost her ability to see and interpret things properly. Was Chutzpah so much of what she experienced?

Once or twice she made the mistake of shaking her head, but it only made matters worse. She might have cracked her head when she went down, but it didn't feel sore. There was just the pounding that went on and on.

Underneath it all lay the great hollow of Chutzpah's absence. Her chest heaved with the thought as she felt her way along the corridor wall.

She heard the low murmur of their voices as she neared the rec area but couldn't make out what they were talking about. As she eased her way through the doorway, supporting herself on the frame, the conversation ceased and both turn concerned faces in her direction. Pellis cleared his throat before asking how she felt.

"As well as can be expected I suppose," she replied. She sighed heavily. "So, where is he? You still haven't told me."

"Not far from here, Mahra. He's in good hands," said Pellis reassuringly. "The prognosis is reasonable, but he won't be out of trouble for some time yet. He can't be moved for a while. It may be up to a week or more before he regains consciousness."

"I've got to see him, Timon."

Pellis looked down at the table and started tracing patterns on its surface with his finger while chewing at his moustache. He seemed to be at a loss for words. It was Jayeer who spoke next.

"Do you feel well enough to travel?" It was as if he had totally ignored the previous exchange.

"Yes, I think so," she responded hesitantly. "But I can't leave before I've seen Chutz. I have to know that he's going to be all right."

"Listen, Mahra, that's all well and good, but in the current circumstances I think you ought to think about what you're asking. We've undertaken to do something and already we've been delayed by over a day. We need to be out of here and away. You know that. Taking the time out to see that animal of yours would only delay us more. We need to leave and we need to leave pretty damned soon."

Timon interrupted him before he could continue further. "Are you absolutely sure you're fit to travel, Mahra? We can't travel unless you're up to it. We've agreed on that much, but at the same time, you have to understand that Jayeer is right. Going to see the zimonette wouldn't achieve anything now. He's being looked after, rest assured."

"So, Mahra," Jayeer interrupts again. "It's up to you. Do we leave?"

Timon looked sideways at her from his position at the table. Jayeer had put the onus on her. She understood the implications of that expectation and she also understood that there was a lot more at stake here than her own personal trauma. It might help her to came to terms with things if she got involved. Though she felt torn, and desperately worried about the affect it was having on her, what they were saying made sense.

She bit her lip. "Yes, yes, I'm sure," she answered after wrestling with the options for a few moments more. She had to be able to deal with this herself. She had to be able to bring these sensations under control. "Just bear with me for a little while longer. I'll be okay. I just need to come to terms with it."

"Good. If you're sure?" Jayeer said with the hint of a question in his voice. He looked at her steadily.

"Yeah. I'm sure."

Mahra moved over to the bench to make herself a mug of kahveh before joining them at the table. She was conscious of both sets of eyes following her and with an effort she tried to suppress the slight limp. She hoped the hot kahveh would do something to clear the strangeness she felt in her head. Her vision was still not quite right, and something seemed to be interposing itself on her thought processes. she had no idea that Chutzpah's absence could affect her so much. She had never really realised before how strong their link had to be.

Cupping the mug between her hands, she took her place between the two of them. Jayeer looked at her for a moment or two after she was settled and then became all business-like.

"The repairs on the ship are virtually done. They'll be finished later this afternoon. The consignment of artwork is all aboard. The items were delivered yesterday when you were out of it. So, I believe we'll be ready to make our departure this night."

Mahra nodded her understanding. Pellis continued to cast sidelong glances at her.

"I've plotted a route that will take us a little longer but it should provide some extra cover," Jayeer continued. "We've logged flight plans as if heading toward Xanthe, but about two hours out, we'll made a sharp detour to take us to our real destination. Timon's feeling was that we should take the opportunity to spend a few days on Kalany after our business is complete. It'll provide us with the chance to get some recuperative relaxation and also keep our heads down for a couple of weeks. Personally, I believe it's a good idea."

"Hm-hm," Mahra responded, only really half concentrating on what Jayeer was telling her. Her mind was filled with images of her missing companion.

"Now, because of recent events, we will need to be especially vigilant on our voyage out. That will require full attention from you, Mahra. Are you sure you're up to it?"

"Yes, I told you I'll be fine," she snapped, and frowned. "I'm sorry, Jayeer. Bear with me."

"That's okay," he said. "I understand. All right then. I suggest you use the rest of the time before this evening, relaxing and getting yourself up to form. Timon and I have some minor checks and preparations yet, but after that we should be ready to leave."

Jayeer pushed back his chair and made his way out to attend to things on the bridge. Timon also stood but waited until Sind was well up the corridor before speaking.

"Listen, Mahra, I'm truly sorry about what happened. I don't know what else to say to you. But I'm certain that he'll be fine. We'll be away for a couple of weeks, and after that, I'm sure he'll be as good as new."

"Thanks, Timon." She was grateful for the sympathetic words.

Timon stayed a moment or two longer, watching her, then also left for the flight deck, pausing at the door to give her one last look. Mahra sat where she was, hands cupped around her mug and head slightly bowed. Neither of her crewmates was there to see the tear that rolled slowly down her cheek. And she made sure that there was no trace of it when she got up and left the rec room.

The remainder of the day passed uneventfully. Final preparations and the routines of pre-flight checks were all that occupied them. Mahra was slowly coming to terms with her anxiety about Chutzpah's health, but was still struck from time to time with waves of sadness. The hollowness within her continued unabated. She was concerned by the lack of improvement in her vision, but said nothing to the other two, not wanting to worry them any further with her troubles. Every now and again the episodes were almost hallucinatory.

As far as she could tell, the only plausible explanation for the continued problem was her body's attempt to came to terms with the loss of her link with Chutzpah. They were probably side effects of her mind trying desperately to readjust to working on its own again. In a way, it was very like the reaction she had felt when she first lost the Old One, but different somehow. But then again, their link had been different too.

The ship took off as planned without incident. Mahra found herself in her normal position, strapped into the couch in the battle pod, listening to the ongoing by-play between Sind and Pellis. It just didn't seem to be the same without her small companion perched upon her shoulder.

Her vision seemed to get worse as they left the atmosphere of New Helvetica. Various geometric patterns picked out in assorted colours superimposed themselves on the vista surrounding her. They trailed off from the light sources represented by the surrounding stars and ships, confusing what she saw. This affliction was starting to become a concern. There was no way she could effectively act as a gunner if she couldn't see what she was supposed to hit.

"Come on, Mahra, hold it together," she said to herself as the images spread. "You're no use to anyone like this. Focus. Find sharpness."

She was talking to herself now in a way in that she'd have conversed with Chutzpah. Her muttered comments brought a response from Pellis over the com, but she brushed off his query.

After a couple of hours, the ship performed the planned diversion, Pellis having judged that they were far enough out from New Helvetian space not to attract attention. With their course locked in, he asked her if she was going to join them in the rec, but she declined, telling him that she wanted to be alone for a while. Her excuse was not too far from the truth. What she really wanted to do was regain some sort of control over her senses.

Three more hours she spent in the pod, tracking the images, and trying to make some sense out of them. If nothing else, she was becoming used to them. Eventually, she felt she had enough control to risk joining the others, and she unstrapped herself and clambered down toward the rec to find them. If she ignored the traceries in her sight rather than concentrating on them, it seemed to be slightly better.

Chapter Twenty-One

Ten days later, with the aid of some of the waygates, *The Dark Falcon* drew in to Kalany space. With ten days of practice Mahra had become reasonably immune to the distractions, but it concerned her, as they still seemed to be there. As they neared orbital velocity, they strapped themselves into their respective positions fully at the alert. They had another six hours at least to wait before the expected rendezvous, but as far as Pellis was concerned it didn't hurt to be at the ready.

They had been sitting in orbit a little over two hours when Mahra's sight went crazy. *The Dark Falcon* suddenly seemed to be the focus of several distinct radiating cones. They were not there and yet they were at the same time. Concentric rings ran down their length toward the ship. Because of her perspective within the pod, she became the direct focus of that movement — as if the universe itself was aiming directly at her. Involuntarily she cried out.

"Mahra, what was it?" came Pellis's concerned voice over the com.

"I, uh, Timon I don't know," she said, trying desperately to maintain her grip on reality. Something seemed to be happening in the space around the ship and she couldn't tell whether it was outside the ship or in her head.

The edges of the surrounding blackness shimmered and slowly began to form other, more solid shapes. It seemed like large bulges were pushing outward from the fabric of the blackness itself. As five large, silver globes formed in the space around her she dismissed them as further hallucinations. Each globe slotted in to one of the cones that radiated from her position, effectively blocking her sight of the pulsing rings that flowed down their length. She was on the verge of panic now. Her mind was failing her. She had virtually convinced herself that she had lost her sanity when she heard Timon's voice over the com once more.

"What the hell are ... Fire! ... Sirona ships. Five of the buggers. Jay old friend, I think we are seriously in it. Mahra, I think you'd better get down here. Don't, I repeat don't fire on them. Just get down here."

Working away under the haze of her confusion, an idea was beginning to take shape. She wasn't quite sure what it was yet, but it was there nonetheless, and she reached for her harness and clambered out of her restraints. The visionary images had faded. All she saw now were the huge, featureless silver ovoids that surrounded them. The magnitude of their size dwarfed *The Dark Falcon*.

So, these were Sirona ships.

Suddenly, she remembered where she'd seen those shapes before and her insides went cold. It was many years ago and it was on a world called The Cradle on the day when she was to take her place amongst the elders of her race. With the dawning of that understanding, with the replay of those memories in her mind, the years of indignity came flooding back to her.

She gripped the edge of the couch and swallowed. Lancing beams of light struck down from the sky and a vast dome exploded into shards. She ran through undergrowth her heart pounding in her chest. She crept backward on a bunk, pressing herself against a wall. She saw the Old One's face and Aleyin's. No! They would not have her a second time.

Gradually she managed to regain some control, and though her breathing still came quickly, she made some sense out of her thoughts. She realised in that instant that she herself had more than a personal stake in the outcome of the CoCee plans. The Sirona! They were the ones responsible! No, Pellis was right. She must not fire. Her teeth were firmly clenched as she clambered down from the pod and made her way forward to the flight deck.

"Well Mahra, any ideas?" asked Pellis as she joined them up front. He looked up at her and immediately his face took on a look of concern. "Are you all right ...?"

Mahra forced herself to remain calm and assess the situation. "Yes, Timon, I'm fine." Her voice didn't sound convincing to her own ears.

Mahra scanned the various monitors clustered about them. *The Dark Falcon* was clearly boxed in and she doubted there was any real chance of making a run for it.

"No, I haven't got any ideas. I don't know, Timon. Have you?" She was finding it difficult to think properly.

"No," he said. "I don't know either. We're not going to be able to shoot our way out of this one. *The Dark Falcon's* good, but not that good. That was why I thought you'd be just as useful down here."

"Why the hell don't they do something?" muttered Jayeer, his eyes flitting from one image to the next. "They're just sitting there. Are they waiting for us to make a move or what?"

"I'm not sure," Pellis replied, narrowing his eyes. "Perhaps they're waiting for our contact to show. We seem to have upset them a bit by our actions on Belshore. Now, one Sirona ship I might have expected, but, five, well that's a bit of overkill. They are obviously fairly intent on making sure that we don't get away." He stroked the ends of his moustache thoughtfully. He glanced up again at Mahra, but she avoided his gaze.

Pieces of a pattern were tumbling into place inside her head. The Old One had taught her patterns, had taught her ways to make sense out of senseless things. He had shown her what fitted and what didn't and it all was starting to come rushing back. She had to reach the pattern and find it — find the way everything fit together. She looked at the vast silver ovoids hanging in the monitors around them and she suddenly became more certain.

"Listen, Timon, Jayeer, I've got an idea. I've just had the answer to a question that's been bothering me for a very long time." They looked up at her, Jayeer with a frown, and Timon still looking concerned. "I'll explain it later, if there is a later. We don't have time to go into it now," Mahra said in answer to their questioning glances. "Look, I'll tell you one thing," she said, suddenly feeling anger start to burn through the fear that pounded through her. "If we can do anything to put a nail in the coffin of those bastards out there, then I'm for doing it. Jayeer, you were telling me earlier about this experimental drive."

"Yes, but I told you — "

"Yes, I know. It's a risk. But what choice do we have. I have a suspicion about something and there's only one way to test it. If this works, then I'll explain it all to you. If it doesn't, well, we're no worse off than we are now and we might just get lucky ... I think we ought to use the drive ... Timon, what do you think?" She had to get his support.

"Well, I don't know ... but we're sure as hell not going to gain anything sitting here waiting to be sent to our next life. What the hell. Jayeer?"

"But we just don't know do we? There are too many unknowns. If we are — "

At that moment events made the decision for them. On the edge of the scanners, another ship appeared, moving slowly in toward them. Its call sign identified it as their contact, arriving just a little before the appointed rendezvous time.

As they watched it creep in, mere moments after it appeared, in concert, a sharp beam of glowing light arced out from each of the surrounding Sirona ships. They found their focus immediately and their contact disappeared from the screens in a glowing storm of energy.

Sind didn't wait. At the same instant as their contact was transformed into nothing more than a glowing cloud of burning gas, he flipped up a panel on the main console and slapped his palm down on the pad.

Instantly their universe exploded.

Chapter Twenty-Two

The jump coursed through every particle of their beings. For an awful moment Mahra believed the move had come too late and she was experiencing her death as the fury of Sirona weaponry consumed them. Then, just as suddenly, the sensation stopped. The other two looked at each other, then back at her questioningly. Then they turned to observe the instrumentation.

Mahra, her hands slick with damp, gripped the back of Timon's couch. Images of those beams of light still played in her head, but she struggled to concentrate and look at what the instruments were showing.

Very little made sense. The normal ship sounds continued. The gentle hum they were normally only partially aware of continued unabated. The slight hiss of white noise filled the com. There were no sounds of traffic or the distant garbled muttering of far-off approach controls.

Mahra realised she was holding her breath and prompted herself to start breathing normally. It seemed as if she was not alone, for Sind let forth a lengthy exhalation and Pellis whistled long and low through his teeth. So far, they seemed to have made it — but made it to where? Outside the screens showed nothing. There was a blanket of greyness and it rolled with snowy haze.

"Well, this is simply fine," muttered Sind.

"Oh, I don't know, Jay. It makes a change from boring black, doesn't it?" said Timon.

"Listen, you two," Mahra said, desperate to get their attention. She was in no state of mind for their banter right now. She had to concentrate. "I want to try something. I'll be back soon. Timon, can you put on the com please. Jayeer, if you just keep an eye on the readings."

They looked at the screens and then at each other with a puzzled expression. Sind shrugged, shaking his head and Pellis reached slowly for the com as Mahra turned and made her way off the flight deck. For some reason, the visual aberrations troubling her sight seemed to have gone away. A further suspicion was growing in her mind and the fact that the images had diminished confirmed it for her. Her sense of purpose grew as she worked her way up into the battle pod and strapped herself into her harness. Piling her hair up and underneath the headset she sealed it into place and took a deep breath.

Immediately her senses were awash with grey. She was suspended in a vast cloud of floating ash flecked with lighter and darker spots. The sudden noiseless light swept over her, overloading her perceptions with blankness. It took a moment to adjust to what she was seeing, but then she could pick out different hues among the visual static — traceries that had form and distance and colour. She concentrated on them and their clarity increased. Some colours ranged through areas beyond her normal visual spectrum, but she could see them anyway. They were colours she couldn't put a name to, but they were there all the same, and *she could see them.*

Concentrating still further, she distinguished a long tube of concentric rings along which they appeared to be travelling. They were definitely moving along its length, and as they travelled, the rings grew steadily smaller. They were the same rings she had seen just before the Sirona ships emerged. In her mind's eye, she concentrated on the point where those rings would eventually converge, and with a certainty, she knew where that point would be. She also knew where that point was, in relation to where they had just come from. It was as if she had a vast map in her head and she could plot the two points relative to one another. She suddenly had her solution.

"Timon. I want you to try something," she said over the com. "Turn her forty-five, would you?"

Pellis responded and turned the ship to the right. As he did so, she lost perception of the rings, their endpoint, and the sense of a long corridor along which they travel.

"Again please. Back forty-five. And be precise."

As the ship turned back to its original heading she was disappointed to find that the rings did not reappear. She muttered a curse and felt her hopes sinking. Just when she thought she had been totally mistaken, they flicked past the edges of her senses and she realised what had happened. She still wasn't thinking straight. She had to find that still place within her and concentrate — concentrate on the patterns just as she would on the patterns of her exercises with the blade. Urgently, she spoke once more into the com.

"Right fifteen, now. Left five, and up the same"

She was right! They were back on their original heading. Those wonderful geometries encircling the ship were back. She could feel their end point and she knew somehow that it was the same endpoint she sensed before. She felt the point behind them again as well. She knew then, without doubt, that it was the point where they made their jump. So far so good. If only Chutz was here to share this with her. Very briefly she wondered if he would have seen it too.

"Timon, take her in a slow swing to the left until I tell you to stop. When I do, try and do it as quickly as possible. Okay? Go!"

The Dark Falcon began a slow turn. Mahra immediately lost sight of the first shapes, but as they turned she began to see others. They swung past a tracery of rings heading in another direction. She could feel them just as easily as the path that they were travelling on previously. With each one, for that briefest instant as they entered the corridor of moving circles, she knew there was a point they led to at each end. These were the corridors that connected space, and she, Mahra Kaitan, could see them. She knew now what they had to do. She'd need maps.

It would be a painstaking search but it was one that she could achieve. Guiding Pellis with her voice, she turned the ship little by little, coming across new pathways and testing them with her new perceptions. Finally, she found one that seemed to end close enough to where they made their initial jump away from the Sirona. It was several worlds away but close enough to get their bearings. With a rush of determination, she tore off the headset and clambered down to join the others up front.

"Timon, Jayeer, I think I know where we were going." She waited while the pair exchanged doubtful glances. "No, listen, I'll explain all of it later. At least what I think I know, but just trust me on this. I want you to keep following my directions. When I tell you, cut the drive. I'm going back up."

She ignored the questioning glances that followed her as she made her way back out toward the pod.

She strapped herself into place, replaced the headset, and her senses were immediately assaulted by the vast nothingness. Gradually her mind adjusted to the input and she began to pick out the shapes in the surrounding field. The transition would have to be something she got used to. Carefully, she began to guide them down the corridor. The shapes that travelled the pathway grew smaller as they went, gradually increasing in frequency until they were pulsing with a rapid and regular beat.

"Jayeer, get ready to cut the drive when I tell you. All right. Now!"

Sind palmed the drive into inactivity at her command and as it died away, her vision flooded with blackness speckled by points of light. Her normal visual senses returned, and with relief, she picked out the steady glowing beacons of worlds and suns sprinkled across the ebon field. The sense of achievement she felt echoed in her voice.

"Jayeer, Timon, cut all drives. I want you to meet me in the rec. I think we've got a lot to discuss. And Jayeer, bring a map pad."

She tore the com and headset from her, fingers fumbling in her haste to get down and tell them what she knew.

By the time she had extricated herself from the restraints and made her way along to the rec room, the other two were already there waiting, curious expressions on their faces. She took her time preparing a mug of kahveh before joining them at the table trying to order her thoughts. Too much was still going on in her mind, and she felt herself trembling. There were too many memories, too much anger. But she couldn't afford to think about the Sirona now, not now. Not just yet.

As she had instructed, Sind had brought along the map pad. She sat across from them and gripped her mug so that the shaking in her hands would not show. She took a deep hesitant breath, then looked slowly from one to the other.

"Timon, Jayeer, I have some news for you," she said slowly. "Mahra Kaitan can navigate in jump."

An immediate expression of incredulity replaced the look of curiosity on Sind's face.

"Mahra, I don't think we're really in any sort of a position to be making jokes."

"No, just shut up and listen for once, Jayeer," she said. "This is hard enough as it is. I'm serious. Deadly serious. Where's your map pad?"

He slid it across the table to her. Thumbing it on, she scrolled through the displays until she located the one she was after. She slid the unit back to Jayeer and leaned across the table stabbing at the screen with her forefinger.

"I would say we were right about ... *here,*" she said, tapping a spot on the display. "Go and check it if you don't believe me."

Sind stood, and carrying the map pad with him left the rec room to do just that. Moments later he returned, an astonished looked on his face.

"Dammit, Timon, if she isn't right. It's exactly where we are. But how?"

Mahra looked at him and nodded slowly, her suspicions finally confirmed.

"This may take a bit of explaining. But I think at the moment we've probably got the time. Nobody is going to know we're here for a while." She took a sip at her kahveh, then a deep breath. "When the Sirona ships appeared before, a lot of things fell into place for me. It strung together some logical connections that I hadn't been able to make before then. I'll come back to the Sirona later, but before I do let me put a few things in perspective. For a start, you both know I've been feeling not quite right since that night in the bar?"

"Uh huh," Timon confirmed.

"Well, for a while I thought it was what happened to Chutzpah that did it. He and I had, well, a special link. It is hard to explain but it's a sort of mental symbiosis, I guess you'd call it. When he cracked his head, it had to have been disrupted in some way. I lost it, and it was as if something was ripped away from inside me. That was almost certainly the reason why I blacked out back there. Anyway, from about the time I regained consciousness, I was plagued with these strange visual distortions, almost like dopplering of everything I was seeing. I didn't say anything about them, because I believed they were the after-effects of what happened. I thought it was just my mind trying to come to terms with his absence. It was quite a shock to me not having him there. Not being able to feel him. I didn't want to worry either of you with something I believed I could deal with by myself."

Sind seemed about to say something, but Mahra raised her hand to stop him.

"Please, Jayeer," she said. "The thing that finally got me to thinking that I was completely wrong about it — perhaps not the cause, but most certainly what I was going through — was the Sirona ships. You see ... I saw them arrive several moments before they actually did."

"How do you mean?" asked Sind. "I don't understand. How could you see them *before* they arrived?"

"That is exactly how it was. It's a bit hard to explain, but it was as if there were these pathways that opened up, sort of overlaid on what I was seeing and then the ships were just there. It happened so quickly. At first, I didn't think they were real, that they were just more symptoms of what I was feeling. And then you saw the ships Timon, and I knew I wasn't seeing things. It was then that the connections started to become apparent. You see they arrived using jump drive and I saw where they were going to arrive *before* they did."

"Uh-huh. I think I'm beginning to see the pattern here." Pellis said thoughtfully. "And that's right. You cried out a moment or two *before* they appeared. I remember thinking it was strange at the time, but there was so much going on ... "

"So, that started me thinking. I made another connection, or thought I had. Really it was a series of connections. There seemed to be a genuine cause and effect there. Now, when I was very young I had a similar link to the one I had with Chutz. It was with, well, I suppose you'd call him my teacher. He died. At that time, I experienced something when he went, and it was similar to what I felt when Chutz cracked his head. But the thing was, there were no lingering after-effects like the ones I was experiencing and that made it somehow different. When the Old One died on Cradle, I felt as if a part of me was lost, but it was over and gone. I felt that same thing in the bar. It was the same, and yet different. I didn't remember it at first."

"Yes, I see," said Sind, now also looking thoughtful and chewing on the end of his thumb. "So, what made you make the connection with the drive?"

"A number of things really. To fill you in properly I need to give you a little bit of the background of where I was brought up. I grew up on a world that we knew as The Cradle. The entire world was sort of an experiment. It was started by a group of psycho-social theorists who had these ideas about furthering the advancement of human mental development. They believed that society and human mental progression were being hampered by society's heavy reliance upon tech. That was the theory anyway. But they didn't stop just there. All the people on Cradle had an operation at a very early age. I've got this set of neural implants that were supposed to enhance the functioning of my brain in certain directions. Everyone on The Cradle had them. Part of my upbringing involved rigorous mental and physical training. Now that physical and mental training was meant to develop those abilities, but we never really knew why we had the implants. Whether it was planned or not, I think those implants are very important to what I'm about to tell you. So, the implants, my upbringing, I guess they're all part of the reason why I am as I am today."

Mahra swallowed before continuing, fighting to hold her composure. "When I was about fifteen, The Cradle was attacked and virtually all of the population wiped out. I was one of the few survivors. There weren't very many who made it off alive. The connection here, and it was one that I couldn't had made until today, was the Sirona ships. I had never seen a Sirona ship before today. At least I thought I hadn't. You see the ships that destroyed The Cradle were Sirona."

Mahra paused for a moment to let that statement sink in before continuing.

"So ... why would the Sirona want to wipe out the population of a world that was basically isolationist, performed very little trade, and had no contact with the rest of the system? Answer that, and at the same time, answer a further question. What have the Sirona got that we haven't got? Answer?"

"The jump drive," Pellis and Sind answered in unison.

"Exactly. The only things that distinguished the population of The Cradle from the rest of the system were twofold. One, the neural implants, and secondly a tendency toward mental training. If you put that together with the things that were happening in my head, and the fact that I saw warning signs of the Sirona arrival before it actually happened then it starts to fall into place. On top of that, I remembered what you told me about the drive, Jayeer. The reason why it remained experimental was because nobody knew where the thing was going to end up when it made a jump. Whatever happened to Chutz must have somehow awakened some latent ability within me. An ability given by both these implants and the training I had when I was young. I'd been told about these things, but had no idea as to their purpose. Seeing the Sirona ships made me remember them. All that bundled together made me think it was right. I had to try it. I've seen what the Sirona can do, and we didn't have much to lose."

"Fire, Mahra, I think you've found it!" said Pellis, slamming his fist into his hand. "Curse me if we don't have some work to do though. So, Mahra," he said more calmly, concern written across his face. "You look a bit shaken up. Do you think you can find our way back to New Helvetica?"

"Yes, I'm almost sure of it. But there's only one way to find out."

"Yes, yes, of course. As long as you're sure? I think we need a few minutes to think about this. If you're right, we have a hell of a lot to do. So too does the CoCee. We might finally have the means to beat the Sirona at their own game. What do you say, Jayeer?"

Sind's eyes were fixed somewhere in the distance. His mouth hung slightly open. He shook his head and seemed slowly to return to awareness of where he was.

"Um, could you make me a kahveh, Timon?" he said distractedly, pulling at one earlobe.

Chapter Twenty-Three

Armed with a clear starting point and a fair idea of the direction they needed to take, Mahra had little difficulty locating the pathway that would took them to the New Helvetian homeworld. She was sure as experience grew, the process would become easier and easier. When she became familiar with the patterns, they would come naturally, just in the same way that her fighting reflexes were a natural extension of her practice with the forms and patterns she did virtually every day. The enormity of what she was about to became involved in hadn't struck her yet but she was fairly sure it would come. There was so much to deal with.

She felt a growing sense of inner satisfaction with the knowledge that what was to come only vindicated the training and care that the Old One took, but also that it would strike a blow at the Sirona. The taste of revenge would be like cold ashes in her mouth after so long. There was no real way it could made up for what they had done, but she was sure it was going to make it difficult for such a thing to occur again.

They weren't there yet, but soon they might be. With all the memories, she suddenly felt very much alone. She ached for Chutzpah's company and that was something she had to remedy very soon.

After discussion among themselves, they decided not to use the jump again if they could possibly help it. The discovery of her new ability was enough. Knowing they had access to the drive if they needed it, gave them a sense of security, but it still took nothing away from the realisation of their situation. They had no way of knowing whether the

Sirona could detect their use of the drive and they didn't believe they could afford the risk.

By the time they re-entered normal space in the region of New Helvetica, Pellis had been working hard. He formulated a lengthy message to his CoCee superiors planetside setting out the situation and what they had discovered.

As soon as *The Dark Falcon* entered the region inside the orbital defence perimeter he sent a high-burst encoded transmission. He didn't wait for a reply but immediately sought permission to dock and arranged a berth before heading the ship in for landing. His message was clear. There was to be nothing planetside to draw attention to the ship or to its crew. They would establish their own contact and took things from there.

Mahra was surprised at the confidence with which Pellis issued his instructions. He clearly had a level of superiority great enough to issue commands and have them followed, for when *The Dark Falcon* eased to a stop, there was no sign of any activity out of the ordinary dockside routines. They sat for a while watching, but there was absolutely nothing to give them cause for alarm.

"Right," said Timon. "I'm going to see some people. Jay, you find us somewhere to stay. I think it's better that we don't stay aboard *The Dark Falcon* for the time being, considering. Mahra, you go with Jayeer."

"Um, Timon," she said shaking her head. "I have other plans."

"What do you mean? We have things to do, Mahra."

"Yeah. So do I Timon, or had you forgotten?"

Pellis paused for a second, then shook his head and grimaced. "Of course, Mahra. I'm sorry," he said contritely, slapping his forehead with his fingers. "I was coming over all efficient and reasonably insensitive, wasn't I? Jay can show you where you should go. We'll meet at the main entrance, what, about six?"

Once he'd organised their accommodation, Jayeer gave Mahra directions and she wound her way impatiently through the back streets to the address he had given her. New Helvetica was fairly well serviced in the needs of animal medicine. The resort set liked their pets.

Eventually she found the establishment and was immediately impressed by what her crewmates had done. The facility was at the upper end of the scale, large, shiny front, and glass all over. It shouted expense. She could barely contain herself as she pushed through the doors at the front and headed for the reception desk.

The girl who sat there was not quick enough for her, but there was little Mahra could do. Nobody could be quick enough for her the way she was feeling at the moment. She could sense Chutzpah close, sense the touches of his familiar alien mind caressing the edges of her senses and felt his presence filling the emptiness within her. She wanted him back so badly.

When finally she reached the room, he was there waiting for her. He launched himself from the table surface at the same time as she rushed across the room toward him.

"Chutz, oh Chutz. I've missed you so much," she murmured into the small ears nuzzling at her neck. She stroked his short fur with gentle caresses, carefully avoiding the patch of skin at the top of his head where no hair had yet grown. "Have I got some things to tell you. So many things."

Satisfied that he was in a fit state to leave, Mahra pulled out her card. The girl told her that everything had been taken care of. She really did have a lot to thank Pellis and Sind for when she saw them.

On the way to meeting the others, people avoided the strange woman talking to the creature perched on her shoulder. Mahra didn't care about the curious stares. She felt almost whole again.

Chutzpah seemed only a little worse for wear. There was, of course, the patch at the top of his head, but apart from that, he seemed to be his old self. He even playfully nipped at her ear once or twice making sure he had her full attention.

While she walked, the shaved patch on Chutzpah's head reminded her. In all the excitement of the last few days, with so much going on, she'd forgotten about the implant in her leg. She'd get Jayeer to take it out once they were secure in the hotel room and that would be that. She doubted they'd be seeing their friend Milnus again, so whatever it was, it was dispensable. There were more important things to think about.

Timon had been busy in her absence and he looked tired when they met. He forestalled their questions, suggesting they retire to their hotel first. They would be met in the morning by some people he had been talking to during the afternoon, but until then, they had their own talking and planning to do.

The hotel Jayeer had chosen was out of the way and small, discreet enough to give them the privacy they needed at the moment. They were aware they were still at risk, but they were less likely to suffer any direct threat soon because of the nature of their escape. If their luck was with them, the Sirona ships may have missed their use of the drive.

They retired to the lounge once they had settled in. Mahra found it difficult to concentrate. So much had happened and she had Chutz back with her. Despite his return, her perception was still dogged by traceries interfering with her vision, but she was becoming used to it. It looked like whatever had been woken within her was here to stay. It was just that she felt such a sense of purpose as a result of her discoveries — about her success and about the knowledge that she had something they might be able to use against the Sirona, that she paid little attention to the sensations. For now, after so long, she finally had a real target for the hurt and pain that had followed her through the years. Even after all this time, and all she had been through, she could find within herself a hunger for revenge.

It was clear to the trio they couldn't stay on New Helvetica. That would present too much of a risk. The Sirona were obviously monitoring what went on around the world and they would be sure to be discovered. The longer they could keep out of sight, the better they'd be prepared to deal with what had to be done. It was even unclear to Mahra what those things might be for the moment. Somehow, they were going to have to fade from view and yet remain accessible to those who needed them.

After discussing the matter some more, and unsavoury though it might be, the choice was fairly clear. There was only one real place in the system where they could disappear while being in the middle of things, and that was Belshore.

Mahra didn't mind that thought so much. In many ways Belshore was her sort of world. Much more than the made-up face of New Helvetica. Despite their experiences there, she could probably feel at home in the rawness of Belshore, at least for a while. She had spent a lot of time on worlds like Belshore. Sind and Pellis however, were a little less enamoured of the idea.

The other thing that was clear was that they had to ditch *The Dark Falcon*, at least in her present state. She was too much of a give-away. The pain was clear upon Timon's face as the decision was made, but he knew as well as they did there was no other choice. So, Belshore it was to be and without *The Dark Falcon.*

Mahra decided that now was as good a time as any. There didn't seem to be any more decisions to make.

"Jayeer, if we're done here, I wonder if you might do me a favour."

Sind raised his eyebrows in query.

"In case you'd forgotten, and I know I had, I'm still carrying this thing around in my leg. Do you want to help get rid of it?"

"Yes, that's right. Of course, Mahra. Look, I'll have to get my kit from the ship, but that shouldn't take too long. I'll meet you in your room later if you want."

Mahra nodded. Sind excused himself and headed off to get his med kit. It looked like she wasn't going to get any conversation out of Pellis; he was brooding and deep in thought. She said good night to him and made her way up to her room to wait.

There was still so much she had to come to terms with. Chutz was back with her, though still a bit fragile, she had this new ability that she had to learn to use — yet another thing setting her apart from everyone else — and then there was the Sirona.

"I just don't understand, Chutz," she told him as she mounted the stairs. "How could they get away with it?"

He clearly didn't have an answer for her.

Sind appeared almost an hour later. "Sorry, for the delay," he said as she let him in. "There were things going on back at the ship."

"What sort of things?" she asked.

"I suppose they're checking it out. They looked like technicians. They were clearly our people and I knew better than to ask, but I tell you, if they do anything ... " He shook his head. "Right, let us get you fixed up. Now, which leg is it?"

Mahra sat on the bed and showed him her thigh. He bent down and examined it, finally locating the point of the insertion.

"Hmm, it almost seems a shame to open it up. It's virtually completely healed. I'll try to be as quick as possible." He hyped the area and proceeded to make a small incision. After digging around for a moment, he withdrew the small package, slapped some plas-skin on the area, and stood. He took a moment wiping the implant clean.

"Well, look at that," he said.

"What? What is it, Jayeer?"

He bent to show her. "See here? This hole here? It must have happened when you took that knife in the leg. Pierced right through. Well, it's of no use to anyone now, and it doesn't seem to have done you any actual harm." He tossed it casually into the waste receptacle. "Right. Well, if you're okay, I'll say good night," he said packing away the rest of his kit.

"Yes, thanks, Jayeer."

He nodded and left, and Mahra went to the shower and let Chutz back out. She found some nuts for him in the room and started preparing for the night. Same old Chutz. He was as greedy as ever. She looked across at him as she prepared for sleep and smiled. It was so good to have him back. It was like a missing part had been restored.

Another night without her patterns. Her leg was going to start looking like a relief map if this kept up. She sighed and made ready for bed.

As she closed her eyes she was thinking about her patterns. Those thoughts drifted to the Old One and Aleyin, and the Cradle and she started to float.

Her flyer descended and behind her the mountains erupted in a sheet of fire. She grabbed her comp. Pieces of the landscape exploded all around her. She turned her head this way and that, looking for a way out. Her heart pounded and her mouth was so dry she couldn't swallow.

There, there was her avenue of escape. A corridor ran off between the flames and the exploding ground ahead. It was so far away. She ran for it, but the closer she got, the further away it seemed. She couldn't run any more, but she had to.

She looked back over her shoulder. There was no way back. She turned, desperately seeking some way out. Then she was there. The thin corridor led on ahead and she rushed up it, her feet pounding into stones and rocks. She gripped her comp tightly in her fist. She mustn't lose it, mustn't drop it. She knew she had to keep hold of it.

The walls of destruction gave way and opened out into a flat smooth place. The ground beneath her feet had changed. Now it was metal, and her feet made ringing sounds as she desperately strove to get to the centre. The pain in her chest was like a knife now, digging into her heart. She had to get to the centre.

The Old One's voice echoed in her ears. "Focus. Reach that place where you feel right."

She stretched as she ran, trying to reach it. But suddenly, the circle was no longer empty. It was full of people. They wore the robes of The Cradle and they sat huddled in the middle. They looked up at her as she ran toward them, pleading expressions on their faces. She stretched out her hands. But then there were others. They wore leather and their hair was long and matted. They carried rifles, and as they strode forward, they used them to club and beat those who sat. The people raised their hands to ward off the blows, but one by one they were beaten to the ground.

"No!" she cried out to them. "You can't do this!"

They clubbed and clubbed until all lay bleeding on the ground. Then they turned. They were coming for her, and they were grinning.

Mahra screamed at them. "No!"

And woke, sitting bolt upright on her bed.

Chapter Twenty-Four

They were met the following morning by a man who joined them for the light breakfast that was normal in these places. At least they had decent kahveh.

The man was crisply dressed and spoke the same way.

"So," he said. "This is Mahra Kaitan." Timon nodded. The man seemed to be studying her, and she was not sure she liked the look. Her nerves were frayed after her troubled night and she didn't feel like putting up with someone who clearly thought he was in authority. "Well, Mez Kaitan, you're CoCee now. You'd better get used to it."

"And who are you?" she asked. Timon raised a finger to still her.

"My name is not important, Mez Kaitan. I just wanted to make your situation clear. All you need to know is that I'm speaking for the CoCee. From now on, you will receive your orders directly from Commander Pellis."

Mahra frowned and narrowed her eyes at him.

"I trust we have your full cooperation?" he continued. Mahra said nothing. The man turned to Timon and started outlining plans. Mahra listened, her resentment growing with each minute.

"You will be leaving here in an hour's time. Passage has been arranged for Belshore. The people there have already been informed of your arrival. Further instructions will be issued when you arrive."

"One hour?" said Timon, "But — "

"Commander?" the man said.

"We need to get some things, and well ... "

"Too late for that. *The Dark Falcon* is gone."

"Damn, so that's what — " said Sind.

"What? What do you mean gone?" said Timon, the disbelief written clearly on his face.

"Commander, I would advise you to moderate your tone," said the man glancing around the small dining room. "Just what I say. Now, we'll expect you at the docks in one hour, as I said."

With that he picked up a napkin, dabbed it against his lips, dropped it on the table and walked out without another word.

"Timon, who the hell was that?" asked Mahra.

"As he said," said Timon, his lips tight, "his name is not important. Suffice it to say that rank has its privileges. *The Falcon's* gone?" He shook his head slowly. "Bloody liberties."

"Now, Timon," said Jayeer. "There is not a lot we can do about it. Things are out of our hands now. It's back to following orders."

Timon grunted and looked away.

"Well, I don't have to follow orders," said Mahra.

"Mahra, you heard what he said," said Jayeer, looking at her over the top of his lenses. "Things are beyond us now. We're part of something much larger. What do you want? You said you had an old score to settle. Well you need the CoCee, and to be clear about it, the CoCee needs you. Please don't make this any harder than it is. Forget about the chain of command and the man who was just here. Think about what you want."

Mahra bit back her reply and thought about what he was saying. He was right. Timon always said Jayeer was the voice of reason in their operation. It surprised her in a way.

"Well, time's slipping away," said Timon. "We had better get our things together and be on our way." He stood and headed out of the dining room with a troubled expression on his face.

"Timon — " said Mahra.

Jayeer stopped her. "No, leave him. He'll be fine. He's right, we'd better get underway." Mahra nodded and they both headed off to their separate rooms to prepare, then made the way to their transport in silence.

They slipped into Belshorian space virtually unobserved as part of a routine cargo mission. Timon was cursing the absence of *The Dark Falcon* all the while. Mahra had little time for his complaints, she had Chutzpah back and although she sympathised, that and making sense of all that had happened was what really mattered at the moment. It was funny the way Chutzpah's absence had shown her how much of a part of her life he really was.

When they at last arrived on Belshore, Mahra didn't even mind that she had to wear her blade concealed. Chutzpah's presence kept her calm. Sind muttered to himself as usual as they travelled in one of the local trans through the wide and then narrow streets of the Belshorian capital. It didn't take them long to reach their goal, and this time the trip was without incident.

Garavenah's place looked exactly the same as it had on their last visit. The entrance to the vast warehouse complex boasted a similar group of guards, vehicles, and rituals. There were no charades from Timon this time. Somehow it seemed the events of the last few days had sobered him. What they were doing was too important.

Garavenah was waiting for them at the top of the staircase when they finally gained admission and she walked down to meet them at the bottom, bidding them welcome.

"So, my friends, twice in such a brief space of time. To what do I owe this honour? Come, come, don't hang around down there. Come up and tell me what has been happening."

Garavenah plied them with wine and hospitality. They took turns filling her in on the drive's details, and Mahra's experience and the Sirona, Garavenah taking it all in and looking increasingly thoughtful as the story unfolded.

"Well, we certainly have been busy, haven't we?" said Garavenah. "You know, Timon, that whatever I have here is at your disposal, but I'm not exactly sure what we can do to help. You know the nature of the operation here. It's not exactly set up to do the sort of things I think we need."

"No Gara, that's not what we need from you," said Pellis. "Basically, we need a place to lie low and out of the picture for a while so we can give time for them, and we know who *they* are, to put the wheels in motion. Hopefully the Sirona don't know, but with the appearance of *The Dark Falcon* back on New Helvetica, we can't be sure. We acted quickly enough when we got there, but we can't be certain. At least we can make ourselves a little bit useful while things are getting ready and stay effectively low profile while we do so. What do you say, Gara?"

"No doubt about it, I could use a few more capable hands at the moment, and ones that I can trust. Not that I suppose I have any real choice in the matter anyway, hey Timon?" She smiled reprovingly at him.

"Well, no, I don't suppose you do," he replied with a sheepish smile. "And nor, really, do I."

☐

It wasn't hard to adapt to the lifestyle on Belshore. There were just three major rules to watch out for, eyes, ears, and lips. It was a bit of a slogan amongst the small group at Garavenah's. You always kept your eyes and ears open and you said nothing. That way you survived. There were two other lesser rules. You never went out unless you were armed, and you never went anywhere alone. These latter two didn't faze Mahra at all. The trio from *The Dark Falcon* were a natural grouping anyway, and she always went armed in one way or another. Not only did she have her blade, but now that she had Chutzpah back, she was regaining some of her confidence, driven away with the shock of her realisations. He too, was still a weapon in his own right.

They had to get used to always keeping an eye out for dusters. The problem with the dusters was they were simply unpredictable. One moment they could be walking unassumingly down a crowded street, the next, some crazy-eyed individual would leap upon the nearest passer-by and start pounding his or her head into the ground. Nobody could plan for something like that, so they stayed alert. The problem seemed to be growing daily.

Mahra quickly developed a deep respect for Garavenah. The short, no-nonsense leader of the group had an unenviable task keeping things together in the adverse conditions provided by Belshore. The world was a haven in many respects, but probably the most violent and dangerous haven ever known. Garavenah had lost many friends and colleagues during her time there, but through all of it she made do. Mahra felt empathy with everything she had been through. The thing was, she did it by choice. Mahra had to admire her toughness and dedication.

Garavenah was hard, and yet there was something about her that was almost maternal. Mahra had little trouble understanding what Pellis liked about her. There was clearly some sort of history going back between the pair, but Mahra didn't think it was necessary to question what. If there was any need for her to know she was sure she'd have been told. She liked the woman for what she was and that was enough. In some ways, she reminded her of Pina so many years ago, full of stout resilience.

Shortly after they arrived, they set about changing their appearance as much as possible. There was not much they could do about Sind, but both Timon and Mahra were able to make some changes. They both suffered short crops, Mahra losing her hair and Pellis his long dark curls. Despite the howls of protest, the famous moustache also went. Pellis turned out to be quite good looking and respectable without the masses of curls dangling around his ears and the growth curling to either side of his mouth. The shock of white in his hair became even more striking, accenting a simply good-looking face, and making it into something more. He also reluctantly dispensed with the famous red boots.

The transformation was a source of great amusement to Garavenah. She chuckled and shook her head every time he reached out of habit to stroke the now non-existent moustache.

Mahra took to wearing shades day and night, though there was not much call to go out by day. Belshore was well and truly a night world. That was when everything happened and when all business of any significance was transacted.

As the weeks wore on, they begin to feel more at home with Garavenah and her crew. They were a tough lot, but disciplined with it and they each afforded Garavenah the respect she was due. Garavenah was in charge. There was no doubt about that. For the moment, Pellis's instructions were to sit put, and that was what they were doing, though Timon had his share of complaints. Wheels had been set in motion and it was going to take time for everything to be put in place.

Inside, Mahra ached with the need to do something, to act somehow to exact a price for what had been done to her and her people. The dreams went on, waking her in the night and making her tired and irritable. She worked hard with her blade, trying to maintain her form, but it was difficult.

Meanwhile, the CoCee plans took shape. Vast cargo ships travelled into Belshore space carrying consignments of machinery and equipment. Small packages were delivered and stowed in various locations around the city. Mahra herself was visited by a procession of medical techs who prodded and poked and probed her until she felt she could stand it no longer. She felt as if there wasn't a single orifice that hadn't been subjected to scrutiny. Chutz was not exempt from the process either, though he suffered it with a little less understanding. Even though she explained to them that he had no neural implants, that he was just what he was, they went ahead anyway. There was more than one bleeding finger by the time they'd finished with him.

Gradually, Mahra watched the CoCee plan solidify. Whether she liked it or not, Mahra had become a weapon in a conflict that she knew little about before the sequence of events that brought them here. She wasn't at all happy about the analysis and attention, but she remembered why she was here. She remembered and she knew it was right.

Although she realised they needed time to get everything ready, along with her frustration, she was becoming bored. Belshore kept her on her toes, but she didn't like waiting for things to happen. Chutzpah was picking up her frustration and he too was becoming tense and irritable. Sind was happy enough. He was involved in the supervision of the project taking place inside various large warehouses around Belshore. It was a different story for Timon. He too felt the claustrophobia and restriction.

It was as much to keep themselves entertained as anything else that Mahra and Pellis began to spend more and more time together. She found that underneath the theatre and bravado was more theatre and bravado, but it was somehow different. It was stuff borne of idealism and the dreams of youth unquelled. He could find spirit and adventure in things where she'd hesitate to look, and, somehow, it had remained untarnished. Without the trappings of his hair and moustache, it was as if he had become more open to her. She knew there was no sense in it but that was the way it felt. The traces of a bond were starting to take shape.

Finally, the CoCee started shipping in trainee pilots and Mahra had something to do. They had found volunteer pilots who were willing to undergo the operation grafting the neural material linking their brain hemispheres in preparation. It seemed that all the prodding and probing was going to come to something after all. Mahra started teaching them about what she knew of jump space and the feelings that accompanied it. There was only so much she could do, because there was no real way to describe it without experiencing it.

She developed a program of daily exercises, similar to those she learnt as a child and drilled the pilots in them. She wasn't sure how much of the routine was essential to the jump ability, but she had to cover every option. Every day she asked Timon to request a ship for her. The only way to train these people was to take them up and show them, she was convinced. She wasn't sure whether proximity to an active jump drive had any part in triggering her own ability, but she had to explore that as a possibility as well.

After much badgering, the CoCee gave in and a ship arrived, fitted for her purpose. It was only a small training vessel, but it was fitted with the drive, and that was what counted. Timon looked the ship over and thought it was good enough for what she wanted, so Mahra arranged to take a couple of the new trainees up the next day. They took off, and when Mahra judged they're far enough out from Belshore to avoid detection, she palmed the drive.

Her senses washed with the patterns and the field outside the ship was covered in streaming flickering grey. She took a few moments to adjust and then turned to her trainees.

"So," she said, "do you see them?"

"See what?" said the pilot called Karnak. He was looking from the holo displays, to the view out of the front port, and back at the displays again, a slight frown on his face.

Mahra shifted their heading to face into a corridor. She sensed the end-point and the start point of that line and she could see the rings clearly pulsing down its length.

"Now?" she asked.

"Uh-uh," said Karnak, looking at her curiously. "What are we supposed to see?"

"Come on. You've both been through the simulations. You know as well as I do what you're supposed to see. Are you sure? Both of you, concentrate. Still your minds as I've showed you. Seek that sharpness inside yourselves."

Mahra waited, watching their faces, and chewing at her bottom lip. After a time, Karnak shrugged and shook his head.

"Stinson ... what about you?"

The woman shook her head.

"Fire!" muttered Mahra from between closed teeth. After all this, was it to come to nothing? There had to be something she was missing. It couldn't be just these two.

"Okay," she said. "I'm taking you back."

The two looked at each other blankly and Karnak shrugged. Well, let them think she was a fool. She didn't care. She'd try it with another pair and then another after that until she worked out what was wrong. And if that didn't work she'd try again. Perhaps the implants needed more time to take. She just didn't know.

Three more times she left Belshore with another set of trainees and each time she returned disappointed. With every attempt, her frustrations grew. She was starting to give up hope.

□

One night, after dinner and a few too many drinks with Timon, events conspired to make something happen.

They were returning to the warehouse glowing in the pleasure of food, drink and each other's company and feeling a little unsteady as a result of their indulgence. They walked arm in arm, enjoying the contact. Chutz was making his disapproval and jealousy felt, but Mahra was ignoring him. At that moment, she just couldn't care less. It was probably because of this that she ignored the first signs of trouble. She felt Chutzpah tense and stiffen at her shoulder but dismissed it. She noticed the low growl growing in his throat, but told him to shut up. By the time she realised there was something wrong, it was too late. The duster was upon them.

The duster had to have been standing hidden in the shadows of one of the small alleys leading from the street they walked, because he appeared suddenly in front of them without a hint of warning. Screaming with full voice, he launched himself at Mahra knocking her back with the weight of his body. Still screaming he grabbed her head with both hands and slammed it against the wall behind her. Then again. Her vision exploded with white light and pain.

The screaming in her ears and the sickly sweetness of his breath were the last things she remembered until Timon's face swam into view, his eyes filled with concern as he gently stroked her forehead.

"Mahra, can you hear me? Are you okay? Mahra?"

"Hmmm," she murmured.

The relief on his face was evident as he leaned down and kissed her forehead.

Suddenly her mind was filled with other images in the semi-dark, and the pain and fear that went with them. Another man was leaning over, reaching for her, fumbling at his leathers.

"No!" she cried, scrambling backward, and pressing herself against the wall.

"Mahra, what is it?" Timon said, reaching for her.

"No!" she cried. "Stay away. Just stay back." She huddled against the wall, her head pounding and her insides gone cold. Her breath caught in her throat, and she had to force herself to take another, then another. She was pressed back against the wall, but slowly she realised that it was a brick wall, not one made of metal. She was crouched back against a wall on a street on Belshore, nowhere else.

"Mahra ... " Timon was standing back now, looking at her pleadingly. "What is it? Tell me?" It was Timon. It was his voice, not someone else's.

Mahra tried desperately to force the sensation of panic from her. Chutz was not helping matters. He stood between her legs, bristling, daring Timon to come any closer.

Mahra reached out a hand to settle him. It was not Timon's fault, she knew, though her heart was pounding in her chest. But Chutzpah didn't.

"Chutz, no," she said with a groan. "It's not his fault. Oh, no ... " Her heart was still pounding in her ears, making the pain in her head worse.

She bit her lip and looked up at him. "Come on, Timon. My head hurts. Let's get out of here," Mahra said with another groan.

"But what was that? What's wrong?"

"I-I can't explain now. Can it wait until we get back? Timon, p-please. We need to get away from here."

Timon spread his hands wide. "Yes, you're right," he said. "We should make ourselves scarce." He pointed over to a crumpled form lying against the wall. "Too many questions."

Mahra staggered to her feet. Timon put his arm out to steady her, but she cringed away. Frowning, he withdrew it.

She didn't want to treat him like that, but something inside her shrank away from his touch. Somehow, when he had been leaning over her, with her head pounding, the pain and violence still with her, it reminded her. It reminded her of other semi-darkness, of faces looming over hers, of a tiny cabin on a transport ship on its way to a mining world. She tried to push the memory away, but it kept coming back to her, making her shrink, small and cold inside herself.

She looked over at Timon as they walked and saw the concern in his eyes. He saw her looking and reached out his arm again, but she shrank away from it, and he pressed his lips together, pulled it away and turned to face the way they were walking.

Later, back at the warehouse, Timon saw her to her quarters and fussed about getting something to relieve the pain in her head. Mahra knew she had to give him an explanation. She owed him that much.

As soon as the painkiller had started to take effect, she lifted Chutzpah and placed him gently outside the door, then closed it behind him. She went and sat on the bunk, then deliberately held out a hand.

"Timon, come here. I need to explain something to you."

After a moment of doubt, he took her proffered hand and she drew him down to sit beside her. She held on to his hand, looked him straight in the eyes, and taking a deep breath, began to talk.

"There are things that happened to me a long time ago, that I need to tell you," she began.

Timon tried to stop her, but she insisted. He sat mutely as she talked, his expression changing from sympathy, to anger, to horror, and back, as she filled in the details of her early life, and beyond. When she had finished, he sat looking at her in silence.

Finally, he looked away. "Mahra, I had no — "

"It doesn't matter," she said. "What's done is done. But there are things that are not easy for me sometimes. I just need you to understand."

He nodded slowly. Somehow, the telling had made her feel better, as if a weight had been lifted from her. She sat back on the bunk, leaned her head back and closed her eyes.

Timon made to withdraw his hand, but she held it tight.

Sometime later, they were sitting together in silence and she relaxed her grip. Gently, the back of his fingers traced her thigh as his hand slid down to the bunk.

"Mahra," he said, quietly.

"Hm-hmm?"

"I'm sorry."

"No Timon, I'm sorry. There's no way you could have known. There are things inside me that go back a long way. Some of them are never going to really go away. It's what I am. I'm different and I have to deal with those differences."

"How are you different?"

"Oh Timon, in so many ways. Look at me. Think about it. What about these things I carry in my head? What about my training? What about my childhood. Why is it that I seem to have this ability and nobody else does? I am different."

"We all carry things around with us Mahra, that doesn't make you different."

Something about what Pellis said suddenly struck a chord. She looked down at where his hand lay on her leg.

"Say that again, Timon," she said.

"What? We all carry things around with us and that doesn't make you different."

Mahra sat bolt upright and stared at him.

"Oh, but it does," she said. "That's it! That's what was missing!" She reached forward with both hands, and threw her arms around him.

"What? What have I said?" said Timon. "Mahra, I can't work you out. First one minute you behave like you don't want me near you, and, oh, I'm sorry ... "

"No, no. That's not important now. Listen. You know the problem we've been having with the trainees. Not one has been able to see the same things I have in jump. They've had the operations with the neural implants, I've been training them, but nothing. Don't you see? Yes, the neural implants are necessary. Yes, the training is necessary, but there's always been something missing from the pattern. Somehow, I knew all the pieces weren't there. When you said we all carry things around with us...."

Timon sat back looking confused.

"I don't see — "

"Think about it. Carry. What did I carry? When Jayeer removed the package from my leg, he noticed that it had been damaged."

"Yes and ... ah, I see. Mahra, we've got to let them know!" He leapt to his feet, hesitated for just a moment, then gripped her by the shoulders. "This could be it."

Without a further word, he rushed out to set things in motion. Chutzpah slipped back inside before the door closed and looked around the room. He sat, just inside the door, his tail bristling as he tasted the air.

"Come on, Chutz. He's gone. And even if it ended up not quite the way I wanted it, it was worth it," she said. She patted the bed beside her and Chutzpah, after a moment, leapt up to join her. Too much had happened in the last few hours, and suddenly she felt exhausted.

She lay back and thought about the discovery. It had to be the answer. It had to be. She also thought about Pellis. Perhaps in time .... She enjoyed Pellis, his company and his humour and his sense of irreverence. It had been a long time since she had felt like this about anyone. Perhaps it would turn into something, perhaps not, but she mustn't let her memories get in the way of their relationship. He was not the same. She knew he wasn't.

She continued to think about him as she lay there, idly stroking Chutzpah with one hand, while the other one propped up her head.

"You know Chutz," she murmured as she finally drifted toward sleep. "I think I like Timon. He's a good man and a good friend. You'd better learn to like him as well."

The next morning, she felt a little the worse for wear. Her head still hurt and the night's memories struggled back hazily. Her sleep had been troubled again by dreams of the Sirona, and of that terrible voyage.

She had taken quite a knock from the duster, but she didn't think there was any permanent damage. Slowly she pulled on her clothes, remembering the side of Pellis that he had revealed last night. Gradually, as she pieced together the happenings of the previous evening, she had further reason to smile to herself, but it was tempered with caution and doubt about whether she was right. She wondered how things would be this morning, whether there would be an awkward embarrassed silence following her revelations, whether it would tarnish her relationship with Timon, him knowing.

Timon made it to breakfast a little after she did and he flashed her a smile as he entered the eating area. He casually nodded to the others assembled as if there was nothing out of the ordinary. Mahra bowed her head and avoided his eyes as he sat, the discomfort of the previous evening still weighing on her mind. She could feel him watching her across the table, and finally she met his gaze. He tilted his head to one side in query, and raised one eyebrow. Slowly, she nodded, and he blinked his eyes at her.

Sind was with them and he caught the interaction, quizzically raising one eyebrow, and then narrowing his eyes as his obvious suspicions started to take shape. Timon gave him nothing to feed upon, launching straight away into a discussion of plans and the news of Mahra's discovery.

It seemed she had at least one more thing to be grateful to him for. Maybe she was right after all. Perhaps in time ...

Chapter Twenty-Five

When he got word that the ship supposed to meet *The Dark Falcon* had disappeared without trace, and there had been no sign of *The Dark Falcon* since, Valdor dropped completely out of sight. He reasoned that the Sirona must know that he had tried to outdo them, despite their conversation. He didn't want them to find him. Not yet. Not just yet. He had to try and do something, and it had to be without their interference.

Marina was most understanding. At least the Sirona hadn't made that connection yet, so he remained where he was. Marina really didn't seem to mind him extending his stay with her, she was accumulating the size of the favour he owed her with each passing day. By the time the Sirona did make the connection, he might be ready for them. If he was right, they wouldn't be ready to play their hand yet, regardless.

Valdor was sitting quietly sipping at a glass and listening to music on Marina's system when the door bursts inward followed by several uniformed guardsmen, visors covering their eyes. He didn't move. It was obvious to him immediately that the odds were clearly in favour of the newcomers. His first thought that this was some new show of force by his alien opponents.

Valdor didn't feel comfortable when he couldn't see people's eyes, but he wasn't going to let them see that. He made a great show of calmly swirling the wine in his glass and looking thoughtfully over its rim as the troopers filed in and stood covering each exit without a word. When they had made the area secure, one motioned outside to the hallway and a tall, white-haired man walked through the door and stood before him. Silvered lenses covered his eyes and he wore a trim grey suit cut high to the throat. There was something about his bearing that shouted authority.

"Is there something I can do for you?" asked Valdor calmly. "Normally it's customary for a visitor to announce themselves."

"Valdor Carr," the older man said. There was no question in his words. It was a simple statement of fact. "Or is it Milnus? But no, that can't be. We have Mezzer Milnus in custody somewhere else."

Milnus in custody? But that couldn't be. No, this wasn't Sirona. This was CoCee.

"All right, point made," said Valdor, carefully placing his glass down on a nearby table. "But I don't see how I warrant all this." He waved his hand in the direction of the scattered guardsmen.

"Possibly not, Carr. But we were eager to talk to you and we weren't sure whether you might have been less than enthusiastic about being around to talk to us."

Valdor didn't like his tone, but at present his visitor seemed to have the advantage.

"So, who are you? Law? Military? I don't know what you think I've done, but I'm starting to think that I'd like an explanation."

"Yes, no doubt you would. May I sit?"

The tall man waited until Valdor indicated a chair with a tilt of his head. The man sat, then looked at Valdor for a while before speaking. Valdor studied him in return. His clothes were well tailored, but somehow severe, and his attitude had the same sort of severity about it.

"Mezzer Carr, it may come as some surprise to you, but we know quite a bit about you and your activities. For some time, we've tolerated you and Carr Holdings because they suited our purposes. Now the time has come to call in the favours."

"Um, just let me interrupt for a moment. Who exactly are 'we'?" Valdor asked. He didn't like the direction this was headed.

"I'll get to that in due course, Carr. First let me fill you in. We've been carefully monitoring most of what you do, particularly the little enterprise you put together with ILGC. We've had step by step progress reports from our own people inside. Unfortunately, it seems you also attracted the attention of another party with your activities. I don't think I need to mention their name. That party has become a shade too interested and far too involved in what's been going on." The visitor stilled Valdor's protests of ignorance before he had time to voice them. "Let's not mess around. We both know what I'm talking about. I'm here to offer you a choice. Either you throw your resources behind us fully and willingly or Carr Holdings will simply cease to exist — every part of it."

Valdor chewed at his lip as the full implications started to filter through the shock. Somehow, he didn't seem to be in a bargaining position. The man sitting watching him had access to a great deal more information than anybody had a right to. It left a hoard of unanswered questions, but he could deal with those later. What he needed now was a solution.

"Who are you? At least give me the courtesy of knowing who I'm dealing with."

"You can call me Aegis, but I don't think that's what you want to know. I suppose there's no harm in telling you. You'll find out eventually, and it might better help you to understand the position you're in. We, Mezzer Carr are CoCee. I presume you've made that connection already, but we are a part of the CoCee rarely seen. There are quite a few of us, and in places you probably wouldn't believe."

"So why would the CoCee be interested in me? I'm not political."

"Ah, but you see, Carr, anybody who wields the sort of resources you do can't help being political, whether they like it or not. That's the nature of the beast. We've been watching your growth and monitoring it for some time. In some ways, we admire the way you have gone about things. We can ignore some of your indiscretions. On occasion, they have actually saved us from having to expend our own resources. Whether you like to think it or not, Valdor Carr, you are not unique in this world. There are others like you and we monitor all of them in the same fashion. You might have carried on for years without us ever having to act. And you would have been none the wiser. But I'm afraid the current chain of events has meant that we need to rein you in."

Valdor reached unsteadily for his glass. There was a sudden dryness in his mouth. He couldn't win. Either it was the Sirona on the one side, or this new face of the CoCee on the other.

"All right, Aegis. Perhaps you can do what you say and shut me down. But even if I'm to believe all this, why offer me a choice? If it's as easy as you suggest, why don't you just do it?"

"Oh, rest assured, Carr, we can do it. You should have very little doubt about that. It's just that it would be a little more difficult. You do not take out the key man in a network without suffering some repercussions. You, of all people, should know that. We just don't have the time at the moment. I'll be honest with you. You have stumbled unknowingly onto something that is of a great deal of importance. You could have no way of knowing just how important it is. We presume the other party in this matter does know, and it's only by sheer accident that we found out exactly how significant it is to them and why. Anyway, I think I've told you enough for you to realise how things lie."

"What if I say no?" asked Valdor, feeling the walls pressing against his back.

"Now, Carr, please don't disappoint me."

Aegis motioned slightly with one finger and the trooper standing behind him dropped the barrel of his weapon a fraction toward Valdor. "I had hoped I had made our position clear. It would be a pity for anything to happen to such a keen mind as yours. Let's not be childish."

If there was one thing Valdor hated more than being made to look less clever than he was, it was being patronised, and this man was doing a respectable job managing both. The position was unavoidably clear and like it or not, he was clearly going to have to play along.

"All right. It appears that you have me… So, what do you want me to do?"

"Oh, it's very simple really. We would like you to continue looking after your operations. Of course, you would do so with our assistance and supervision. That's the easy part. The problem is that they've became a little exposed here on New Helvetica. For that reason, we're suggesting a move to a more convenient location. Have no fear though, I imagine you will find everything you need to satisfy you there. And, Carr, I'm glad you've chosen to be sensible."

"Now hold on a damned minute," he said, ignoring the weapon that started to track him as he rose from his seat. The full implications of what Aegis was suggesting were starting to hit home. "How in the hell do you expect me to run my 'operations' as you call them, from somewhere else. I have everything I need here."

"Oh, don't worry. I thought I told you. That will all be taken care of. You cannot expect us to allow things to continue under the watchful eyes of our friends do you? Now, I suggest you *sit down* and *listen*."

Valdor glared at him but grudgingly resumed his place on the sofa.

"We've already put steps in motion to move your centre of operations to your new location. I can assure you, you will have everything you need. And if you don't, we'll provide it. For the most part, your business dealings will be taken care of while you're away, but you will have direct control over the parts that really matter. And for once,

Valdor Carr, you might be doing something worthwhile with your talents."

"So why the hell is your offer any different from theirs," Carr spat. Whatever way he looked at it, he just couldn't win.

"Because, Valdor Carr, for once in your life you'd be working on the side of right."

That really was it. He was dealing with a moralist as well. But the way things looked, he had little option. He sank back into the sofa, and with a sigh, ran his fingers back through his hair. "Fine. It looks like I really don't have much of a choice."

"Good, that's settled then. I didn't believe you were a stupid man, Carr. If we've finished talking we can get under way."

"Wait! There's a lot more I need to know first, and I have things that need to be put in order."

"All that will be taken care of and you would be briefed on the way."

Valdor bit his lip, drained the last of his wine and moved toward the door, running his eyes one last time over the familiar trappings of Marina's apartment. Aegis stood and followed behind. As Valdor made his way into the corridor outside, guardsmen fell in to either side and to the front of him. It was perfectly clear he wouldn't be slipping away. He wrapped his arms about him as he walked within the cocoon of uniforms.

He felt suddenly very cold.

☐

With the increasingly frequent visited of aligned ships and crews, the information flow to the small base on Belshore improved. They started to receive regular updates about events around New Helvetica. There had been a marked increase in Sirona activity and that was of some concern. Mahra wondered whether it meant the Sirona knew about their escape. There was no way of knowing. It wouldn't affect their plans though. The Sirona would find out in time. They were all sure of that.

The CoCee had arranged for the acquisition of a number of factory sites on Belshore. Gradually the freighters that had been coming and going over the past weeks had shipped in consignments of parts and equipment, ready for their ambitious production plan. Jayeer's role was to supervise that process and make sure it all went without hitch. He had logistical support of course. That was provided with a rotating staff who came in and out as needs dictated, but Sind himself provided overall continuity. His primary input was for the technical aspects of the plan and he had overall supervision of that area.

The core idea was that Belshore was to become the site for the refit of a number of ships with the new drive. The ships would land on Belshore routinely, and, one by one, their drives would be enhanced, ready for the day when they could be piloted by those who would eventually have the ability to navigate through jump. *The Dark Falcon's* experiences had proved the drive was viable.

A few days later they received something other than a piece of news.

They were due an incoming shipment of information and parts along with the courier. They were all sitting round chatting about this and that when the guardians at the door put them on immediate alert. Garavenah motioned for quiet as she spoke rapidly into the com.

"Weapons everyone," she ordered. "We have company."

They waited expectantly while Garavenah listened to the proceedings outside the vast warehouse door. With rapid hand gestures, she ordered coverage of vantage points and the group members scattered, taking up position behind protective crates and girders. Keenly they watched the narrow passageway that led from the building's front. Two raced quickly up that same artificial hallway on silent feet.

There was the sound of metal scraping against metal as the inner door was pushed inward and then silence. Everyone held their breaths in anticipation.

The two who went to check at the front return herding three more people in front. Two of the newcomers were regular CoCee crew and they were known to Garavenah's group. The third looked vaguely familiar and Mahra and Timon exchanged a glance across the intervening space. One by one, the group members emerged from their defensive positions and joined the three newcomers in the centre of the open communal area where they waited.

Garavenah stepped forward first, acknowledging the two crewmen with a quick nod of her head. She took her time over the vaguely familiar stranger, scanning him slowly from head to foot and then back again.

"So, what have we here then?" she asked speculatively.

The hawk-faced man standing before her returned her gaze through heavily lidded eyes, a slight sneer upon his lips as he spoke.

"Indeed, what have we here?" he said contemptuously as his gaze left Garavenah and roved over the warehouse interior. Mahra recognised the voice and the manner as soon as he spoke.

"Milnus," she and Pellis said in unison.

"Ah, you two," he said, gaze flicking now in their direction. "For a moment or two your appearances kept me from seeing it. So, where's your fat little companion? And just out of interest, the name is Carr. Valdor Carr. And it's thanks to you, no doubt, that I'm here."

Suddenly a whole lot of unanswered questions fell into place for Mahra. She knew the connection between the events leading up to their involvement with the Sirona and Carr Holdings. The fact that the man they knew as Milnus turned out to be the head of Carr Holdings made a lot more sense.

One crewman accompanying Carr handed Garavenah a small package and waited while she tore it open and read the contents. She nodded and the two crewmen withdrew.

"Well, my friends," she announced. "It appears we have a new recruit to our humble group. Allow me to introduce the illustrious Valdor Carr, head of Carr Holdings. He has generously agreed to assist our efforts here on Belshore. For the duration, he is to be a guest of our joint benefactors."

Valdor rolled his eyes heavenward, and hissed between closed teeth, obviously not too pleased to be among them. Garavenah immediately became more business-like.

"Saran will show you to where you sleep. You eat with the rest of us. I don't know what you're used to, Mezzer Carr, but we all have things to do here. You strike me as a man with attitude. Now for as long as you're here, you will keep that attitude to yourself. We don't need it. Be damned sure I'll be watching you. Now, I suggest you get settled."

She watched his retreating back as he was led off to his quarters. No doubt he'd be unlikely to find them to his satisfaction.

As he left, the others drifted off to whatever they were doing. Garavenah called Mahra and Pellis over to her.

"So, you two know him, do you?" she asked, the tone of authority not having left her voice.

She waited as they explained the circumstance of their meeting. Garavenah looked thoughtful for a moment or two and then spoke.

"Yes well, that all makes sense. But I'll tell you now, I don't like the looks of that one. He seems like trouble. That communication I had suggested as much. Carr's here for a specific purpose. He has access to a range of people and processes that have started to provide us with the tools we need to master your little discovery, Mahra. The problem is that the Sirona were, or are, very interested in him too. Somehow or other they managed to become aware of what he was up to and took a more direct interest in his operations. The CoCee have moved him here because they decided to take him out of the New Helvetian picture, but remain in control of the biolab side of things. Now even more than before, with what we need, that side of things is crucial. The delay in his arrival was because they needed time to set things up for him at this end."

"But is that wise, Garavenah?" asked Mahra. "If the Sirona are so interested in him, isn't he just going to draw their attention here?"

"Who am I to question the wisdom of the CoCee, Mahra? I guess they know what they're doing. He won't be operating without appropriate supervision. Most people involved in the project were already well and truly his to start with. It suits the CoCee purposes better if he remains in control. Don't ask me why we have to put up with him in the meantime. I guess they want us to keep an eye on him as well. He's a bright boy by all accounts," she said with a sigh, rubbing the back of her neck. "As if we don't have enough to contend with."

☐

As soon as the biolab side of things had been well established, four trainees were selected to have the material inserted. The implants were made, and within two days, the first batch of subjects had healed well enough to recommence their training. She took the first two up as soon as she could.

Outside Belshore space, she felt the adrenaline coursing as she prepared to palm the drive. Chutzpah rode with her, and she could feel him sensing her tension, for he fidgeted on her shoulder and jumped from left to right.

"Chutz, sit still would you?" she snapped, but it did no good.

Mahra hesitated for a moment. So much was dependent on what she was about to do. If this worked, then they were on their way, but if it didn't ....

Quickly she reached forward and hit the drive. She watched the two pilot's faces intently as the transition occurred.

Their reaction was immediate.

"Yes!" she breathed. Her missing key had been found. The pattern was complete.

She wasted no time getting the ship back to Belshore and informing the others. Timon was as ecstatic as she was.

"Mahra, you're sure?" he asked her.

"Absolutely no doubt, Timon. We've now got more like me. If we can get enough pilots ready and familiar with the transition into jump space, then we'll be on an even footing. Perhaps. I've still got to test it with a few more, but I can feel it's right."

"Mahra, that's wonderful. Sure, I'm itching to get out of this place. I don't care what it takes."

Mahra found increasingly more of her time monopolised by the needs of the program. First, she had to nurse the new pilots through the transitional phase where their perceptions were interfered with, and then, once they had become used to it, proceed with their training. Her days began to be taken up by the training sessions and Timon filled her nights. They saw very little of either Valdor Carr or Jayeer Sind. Both were more than fully occupied with their own assignments.

Carr was trouble to begin with. Barely a day went past without a sneering complaint or cynical comment. More than once Garavenah was forced to step in to forestall imminent violence as one or other took exception to his superior attitude. It took him several weeks to get used to the absence of the sort of conditions he had on New Helvetica and the ready touch of power that lay within his grasp. Even though his attitude eased, he still made it plain that he'd be nobody's servant but his own and he worked to the CoCee desires reluctantly at best.

Timon was little better. As the days and weeks progressed, he complained of feeling more and more like a superseded part and his temper deteriorated with it. He and Mahra still spent a deal of their time together but he was becoming snappy and irritable, even with her.

Mahra did all she could to calm him, but her own successes with the new pilots made it difficult for her to relate to his frustration. He begged her to allow him to come along on some of her training jumps, but orders would not permit it.

One afternoon, he burst into Mahra's quarters, out of breath.

"Come on. She's back," he said excitedly as Mahra sat on her bed looking at him blankly. She had no idea what he was talking about.

"Who's back Timon? What's the hurry?"

"Come on. Don't just sit there. It's *The Dark Falcon*. She's back!"

The change in him was undeniable. She wanted to share in his excitement, in what was obviously a great moment for him, so she quickly strapped on her blade, called to Chutzpah, and made her way down the corridor after his rapidly retreating form.

They caught a trans to the port and, all the way, Timon could barely contain his excitement. He was like a small boy all over again. The roads were relatively clear and they made good time to the port. As soon as they were there, he could hardly restrain himself long enough to pay the driver, before leaping out and striding off toward the docking bays.

She finally caught up with him standing open-mouthed before a sleek silver ship. The lines were the same, but the colour was all wrong. There didn't seem to be any mark on the outer hull and there, in old style script upon the nose sat a name; *The Pilgrim*.

Pellis slowly shook his head from side to side. Mahra could feel his stunned disbelief and she reached for his hand.

"Oh, what have they done to her, Mahra? What have they done?"

Gently she led him to the ship and the open hatchway. She had to guide him up inside as he traced a finger over the shining surface.

Once inside, there was no doubt. It was *The Dark Falcon* right enough. The familiar passageway led off toward familiar doorways. Pellis slowly walked forward to the bridge still shaking his head. Sind was there already, glued to his rapidly scrolling screens.

"Well, Timon, what do you think? I would say as good as new. Better in some ways," he said, barely looking up from the displays.

"Jay, how could you? Look what they've done to her!"

"Oh certainly, a few cosmetic changes, but that was inevitable. There are a few interesting additions though. Timon, come and look at this."

"Aughh!" was the only response as Pellis turned, slapped his forehead, and strode off the bridge and down the corridor.

"Timon!" Mahra called after him, but it was too late. He had gone.

"Oh, don't worry about him, Mahra. He'll get over it. But seeing as you're here. There are a couple of enhancements they've made to the weaponry that might interest you. I'd take the trouble to go and familiarise yourself with the pod if I were you. From what I understand, we have only a couple of days before we have to leave."

"Why, Jayeer? What do you know that I don't?"

"Nothing really. Just that we're leaving, Mahra. We have something to do and plans have already been set in place. It requires us to be elsewhere. I have only a few more checks to make and then I'll join you for a kahveh and we can talk about it. I suggest you go and have a quick scan of the pod while I finish up here. Maybe by then, Timon might have come to his senses and we can all discuss it together."

Mahra did as Jayeer suggested and made her way up to the pod. Most of *The Dark Falcon* seemed pretty much as she remembered it, but Jayeer was right. There were changes in the battle pod. Somehow, she could tell the weaponry was different without having to test it. The most obvious thing was the headset. The familiar arrangement was gone. In its place were a simple throat mike and earpiece. Whatever they had installed here would require practice. Looking at it, she knew without doubt where she'd be spending her time for the next couple of days.

By the time she was finished playing with the new apparatus and had returned to the rec to join Jayeer, Pellis was already in place. He sat with a mug of kahveh in front of him, head buried in his hands.

"Look Timon, I know how you feel, but what do you expect?" she said. "What are we going to do, wander up to whoever in a ship that was supposed to have been blasted into nothingness as if nothing had happened? It would do our cause a lot of good, wouldn't it?"

"Yes, I know, I know, but can't you understand the way I feel?"

She could, but she wasn't going to pander to his self-pity by agreeing. She patted him on the shoulder and took a seat. They both lapsed into silence and waited for Sind to appear.

Finally, Jayeer emerged and took his time preparing a fresh brew before sitting at the table to join them.

"So, my friends. Like old times, isn't it?"

Pellis merely humphed in reply. With the mood Timon was in, Mahra also found it difficult to be as cheery as Sind seemed to be and seemed to expect them to be.

"Well, we have new orders," said Jayeer. "As you both know, I've been involved in the refit of a number of ships. Most have been warrior class or better, and most are fairly well armed. I myself have been surprised by the level of some of the things those ships are carrying. More than enough of a match for our alien brethren I would hope. But that remains to be seen. The CoCee has spared nothing on this one. And now, I think we're finally ready. With your work Mahra, and with the rather reluctant assistance of our friend Carr, we now have probably enough trained and equipped personnel to crew those ships. Even if we don't, there are enough people versed in what is needed to continue the work."

"So, what are you telling us, Jayeer?" asked Mahra. "That we've become dispensable?"

"Perhaps I should explain," said a new voice from the doorway. "No, remain seated. Mez Kaitan, I'm sorry we've had no time for formal introductions. These two know me already. You can call me, Aegis."

The tall, white-haired man helped himself to a kahveh before joining them at the table.

"What Mezzer Sind is telling you, is that we are now ready to put some plans into effect. This is where you three come in. We are confident that with the right situation, we just might have the ability to determine the exact location of the Sirona homeworld. That is dependent however, on your skills, Mez Kaitan. As you have no doubt been hearing, since Mezzer Carr's disappearance from New Helvetian public life, there has been a marked increase of interest in the area by our friends the Sirona. They are starting to visit more and more frequently. We have let them do so unmolested up to this point, but now we believe we are ready."

"But ready for what?" asked Mahra.

"What we want you to do, is to wait for the appearance of one of their ships and track it to its origin. Do you think that's possible?"

Mahra nodded her head hesitantly. "I think so," she said.

"If you think you can do it, then we believe you probably can. Once you have that location, then, and only then, will we be in a position to act. The task fell rather naturally to you three as most of our newer crew were reasonably inexperienced. We've been able to muster some simulations of the process since all this began, but not enough to trust straight away. I wouldn't suggest the operation is without its risks, but we're expectant that you'll succeed. So, no, you have not become dispensable, Mez Kaitan. We need you now, more than ever."

Mahra studied the man, and he watched her in return.

"But what use would that be?" she asked. "What good would it do us knowing where their homeworld is?"

Aegis nodded. "I know it might not seem like much, but we're going to prepare a little surprise for the Sirona. You'll be informed of the details as soon as we have some other things in place. I'm not in a position to tell you any more at this point, but the information will be passed on to you at the proper time."

Mahra looked over at Timon, who simply raised an eyebrow.

"One last thing," said Aegis. "We want you to know how much we appreciate the work you've been doing here. Without you, so much of what was about to take place would not have been possible."

Mahra could hear the sincerity in the man's voice, and a warm flush grew in her cheeks. Timon glanced over at her and gave her a slight smile, which only made matters worse.

"So, Mez Kaitan, do you think you're ready to put the first step of our plan into operation.

Mahra looked at him steadily. "Nothing would give me greater pleasure," she said.

Aegis returned her gaze. "Good," he said. "I was hoping you'd say that."

With that last note Aegis nodded to each in turn then stood and left. The three were left looking at each other across their mugs of kahveh. For the first time in a long time, Timon Pellis had a wide grin upon his face.

Mahra felt a touch of trepidation mixed with excitement. Now that the prospect of facing the Sirona had finally arrived the fear was starting to work inside her, but she knew how much this meant. Despite her unease, she looked at Timon, and she couldn't help grinning back.

Chapter Twenty-Six

Their instructions came through to them two days after their meeting with Aegis on board *The Pilgrim*. They sat together in the rec and discussed it. There was a lot that could go wrong, but they decided that the CoCee plan had the all the marks of one that was likely to succeed. It was simple. A lot depended upon Mahra's ability to track navigational references in jump, but she was fairly confident she could do it. In a way, she knew she had to.

For the next few days the three were stationed aboard *The Pilgrim,* well enough away from Belshore to avoid detection, but close enough that they might make a run for it if they got into trouble. What they were doing in that less than populated sector of space was getting practice. The new weapons tracking system didn't take much for Mahra to get used to. It employed the same principles; there was just less equipment to surround her. The real reason for the practice had nothing really to do with the weapons system. it was to gain a deeper familiarity and understanding of jump space and the mechanisms of getting in and out of it quickly. That was fundamental to what they had to do and a key part of the CoCee plan.

The closeness that had developed over the last few weeks between Mahra and Pellis helped them co-ordinate their movements, because somehow, they almost seemed to be able to second-guess what the other was thinking. Mahra wondered if finally, she was getting close enough to someone to develop a rapport, but she kept the speculation to a minimum. Whatever the reason, it kept the need for spoken communication to a minimum and made the interaction between pilot and navigator much smoother. Of course, they had taken the opportunity for smaller practice jumps during the brief time after they took delivery of *The Pilgrim*, but it was not quite the same as really getting in touch with jump space.

Mahra had benefited from the several jump experience simulations with the trainees in the weeks before that, so she was a little more at home with it than Timon. Her initial input had been vital to the creation of those simulations and she helped to populate them with as much as she could remember. She reminded herself to update that information when she had a chance, as her familiarity with that place beyond jump grew. Everything she could add would help the new trainees understand the mechanisms of what they were planning to do.

Finally, they felt they were ready. The CoCee had had a number of elements of their plan to put in place and they hadn't been idle during the time while Mahra and the others were stationed away from the surface. The crews were ready, and one by one the CoCee had upgraded a vast number of the combined fleet's ships. As soon as they received confirmation, *The Pilgrim* laid in a new course, to the space around New Helvetica.

A few days later, they reached their destination — one of the orbital security stations that circled the perimeter of New Helvetian space. Their orders were to wait there, doing nothing until the right opportunity arose. For a time, there was little to do but watch and feign patience.

Timon eased *The Pilgrim* into a stationary parking position lying in the platform's shadow. The orbital station was large enough and the ship small enough that there was enough protection to keep them out of sight of curious eyes. The orders required them to maintain complete silence during their vigil. They were left to simply monitor the activities taking place in the region below them and keep an eye on the emptiness beyond.

At long last, the hours and days of patient waiting were rewarded.

Mahra felt it first, the slight rippling of her senses and the overlay of patterns that alerted her to a ship emerging from jump somewhere close to them. Chutzpah sensed it too, because he chittered in her ear. She paid careful attention to the convergence of patterns, seeing if she could pinpoint the exact spot where the ship would appear. As soon as she had no doubt at all, she relayed the information over the com.

"Timon, Jayeer, ship coming. About sixty degrees and up."

A moment more and she was proved right. There was a slight shimmering in the region she had pointed out and that was followed by the appearance of the large silver ovoid of a Sirona ship. As it had before, the huge silver shape appeared to coalesce out of the empty blackness. There was no other way to describe it. Mahra felt the bottom drop out of her stomach. She felt cold within, and for a moment, those nightmare images chased through her mind again. Pellis's voice snapped her back immediately.

"Well done, Mahra. Now keep whatever it is you keep open. Tell us if there's the slightest sign that it's going to move."

Mahra knew she couldn't afford to let her memories and emotions get in the way. She had waited too long for this.

"Understood," she responded calmly, feeling nothing of the sort.

The hours wore on and the cold feeling in the pit of Mahra's stomach gradually eased. She found herself grinding her teeth as she watched the Sirona ship. Why didn't they do anything? They still didn't have any idea how the Sirona managed to get from place to place, so the ship's inhabitants could have been anywhere at that moment.

Perhaps that was another thing that would cease to be a mystery within time, just as the Sirona drives had. She watched the ship, willing something to happen.

More time passed and Mahra caught herself drifting, running her mind over all the things that had happened over the past few weeks. It was strange how fate had conspired to bring her full circle, back to the teachings of the Old One. Just for a moment, Aleyin's face appeared in her mind, and she felt a touch of sadness. She wondered what had happened to him. In many ways, it was as much because of him as well as the Old One that she was where she was today.

At that moment, a sense of discomfort grew in her stomach and the edges of her vision started to waver. At last, something was about to happen. The Sirona ship was about to move.

"Heads up, my friends," she announced. "Timon, get ready to hit it."

The area around the large silver ship started to shimmer. Mahra felt the energies moving toward a point in the distance beyond the vast metallic bulk and she tensed, ready to give the command. It had to be at the right moment or they'd lose the opportunity completely.

"Now Timon! Now!"

The Sirona ship shimmered and disappeared. Pellis had hit the conventional drive as soon as Mahra yelled her warning and *The Pilgrim* shot out from behind the concealing platform. On Mahra's command, Pellis jammed down hard on the jump switch and they immediately made the leap into that place of familiar grey blankness.

Again, Mahra's senses were awash with the shapes and patterns of jump space, but this time it was different. She knew they were not alone. She could feel the vast ship's wake in front. It acted like a pointer for her and she followed it unerringly, tracing its path without difficulty. She only hoped the ship in front couldn't sense *The Pilgrim's* presence in the same way. Even if they could, she thought, it was unlikely that the Sirona would be expecting another ship to follow them. Hopefully, if they had planned well enough, the Sirona wouldn't be looking.

There were elements of a gamble in what the CoCee planned, but so far it seemed to be working. The Sirona had arrived and obviously observed the vast gathering of ships taking place around New Helvetica. That gathering couldn't mean anything good for a place that the Sirona had so much interest in, and it seemed to have prompted the desired reaction.

They travelled a long time through the vague void's blankness. Mahra could see and feel, but the others had little sense of what was taking place. She strained forward on her couch, waiting, waiting, barely daring to breathe in case she missed the instant of their reappearance in normal space.

Then Mahra felt the change in front and she knew without thinking, that the Sirona ship was about to re-emerge from the non-space they both moved through.

"Timon, Jayeer, get ready to cut the drive on my word. I think we've arrived. Wait .... Wait .... Now!"

They cut the drives and *The Pilgrim* popped into normal space. They had emerged in a place that Mahra knew no human had willingly been to before. For a moment, their vision was obscured by the Sirona ship's bulk in front, but then the other details started to become clear.

They were inside a new system — that much was clear. Mahra looked around, trying to accumulate as many details as she could, and to guard for potential threat. Chutzpah seemed at ease, so she thought they had a few moments yet.

A huge red globe sat filling one side of the darkness to their right. In the middle distance hung a collection of silver globes clustered in numbers she could barely guess at. Mahra heard a low whistle from down below. She too was awed by the display. Jayeer's voice barely registered as he spoke.

"Hmm, very interesting. According to the displays there is not a single world in sight. One large star and several groups of ships. That's it. There has to be about thirty in that group up ahead and it looks like there are several other groups, just as large, besides."

"This is it!" said Mahra. "Well, some of the stories seem to have been right. It's not a home world. It's a home system ... But there are so many of them."

Mahra suddenly realised how exposed they are, sitting in the emptiness. There was nowhere at all to hide. Jayeer was still muttering observations and there was nothing but stunned silence from Pellis.

"Timon, come on. We've seen enough. Hit it now!" she said urgently. The group of silver ships in front was starting to separate into its component parts and she didn't want to be around when it did. "Come on, Timon," she muttered. "Come on."

It was clear they'd been spotted. If he didn't activate the drive soon, the Sirona ships would be upon them.

"Now!" said Timon, and her senses surged with their entry into jump space.

They had the information they needed and as soon as they were secure in jump, Mahra let out a deep breath and started reading off co-ordinates to Jayeer through the com. The system was a long, long way from New Helvetian space. But now they knew how to get there. All they had to do now was get back in one piece.

Jayeer busied himself compiling the information into a broadcast message they would release as soon as they re-entered New Helvetian space. They would have to do it quickly. Mahra could feel the energies in the void behind them shifting. They had company, and Mahra knew, without doubt, that more than one Sirona ship had jumped into the corridor behind.

"Timon, they're following. I hope everything's in place when we arrive. There's about a dozen of them behind us."

"I hope so too, Mahra."

She could remember all too vividly what happened to their contact off Kalany. Desperately she tried to sense if the ships were getting closer, but all she could tell was that they were behind and following. She reached inside herself, calming and achieving focus. She concentrated on the patterns she was sensing, pushing emotion to one side.

The Pilgrim popped back into normal space virtually at the same point they disappeared. Jayeer immediately sent his broadcast and the figures and co-ordinates streamed into the memories of dozens of battle-ready ships. Mahra still brimmed with visions of the space beyond void, but they had no time. The moment was too close. Months of planning was about to came to fruition. If only it would work. Mahra had done her part and now it was up to the rest of them. Timon opened a channel and broadcast to the collected ships below.

"All right. Each one of you knew why we're here. Take your lead from our ship. You have the co-ordinates and each of you is as ready as you'll ever be to do this. Battles one, two and three take up your positions. We haven't got long."

Mahra heard the tone of command in his voice. The traces of his accent were back, so she knew without having to be told that he wasn't altogether comfortable. None of them were. What they were about to do was going to be hard.

Mahra's perception started to shift. Line upon line of intersections converged on the space around them. The Sirona were coming to see and there were many, many of them. They were arriving in numbers greater than she first thought. More must have followed the initial pursuit.

"Here they come," she said pointlessly as thirty or so separate shapes shimmered into existence in the space in front. They had to time this just right. Mahra swallowed, waiting for Timon to give the order.

"On my command," came Pellis's voice over the com. "Now!"

As one, three separate wings of CoCee ships accelerated and suddenly faded out of existence, The Pilgrim in the lead. Just before they winked out, chaos erupted behind them. The Sirona ships had spread when they emerged, moving to mark the borders of the CoCee fleet gathered below. The first large ovoid moved sideways toward the outer edge as the CoCee ships moved up to meet them. At the same moment, a burst of killing light struck from the sides, above and away from the converging CoCee fleet. It played across the surface of the outermost Sirona ships until they glowed with fury. For the briefest of times it appeared the Sirona ship was unaffected, that it could swim through the energies that bathed it. Then, in a sudden burst of orange and glowing debris, it ceased to be a ship. In its place was a glowing ball of debris. It was joined in an instant by another. The power of the orbital platforms was doing its job. The CoCee had chosen their place well.

Immediately the Sirona recognise the threat and started to return fire, but by then, the fleet had joined the fray. Mahra just had time to see the start of the assault as the images disappeared from her senses behind them.

They were on their own now. In the space beyond jump, *The Pilgrim* and its companions moved toward the Sirona system. Because they could no longer see the violence erupting behind them and they had no way of knowing which way it was going. Mahra knew there would be losses, but there was no way she could influence that outcome any more. She only hoped that now they could do their part.

Battles one, two and three numbered forty-six ships in all. She knew they were not enough, but they had surprise on their side. The Sirona couldn't possibly be expecting their arrival, but when they did, their message would be clear.

As a group, the CoCee ships emerged on the other side of jump. The huge red star filled their view. Fortune was with them. None of the spherical groups of Sirona ships were in the immediate vicinity of their emergence.

Mahra's heart was in her throat as they popped into normal space, expecting nothing short of the reception they had prepared for the Sirona ships around New Helvetica, but nothing moved around them. Jayeer reported that there were a few Sirona clusters present, but none close enough to cause concern. All they had to do now was wait.

They were ready when Mahra felt the first sensations of an approach through jump. She could feel five ships approaching back through the corridor — only five. If they were part of the same group that had emerged over New Helvetica, then the battle had gone better than expected for the CoCee forces. Mahra knew she was making assumptions, built on nothing but hope, but for now, things seemed to be working in their favour.

"Timon," she said. "There's only five of them. Maybe there are more coming, but I can only feel five at the moment."

The five ships solidified before them. Each wore the marks of battle and Mahra knew she was right. She strained to sense any more, but she felt nothing.

Pellis barked the command and the CoCee ships opened fire, their weapons targeted on the emerging Sirona. One by one the retreating Sirona emerged. One by one they met a wall of fire and erupted, blossoming into balls of spinning debris.

"Right," said Sind over the com. "We have movement. A couple of the clusters are starting to break up. No, make that several. Here they come! They're starting to head this way!"

"All ships. We have company again," announced Pellis to the assembled fleet. "Let's stay around long enough for them to see us and know who we are. Then we leave. No engagement. Let that be clear. No engagement."

The first Sirona ship moved into view, then another and another. A vast wave of silver ovoids trailed around the edge of the dull red disk taking up so much of their view. Silently the Sirona edged closer toward the small CoCee fleet, nearing the limits of effective firing range. Timon must have known it would have no effect. The ships were well outside the range of even *The Pilgrim's* weaponry, but he fired all the same. Three short bursts of blue light arced toward the approaching Sirona. Yet still the ships came on.

With the afterimages still glowing in their sight, he yelled the command, and the fleet jumped, leaving the Sirona behind with their message.

What the alien creatures made of the wreckage of their returning ships and the parting burst of ineffectual fire, they could only guess. When their group of jump ships emerged from the long tunnel, the CoCee fleet was ready, but none of the Sirona followed. Mahra felt not a trace of their movement behind. Apparently, their message had been clear enough for now.

When the ships re-emerged in New Helvetian space, the battle's devastation was clear to see. Pieces of wreckage floated around the world and just three of the five orbital platforms remained. Mahra did a quick count, but only two-thirds of the vast fleet they left behind seemed to have survived. She scanned the surrounding space, but there was only debris.

"Timon, Jayeer," she said, surprised by what she was sensing. "I can't feel anything behind us. They're not following."

"It's too soon to tell, Mahra," said Jayeer.

"Well, at least we got through this part of it," said Timon. "And we showed them a thing or two as well. The Sirona are going to have to think twice before going ahead with anything else."

"But what about the losses?" said Mahra.

Timon's voice sobered. "Yes, we'll be hurting from this one for a while. But with what we know now, we should get the backing of all of the worlds behind us. I don't care how deep the corruption goes. The Sirona are going to find themselves a little short on welcome from now on."

Mahra thought about this, and she knew he was right. She could hear the noises of the fleet as a background over the com, but there were other things on her mind.

"What now?" she asked.

"Well," said Jayeer. "We wait here long enough to be sure that things are truly over for the time being. After that ... the real work begins."

"What say you, Mahra?" said Timon. "Are you ready?"

Mahra knew then, without even having to think about it, that her place was here. She knew without doubt she'd see the Sirona again, but the next time, the odds would be very different. To know that they were different, and she had helped make them that way, satisfied her for the moment. Things weren't going to be easy for the Sirona from this point forward. And with her help, the legacy of The Cradle would live on.

Finally, she was in a place where she belonged. She could sense the rightness — a rightness that had been missing from everything for years. She thought back to the last time she felt that rightness, of the years of harmony she had spent with the Old One and she breathed a silent thanks.

She reached up to tickle Chutzpah beneath his chin and smiled.

"Yes, Timon. I think we're ready now," she said.

The End

About the Author
Hartley James

Hartley James writes science fiction, though sometimes he thinks that the science fiction writes him. He grew up on speculative fiction of all sorts, though it was the greats, Asimov, Herbert, Dick, Clarke, Wolfe, Heinlein that shaped his perception. In his real life, he does other things, apart from writing, following the principle laid down by Robert A. Heinlein, that specialization is for insects. So, he strives not to be an insect.

Also Available

The Sirona Cycle

Mahra Kaitan, her zimonette companion and the CoCee crew struggle against the deep and growing threat of the alien Sirona.

The Jump Point (This book)

Dragged from her homeworld, young Mahra Kaitan must discover the key to fighting an insidious alien threat. The Sirona promise to subvert and control humanity, but it is Mahra alone who holds the solution. She just needs to find out what it is before it's too late.

Daughter of Atrocity

Back from their encounter with the Sirona, Mahra and her team must employ their newfound knowledge to counter the ongoing threat. After the Sirona start showing their hand, the time to act is upon them. Mahra must find out more about her new abilities, and also discover the source of the mystery that is starting to follow her. It is now becoming much more than revenge. It's about all of their futures.

Benevolent

Mahra Kaitan has a new challenge now that she has separated from the crew. The Sirona present an ongoing threat, but who or what are the Sleeth. They are like nothing they've ever seen before. And what is Chutzpah's role? On new worlds and with a new company, Mahra finally finds the clues that will eventually lead to the truth.

Standalone Novel

The Serpent Road

Aliens, ancient civilizations and the ultimate road trip. No one knows where the Seelee came from or where they went. All Tohil knows, is that he and his companions must find a way to stop them. His journey of discovery raises as many questions as it has answers. The clues to the alien technology that threatens them lie deep within himself.

Printed in Great Britain
by Amazon